A FATAL SILENCE

A DETECTIVE KAY HUNTER CRIME THRILLER

RACHEL AMPHLETT

A Fatal Silence © 2025 by Rachel Amphlett

The moral rights of the author have been asserted.

All rights reserved.

No part of this book may be reproduced in any form or by any electronic or mechanical means, including information storage and retrieval systems, without written permission from the author, except for the use of brief quotations in a book review.

This is a work of fiction. While the locations in this book are a mixture of real and imagined, the characters are totally fictitious. Any resemblance to actual people living or dead is entirely coincidental.

ONE

It was the morning after the night before when they found the mutilated body.

The park was quiet at seven o'clock, a stark contrast to the bright lights and pounding music that had filled the air until six hours ago.

The two enormous stages that had been built over two days last week were silent, the U-shaped lighting rigs arcing above them darkened, and – mercifully, given the antics of the Australian band that had taken to the international stage and delivered a Friday night headlining act that was all over social media this morning – scrubbed clean of dried-up exploding foam and streams of toilet tissue.

Now, the soft chirrup of larks carried on the light summer breeze at the far end of the undulating parkland, punctuated by the rhythmic *tap-tap-tap* of a woodpecker.

A soft hue of pink and blue hugged the horizon, muting the harshest of the sun's rays for a few hours and casting a soft dew across long grass that threatened to wither if the heatwave continued any longer than the weekend.

Lilac and ghost-like white petals dotted the grass, with wild clover thriving alongside vetch and yarrow to create a heady scent that attracted a myriad of insects that happily buzzed amongst the foliage despite the dive-bombing antics of swifts and chaffinches. Tall horse chestnut and beech trees cast dappled shadows across the old carriage paths that criss-crossed the undulating landscape of the old country estate, the bases of their sturdy trunks littered with empty beer cans.

In the distance, over by the car park, a dozen or so uniformed police officers fresh out of training milled around one of the food wagons that was doing a brisk trade in strong coffee and bacon sandwiches, the aroma of Arabica beans and grease wafting over the slumbering festival-goers.

A thin line of ragtag T-shirt-clad twenty-somethings eyed them suspiciously from their position next to the opening of a drugs advisory charity's tent until their attention was taken by a young woman emerging, her slight frame enveloped into a reassuring hug by the nearest male before she was led away.

The campsite next to the car park began as a sprawling rainbow of polyester tents in all different shapes and sizes that, after a few hundred metres, gave way to the more expensive pitches and purpose-built luxury end of the accommodation options. Here, billowing white canvas housed double beds and en suite bathrooms, bespoke thick woollen rugs lining the waterproof flooring.

The police constables were soon joined by a group of

St John's Ambulance volunteers, a mixture of bright orange and yellow high-visibility vests jostling for position next to the trestle tables laid out with complimentary sugar sachets and wooden stirring sticks.

More crap to pick up later, then.

Andrew Bressett turned his back on the temporary stages and towering lighting rigs, clucking under his breath as he used a pair of extendable aluminium tongs to fish another spent cigarette butt out from under a thorny shrub.

He wrinkled his nose, then dropped the offending article into the black bin liner he carried.

The gloves he wore provided a modicum of protection from sharp objects and germs but, like yesterday, he would slather his hands with antiseptic soap once he and the other volunteers were done here.

'Jesus, another bloody needle.'

He turned at the woman's voice, and saw Susie Hinsen clasping a spent syringe carefully between her gloved fingers.

'Lewis has got the biohazard bin,' he said. 'I've already found three this morning.'

'I'm winning – this is my fifth.' She beckoned to a stooped man in his sixties farther along the path and waited until he joined them. 'Thanks, Lewis. I thought everyone was taking pills these days anyway?'

'Different generations,' said Andrew. 'I heard one of the first aiders saying yesterday that the older ones still go for needles, and the younger ones are too scared. They think the pills are the safer option.'

Susie rolled her eyes in response, then popped the needle through the letterbox-shaped hole in the top of the box and gave Lewis a grateful smile. 'How's your back holding up?'

'Okay.' The sixty-something shook the biohazard bin, rattling the contents. 'I'm going to go and empty this.'

Andrew watched while the older man shuffled away, shielding his eyes against the glare off the car windscreens. 'Remind me again why I agreed to do this? I could be in Brighton, windsurfing right now.'

'Because you love me.' Susie raised herself on her tiptoes, kissed him and then grinned. 'Besides, there isn't enough wind.'

'Not here.' He wiped his forehead with the back of his arm, then eyed the path snaking off around two beech trees before disappearing over a slight rise in the grass. 'Another twenty minutes, then we'll head back and get some water, sound good?'

'Works for me. The first band won't be on until ten anyway so we could probably get another hour done before then.'

Andrew groaned. 'Great.'

He trudged after her, the steel-capped safety boots she insisted he wore scraping the dry earth and weighing down his feet that were already sweating in the morning heat.

If he were honest, the chance to volunteer at the music festival in return for subsidised tickets had been a good one – he just hadn't factored in the early starts on top of partying along with all the other revellers and then trying to sleep while most of the other festival-goers continued their celebrations.

When his phone alarm had gone off at six, he had nearly tossed it out through the tent flap in disgust.

He wouldn't be here if it wasn't for Susie.

They'd only been seeing each other for four months but already he was captivated by her, and she knew it.

Hence why, when they missed out on securing tickets through the online agency and she suggested an alternative way to get through the gates and see their favourite bands, he'd gone along with the idea.

He stabbed at a foil crisp packet, wondering for the nth time why salt and vinegar flavour was in *that* colour these days, and exhaled.

If this morning's clear-up was anything to go by, then tomorrow would be worse.

Raising his head to peer across to the far side of the park, he could see cars already queuing to enter the festival site, adding to what would be a full capacity crowd for the headlining act tonight.

'They're going to be awesome,' said Susie, pausing to shield her brow with her hand. 'I just know it.'

'Hope they've been practising. It's been fifteen years since they were last on a stage together, and that didn't go well.'

'Wasn't that Frankfurt, where Joey punched Thommo after the fourth song?'

'Yeah. Apparently Thommo tried to trip him up for a laugh.' Andrew grinned. 'I wouldn't have minded being a fly on the wall when this tour was suggested.'

On cue, the sound of a drum kit being thumped at odd beats carried across to where they stood, the gentle rise of the hill providing a clear view to the stages. A guitar technician started noodling up and down a fretboard, the well-known riffs and fills providing a potent concoction of memories.

'Like you said, maybe they all need the money.' Susie jerked her chin towards the hedgerow lining the path in the distance. 'Come on, the sooner we get this done, the sooner we can get back to the tent and get changed.'

'Having second thoughts about volunteering?'

She moved closer to the tangled hedgerow, the sound of her aluminium picker stabbing at the ground carrying across to where he worked. 'My head hurts. I'm staying off the cider today, that's for sure.'

He laughed. 'I told you it was strong.'

Pausing beside a thicket of tangled holly and a blossoming blackthorn bush, he reached out with the pincers and snatched up a pair of discarded knickers, turning his face away as he dropped them into the bag. 'Jesus, some people.'

'Hey, do you think I should hand this in?'

He looked up at Susie's voice to see her holding aloft a blue cotton scarf, the sort he'd seen a lot of the women wearing in the evenings to keep the chill off their shoulders while strolling around the various food and beer tents.

Wrinkling his nose, he wandered over, noting the dirt-streaked material. 'I don't know, it could've been there a while. Where was it?'

'Right here, on the ground.' She gave it a shake, loosening some of the dirt. 'It's good quality. I reckon someone's lost this recently. Even if they haven't, the lost property lot could bundle this up with the rest to donate afterwards.'

'Go on then.' He watched while she tied it around her waist for safekeeping, then peered over her shoulder, his gaze taken with something catching the sunlight beyond the tangled trunks of the hedging.

He brushed past her, unwilling to take his eyes off the glistening item in case he lost it.

Something like a tin can or a discarded crisp packet, or—

'Jesus Christ,' he managed, before spinning around, the back of his hand to his mouth as he gagged.

'What's wrong?' Susie started to walk towards him, concern etched into her features. 'Babe?'

'Don't come any closer,' he said, his voice trembling. He tugged his mobile phone from his pocket with a shaking hand, the other grabbing hold of her wrist and pulling her away, putting as much distance as possible between them and the thorny brambles. 'Don't look.'

'Andrew, what's going on? You're scaring me.'

He let go of her as the call went through, his stomach lurching as the operator answered.

'I-I need the police,' he said. 'There's a woman… There's so much blood… I think she's dead.'

TWO

Detective Inspector Kay Hunter drummed her fingers on the steering wheel of the scratched and dented silver pool car and fought back the first words that sprang to mind.

For a start, the air conditioning in the vehicle had ceased working two days ago when she and her colleague, Detective Sergeant Ian Barnes, had been stuck on the Sittingbourne Road after a four-hour meeting at Kent Police headquarters in Gravesend.

Then, the electric window mechanism had refused to work when they left the Palace Avenue police station this morning, encasing them within a metal canister that was slowly cooking them as the queue of traffic inched forward.

A dismal May had given way to a blistering June, the county town heaving with tourists and the pubs and nightclubs full to brimming every night as people began their summer holidays.

Another few weeks, and the schools would close as

well, adding another disruptive element to the town centre as bored teenagers hunted in packs for easy distractions.

Kay huffed her fringe from her forehead and eyed the junior constable beyond the windscreen who was manning a hastily erected security cordon, his face flushed while he tried remonstrating with a drunken festival-goer who was old enough to know better.

'Go on, say it,' Barnes murmured. 'I dare you.'

The older detective put his mobile phone in his shirt pocket and rolled up his sleeves, a waft of whatever deodorant he was wearing these days carrying across to where she sat.

'They're doing the best they can in the circumstances,' she said.

'Spoken like a true leader.'

'Hmm.'

The junior constable spotted her then, his eyebrows shooting upwards before he waved two more cars through and stooped to her window.

Kay sighed, opened her door and waited while he stepped back in surprise.

'Don't ask,' she said. 'Where's the outer cordon?'

He turned and pointed beyond the park's permanent snack bar. 'If you park over there, guv, and follow the path taking the right fork, you'll find DC Piper at the crime scene beside a copse of trees at the top of the hill. The pathologist got here fifteen minutes ago.'

'Good, thanks.'

Kay slammed the door shut and eased the car forward, weaving it carefully around a party of forty-somethings wearing a variety of branded T-shirts that echoed her own musical tastes.

'Jesus, I thought that lot broke up years ago,' said Barnes, craning his neck to stare at one of them as they passed.

'Maybe the pension coffers needed a top up.'

'Don't tell me they're playing here this weekend?'

'They were. They're meant to be the headline act on the main stage tonight.' Kay grimaced. 'I'm glad I'm not going to be the one telling their manager they'll be rescheduling for another year. If they last that long. Did you see the drummer's photo in the paper last week?'

Barnes chuckled. 'Don't tell me – you gave Laura the job of telling them, didn't you?'

'I figured her charms would perhaps soften the blow.' Kay turned the car into a space beside a plain off-white van and switched off the engine. 'Christ, Ian – what a way to start a weekend.'

She reached over, plucked a lightweight grey-coloured summer jacket off the back seat and climbed out, falling into step beside her colleague as they walked past the snack bar.

A crowd had gathered beside the serving window, all eyes turning to watch them accusingly, as if it were their fault that the weekend had been ruined.

A woman in her twenties with tangled brunette hair down to her waist, denim shorts and a green tank top stumbled over to them, a half-empty alco-pop bottle in her grip and a smouldering roll-up squished between the fingers of her left hand. 'You sha be gettin' shome-one to sor' this out. We paid 'undreds for our tickets, y'know.'

A FATAL SILENCE

Kay reeled back from the stench of alcohol and unwashed skin, and waved the woman away. 'There'll be an announcement from the main stage in due course. And you might want to go easy on that stuff. It's going to be a long day.'

'Feck off.' The girl snarled, then pirouetted and wobbled back to her friends.

Kay gritted her teeth. 'At times like this, I wish we could tell them. At least then they might be more cooperative.'

'It'll be all over the news before long,' said Barnes.

She peered over her shoulder to where a television crew were setting up beside the queuing traffic, the presenter thrusting her microphone under the noses of infuriated ticket holders who were being turned away. 'Christ, this is going to go national too, isn't it?'

Her mobile phone trilled in her pocket, and she pulled it out, sighing at the familiar name on the screen. 'Hold on, Ian. I'm going to have to take this. Guv?'

'Are you on scene yet?'

The familiar bark of Detective Chief Inspector Devon Sharp carried easily over the phone's speaker, and she hastily turned down the volume before following Barnes towards the path leading away from the snack bar.

'Just got here, guv. The perimeter cordons have been set up, and Traffic have officers here diverting vehicles away from the site. It's taking a while by the look of things though, especially as people want an explanation that we can't give them.'

'I've spoken to the Chief Super. She's agreed to release

another twenty officers from Ashford and Sevenoaks to assist on scene—'

'Guv, with respect – any chance you can make sure they're experienced?' Kay turned around, slowing while she walked backwards and watched the newly qualified constables who were trying to calm the increasingly fractious crowd. 'Things could kick off any moment here.'

'We'll send four mounted patrols as well, then,' said Sharp. 'About time those bloody horses got some exercise. They're costing us enough to feed.'

'That'd be great, thanks.' She hurried after Barnes, who had reached the lip of the hill and was waiting for her beside the next cordon of blue and white crime scene tape. 'We're about to get suited up, so I'll give you another update in an hour or so.'

'I'll be waiting,' said Sharp. 'We'll hold fire on sending out the press release until I hear from you in case we can share any more details to help with the investigation.'

'Thanks, guv.'

Barnes raised an eyebrow when she caught up with him. 'Is he sending reinforcements?'

'And the cavalry.'

'Blimey, you must've done something right in your review this week.' He held up the tape for her to duck under, then paused while a familiar uniformed constable crossed to where they stood, a clipboard in his hand. 'Morning, Aaron.'

'Morning.' Aaron Stewart removed his cap and ran his hand across short cropped brown hair that was already damp with sweat, then thrust the clipboard at Kay together with a black pen. 'Guv, we've set up a second cordon around the crime scene – this one's just to keep the rabble away. The two people who discovered the woman's body have been interviewed, and we've got them down at one of the St John's Ambulance tents to give them a bit of privacy. Gavin figured you'd want to speak to them yourself before he sends them home.'

'Good, thanks.' Kay scrawled her name and handed back the formal record sheet. 'Where's home for them?'

'She's from Burnham, he lives on that new estate off the Loose road.' Aaron tucked the clipboard under his arm. 'I've also had a couple of constables make a start going through the bags of rubbish that had been collected from this area prior to them finding the victim. Looks like they possibly picked up some of her clothing – a scarf – hence that extra cordon in case there's anything else lying around. I'm just waiting for some more officers so we can start a fingertip search.'

Kay nodded. 'Sounds like you've got it all under control. Where d'you want us to walk?'

In reply, Aaron pointed to a line of tape that had been weighed down with stones, its snake-like route leading across the grass towards a small white polyester tent. 'Just follow that, guv – Gavin popped a few spare protective suits in the tent for you.'

Barnes led the way, the pair of them lost in thought as they hurried over to the tent and took turns pulling on the all-in-one white suits over their clothes.

Balancing on one leg then the other to tug plastic

booties over her flat shoes, Kay paused to scratch at the trickle of sweat that was forming under the hood, making her scalp itch.

The sun was now beating a fierce path across the morning sky, and it would be several degrees warmer before she was finished here.

She heard murmured voices beyond the tent flap, and opened it to find Barnes talking on his mobile phone, his brow furrowed.

'What's up?' she said when he ended the call. 'Problem?'

'Headquarters are only going to be able to provide an extra five admin staff from tomorrow,' he replied, tucking the phone back in his shirt pocket and rezipping his protective suit. 'And two of them are part-time contractors so we could lose them at any minute.'

'For f—'

'Guv, got a minute?'

Kay turned at the familiar voice to see Detective Constable Gavin Piper encased in a similar suit to her own, marching across the grass towards them.

As he approached, he pulled back his hood, his normally spiky hair flattened against his forehead, and there was a determined expression in his eyes.

'Aaron told us about the couple who found the victim,' Kay said. 'What have you found out about her so far?'

'Lucas reckons she's in her mid-twenties to early thirties,' said the younger detective. 'Obviously he won't commit to anything formally until he does the post mortem, but there are strangulation marks around her neck and bruising to her inner thighs...'

He broke off, his eyes troubled, and Kay frowned.

'What is it, Gav?'

'Her fingers, guv. Whoever did this to her, they've sliced off her fingertips.'

THREE

Kay stared at her colleague for a moment, stunned.

The musical chirp of a song thrush echoed around her, the noise tracking back and forth between the branches of the beech trees that rustled in a gentle breeze now carrying up the hillside towards them, the light notes at odds with the weight pressing on her chest.

Throat dry, she glanced at Barnes to see a horrified expression creasing his face.

'She's got bruising to an eye socket and cheek bones too,' Gavin said, his voice dropping to a murmur. 'There could be more, but Lucas is still with her.'

'Any ID?' Barnes said, the desperation in his voice tangible.

'None on her. She's only wearing a summer dress. The two who found her – Susie Hinsen and Andrew Bressett – found some underwear over there in the grass on the other side of the hedge shielding her body from the path, and a scarf. We've also found a pair of sandals thrown amongst the ivy just over by that dip in the grass.'

Gavin tugged at the puckered polyester collar of his suit and exhaled. 'We haven't found a bag, or a phone, or anything else yet. The bags of rubbish they'd been collecting prior to finding her have been taken by the CSIs for processing, just in case there's anything else that can be connected to her.'

'How far has Lucas got with his initial examination?' said Kay.

'He's covered her hands to preserve any evidence of her attacker. There's traces of blood splatter up her arms that may be hers, or perhaps her killer's if she managed to lash out at them.'

'Only traces?'

'The blood on her arms and hands has been smudged, guv – perhaps her attacker tried to wipe it away afterwards, something like that.' He glanced over his shoulder. 'Hopefully we'll find what was used to do that once we widen the search but I've heard that could take a while…'

'Aaron mentioned he's waiting on some help, so that might change over the course of the morning.' Kay peered around him towards the crime scene tape stretched between two stainless-steel stakes. 'Do you want to show us what we're dealing with?'

'Sure, follow me.'

Gavin trudged back over to the inner cordon, Kay following as he then weaved between a series of brightly coloured plastic markers dotted about the demarcated path.

The long grass swooshed against the polyester fabric of her suit, brushing against her legs as she drew closer to a group of four crime scene investigators, their heads bowed as they conducted a meticulous analysis of the immediate area.

She forced herself to batten down her emotions, the anger that a woman had been brutally slain. The despair that a human life had been taken, and now represented a scientific specimen to be recorded and analysed to find the answers they so desperately sought.

'Kay.'

She blinked, giving herself a slight shake as a figure rose to his feet, keen brown eyes peering at her over a mask that obscured the rest of his features.

'Lucas. Thanks for getting here so quickly.'

'It was my rostered weekend off, but in the circumstances...' He glanced down, and sighed. 'I couldn't say no, could I?'

Kay moved closer, hearing Barnes's sharp intake of breath.

The woman lay on her back, one arm thrust away from her body as if trying to break a fall, the other bent awkwardly under her hip. Her red hair was chopped into a stylish shoulder-length bob, the bright colour a stark contrast to the blue-grey hue of her skin. Three studs pierced her right ear, each a perfectly formed silver star, and a slim silver ankle bracelet curled around her foot where it had slipped.

Then Kay's gaze moved to the woman's fingers encased in plastic protective bags, and she took an involuntary step backwards at the dried blood running down them.

'Gavin told you about these then,' Lucas said. 'I've checked – every single one of them has had the tip sliced off, but in a hurry. Maybe it was done to make it harder to identify her.'

'Did her killer do that before or after…?' said Barnes, his voice gruff.

'I can't say, not until I've conducted the post mortem.' The pathologist dropped to a crouch once more, and gently picked up the woman's hand, his gloved fingers cradling her wrist. 'I'll run swabs on these wounds too, in case there's any trace evidence from her killer, but—'

'If whoever did this was determined to stop us finding out her identity, then they'll have also been careful to hide theirs,' Kay said. She frowned, her thoughts already tumbling over one another. 'Why go to such extremes I wonder?'

Lucas shot her a look, the skin at the corners of his eyes crinkling with a sad amusement. 'I'll leave those sorts of questions to you to solve, Kay. In the meantime, I need to finish here so Harriet's team can get to work.'

'Okay. Thanks. When do you think you'll be able to do the PM?'

'I'll give Simon a call when I've finished here and ask him to check the diary. As early as possible next week.' Lucas's gaze returned to the dead woman. 'She'll take priority over any of the hospital cases, I can promise you that.'

Kay paused while Barnes turned away, taking in the brutalised features of the young woman, committing them to memory.

After a moment, she clenched her fists, then turned to Gavin. 'I need to speak to the couple who found her while you finish here.'

'No problem, guv. Like I said, we put them in one of the St John's Ambulance tents away from prying eyes. I was going to arrange for a car to take them home too, given that the media are here now.'

'Not to mention everyone with a mobile phone will be posting about this to social media the minute they get a whiff of what's going on.' Kay sighed. 'We can't really afford the manpower to act as a taxi service, but I agree it makes perfect sense in the circumstances.'

'Leave it with me, guv. I'll wander down there when I'm done here. That should give you plenty of time to speak with them.'

'Okay.' She turned to go, then paused and glanced over her shoulder. 'And, Gav? Good work getting all of this organised so quickly.'

He straightened then, a modicum of stress leaving his tanned features. 'Thanks, guv.'

FOUR

By the time Kay and Barnes disposed of their protective suits in a designated biohazard bin and walked back to the snack bar, the crowd had grown considerably.

Most people wore perplexed expressions, some talking to volunteers that were milling about with an air of distraction, their movements nervous while they busied themselves with seemingly mundane tasks, anything to avoid eye contact with the ticket holders.

One of the television crews had braved the ruckus, a cameraman and sound engineer facing a reporter who was attempting to interview frustrated ticket holders while looking distinctly out of place in his suit trousers and shirt. He wore a fixed smile while listening to two men who were singing at the top of their voices in between answering his questions and waving tin cans in the air, slopping beer over themselves at regular intervals.

The woman who had accosted Kay earlier now sat cross-legged on one of the wooden picnic tables, gesticulating wildly with her hands while shouting at one of the men who crowded around her.

A couple with a toddler in a pushchair hurried along the path, the man casting a sideways expression at the reporter and the growing crowd before holding up a hand to stop Kay as they passed.

'Are you police? What's going on?' he said. 'We had a family pass for the festival but someone said something about a body being found. Is that true?'

Kay felt an almost imperceptible shiver as heads turned to face them, curious expressions on the nearest revellers.

The reporter lowered his microphone and stared for a moment. Then a predatory smile appeared, and he beckoned to the cameraman and sound engineer before pushing his way towards her and Barnes.

'I'm unable to comment at the moment,' she said to the man and his worried-looking wife. 'There'll be an announcement by the organisers in due course.'

'Your lot said that an hour ago,' another man yelled across, his skin an angry shade of sunburned pink. 'We're still fucking waiting. Who's dead?'

'Guv, over here.' Barnes glared at the news crew, stopping them in their tracks, then gave Kay a gentle nudge, pointing to a large blue canvas tent closer to the car park.

'Those reinforcements and horses better bloody turn up soon,' she said through gritted teeth. She cursed as her heel turned in a deep pothole, nodding her thanks to him when he reached out to steady her. 'Things are bound to kick off if this lot don't get some answers, and that reporter isn't going to help. We'll need more manpower to interview as many people as possible as they're leaving too, just to make sure we get names and contact details.'

A familiar face greeted her outside the tent, his height lending an extra air of authority and his stance one of high alert for anyone tempted to approach. He nodded as they drew near.

'Guv. Do you want to speak with the couple who found her?'

'In a minute, Kyle.' Kay lowered her voice and pulled him aside while Barnes took his place and glared at the crowd. 'What have they said to you so far?'

Probationary Detective Constable Kyle Walker turned his back to the crowd before continuing, and Kay appreciated the gesture – it would stop any would-be lipreader from eavesdropping on their conversation.

'They're both shaken up, as you can imagine,' he said. 'I had the first aiders check them over when we brought them here, but I think the initial shock is starting to wear off. They've confirmed neither of them recognised the victim, and after speaking with them I checked out their alibis for the past twenty-four hours. Everything's okay on that front. As for where the victim was found, the bloke – Andrew – said that the woman organising the clean-up volunteers simply allocated that part of the park to them this morning when they turned up.'

'Have you spoken to her yet?'

'She's on the list, a Dana Schuldberg. There wasn't anyone else available to stay with these two, so…'

Kay nodded. 'Don't worry. Give me her details, and I'll speak to her.'

'Thanks, guv.' He pulled out his notebook and held it out.

Taking a photo of the open page on her phone, Kay craned her neck to peer around the side of the tent. 'Where do I find her?'

'There's a central administration tent two rows behind this one, before you get to the car park.' Kyle jerked his chin towards the swelling number of people gathering around. 'She's probably in there because they're having to organise getting this lot off site without starting a riot.'

'Okay, thanks.'

Stepping over a taut bright red guy rope, she passed a signboard with the familiar logo of the St John's Ambulance first aid volunteers' association and pushed her way into the tent, Barnes at her side.

A soft blue hue enveloped her, dulling the harsh light from outside, the thick canvas soaking away some of the noise from the revellers.

Reminding herself to remain professional instead of emitting a sigh of relief, Kay cast her gaze about until her eyes adjusted, noting that the tent had been set up such that the front of it provided a rough reception-like area with two trestle tables. Beyond those, three cubicles were sectioned off by more canvas, the flaps pulled back to reveal camp beds and first aid equipment neatly organised into plastic boxes of various sizes. Labels were stuck to the outside of the boxes clearly denoting what could be found where in a hurry.

Movement out of the corner of her eye caught her attention, and she spotted a couple sitting on a pair of canvas camping chairs off to her right, the woman's face blotchy while she dabbed at her eyes with a paper tissue.

The man beside her had been leaning his elbows on his knees but straightened as Kay and Barnes moved towards them, his face inquisitive.

'Are you detectives?' he said.

'Yes. I'm Detective Inspector Kay Hunter, and this is my colleague, Detective Sergeant Ian Barnes,' she said, holding out her warrant card. 'I realise this is a difficult time for you, but we're going to need to ask you some more questions.'

'That's okay,' the woman sniffed. She reached out for the man's hand, their fingers entwining. 'We want to do anything we can to help.'

Barnes crossed to where a rack of wooden chairs had been propped against the side of one of the trestle tables. He returned with two and unfolded one of them for Kay.

She murmured her thanks, waited until her colleague had pulled out his notebook and then turned her attention back to the couple. 'Okay, so it's Susie and Andrew, is that correct?'

The pair nodded in unison.

'Take me back to first thing this morning,' she said. 'Were you staying on site overnight?'

'Yeah,' said Andrew. 'That was part of the deal for volunteering with the clean-up. Susie found the details online after we missed out on getting tickets. It meant we got a weekend pass for half price. It seemed like a fair swap at the time...'

He broke off, forlorn.

'I knew someone who did this last year,' said Susie

quietly. 'We were given a tent pitch away from the main section so it was a bit quieter. It meant we could – sort of – get a few hours' sleep before getting up in the morning to start tidying up before the music kicks off again at ten o'clock.'

Andrew emitted a strangled snort. 'Not that we got much sleep. The music might've stopped at midnight but most people were still partying until the sun came up.'

'What time did you leave your tent?'

'Just after six,' he said. 'There was a team meeting at half past six, same as yesterday, just to go over basic health and safety stuff—'

'There are a few needles around, things like that,' Susie added. 'And the organisers are paranoid someone might get sick so there's a whole raft of rules about those. And of course there's a risk of sunstroke this weekend, so they were doling out those half-litre bottles of water for us too.'

'How long did the meeting last for?' said Kay.

'Only fifteen minutes or so,' Andrew said. 'We all had to take part in an induction meeting on Wednesday before the VIP pass holders turned up on Thursday so the morning meetings are basically just to reiterate what was said then, and for us to raise any concerns.'

'Have any volunteers raised concerns about anything?'

'No, not that I know of.'

'Susie?'

The woman shook her head. 'To be fair, it's been really well organised.'

'Okay, so what happened after the health and safety stuff was dealt with?'

'We were told which areas of the park to go and clean

up,' said Andrew. 'They change it around every day so you don't get the same area as you cleaned the day before.'

'That's because some areas are worse than others,' Susie explained. She gave a slight shrug. 'Makes it fairer, so one team isn't stuck with the same place every day.'

'Yes, that makes sense,' said Kay. She glanced at Barnes. 'We'll need to speak with whoever tidied that area yesterday.'

He nodded in response, his head still bowed to his notebook.

Kay turned back to the couple. 'What time did you leave the team meeting?'

'We were probably on our way by seven,' said Andrew. 'They wanted us to get a head start before it got too hot. That's the problem this year – apparently the clean-up didn't usually start until half seven in previous years. We would normally have had an extra hour in bed.'

'Which way did you approach the slope and the hedgerow where you found the victim?'

'We used the path, the one that takes a right fork away from the lake. It takes you up to the top of the hill, and then you can follow it round in a big loop around to the right before it curves back down to where all the stages are.'

'Did you see anyone else while you were walking towards the top of the hill?'

'No,' said Susie. 'We were the first ones to get to the top of the hill. Lewis, who was following us, was quite a way behind—'

'He's in his sixties and loves the music but can't afford a ticket so he's been volunteering for years at different festivals.' Andrew managed a smile. 'He's a right character – some of the regular bands know him well.'

'The woman who was organising us all got him to take the biohazard bin around to the different volunteers who are dotted around the park,' Susie continued. 'But like I said, he wasn't that close when we first got up there…'

'But then you found that needle,' said Andrew, 'and Lewis joined us for a minute before he wandered off to empty the bin because it was getting full.'

Kay rose from her seat and eyed the couple. 'We're waiting for reinforcements to help with crowd control, but you're free to go. We'll probably have more questions as our investigation progresses, so if we could contact you again…?'

'Absolutely.' Andrew reached out for Susie's hand and gave an involuntary shiver. 'We gave our details to the other detective out there, so…'

'All right, we'll be in touch.'

Pushing her way out of the tent, Kay squinted in the harsh sunlight and eyed the brightly decorated stalls selling branded merchandise and clothing.

'We'll speak to that Dana Schuldberg,' she said, 'and then we'll head to the incident room and update the team there. In the meantime, can you—'

'Excuse me, are you in charge here?' A man in his late sixties wearing a black suit jacket over a white T-shirt and blue jeans barged a younger couple out of the way and elbowed past Kyle. 'I need a word.'

Kay cocked an eyebrow. 'And you are?'

'Brian Kasprak.' He thrust out a hand, which she ignored. 'I'm the manager for the headline act.' Kasprak looked at each of them in turn, emitting a nervous laugh. 'You've heard of them, right?'

'Vaguely,' said Barnes.

'Right, right.' Another splutter of laughter.

'Brian? You in there?' A voice cut through the canvas wall, and then a woman appeared beside Kyle, shading her eyes. 'You need to let me have some more photographs for social media. And there's a Polish radio station wanting a quote from you for their lunchtime news segment. Like, now.'

'I'll be there in a sec, Melanie. Hang on.' He turned back to Kay. 'See, the thing is, the lads are due to headline tonight, and they're really excited about it, and well... this is all a bit of an inconvenience, isn't it?'

'An inconvenience?' Kay said.

'All these people, all with tickets and supporting live music,' Kasprak continued. 'It'd be a shame to disappoint them, after all, the band's only been out of retirement for six months and this is—'

Kay held up her hand. 'Mr Kasprak, we've yet to speak with the festival organisers and we're still conducting an active investigation. As our colleagues have no doubt already told you, there'll be an announcement in due course. Until then, if you wouldn't mind...'

The manager's face fell as he stepped aside, but then a hopeful expression filled his eyes. 'Did you get a ticket?'

'I didn't need to,' Kay said. 'I could hear it from my place with the windows shut just fine, thanks.'

FIVE

Detective Constable Gavin Piper tugged the sleeves of the protective polyester coveralls from his arms, then muttered his thanks as he dropped the damp suit into a biohazard bag that a junior CSI held out.

Beside the tent that had been set up to house a temporary base for the forensic team, there was a plastic crate of water bottles that someone had scrounged off the festival organisers, and he twisted one open, gulping half of the warm contents in seconds.

The tent was several sizes smaller than the colourful ones peppering the campsite below the gentle slope, and its purpose more sombre.

He felt a growing sense of unease while a steady stream of investigators moved back and forth in their bulky protective suits, their focus on the various testing kits and samples that were being recorded and bagged as their search continued.

They ignored him while they worked, their concentration too great on the task at hand and the need for answers growing more urgent as the morning progressed.

Slicking his hand over his hair, feeling the damp between his shoulder blades, he watched while Lucas oversaw the woman's broken body being gently rolled into a black nylon bag, her features disappearing from view as it was carefully zipped shut.

He swallowed, realising that she wasn't only someone's daughter, perhaps someone's wife or girlfriend, but another victim whose brutal end demanded answers – and justice.

Gavin's jaw clenched, and he spun on his heel, pitching the empty bottle into a pile that was steadily growing in a cardboard box beside the open tent flap.

It missed, and instead landed at the feet of a CSI technician who had at that moment stuck her head out through the flap and was looking at him with some concern.

'If everyone threw something at me when I tell them something they might not want to hear…'

'Sorry, Harriet.' He shot her a bashful smile, then scurried over and deposited the empty bottle in the box. 'I heard you were looking for me.'

'Indeed. Come on through.'

Harriet Baker, lead crime scene investigator and veteran of several years with Kent Police, turned without waiting for him.

Entering the stuffy confines of the tent, he saw that the bonnet of her coveralls was now pushed back, revealing dark brown hair that she had tied back into an efficient ponytail, while her mask dangled around her neck. She moved towards a folded-out table that took up one length of the small box-like tent and was covered in evidence bags of various sizes.

She seemed oblivious to the effect of the warm weather, and instead turned her attention to the evidence bags, her gloved hand hovering over them as she spoke.

'This is what's been found so far within a one hundred metre radius of where the victim was found, and we've yet to process the outer cordon.'

Gavin's eyes widened. 'That's more than I thought there would be.'

'And I think it's safe to assume that not all of it will belong to our victim, but I wanted you to see how much we've got to get through here before Kay starts asking you to chase me up for a progress report.' Harriet lowered her hand and sighed. 'This is going to take a while, Gav. There're things here that could've been dropped over any number of years.'

He moved closer, running his gaze over the contents of the bags. 'Jesus, is that a wedding ring?'

'Yes, and there's an engagement ring somewhere in amongst this as well.' Harriet shook her head in wonder. 'And you don't want to hear about some of the other stuff we've found. Needless to say, we're going to be here until sunset, and then we'll probably have to continue in the morning as well so we'll need to secure the area.'

'I'll have a word with uniform to get that organised.'

'Thanks.'

'Once those reinforcements arrive, where do you want me to have them search?'

'From the tree line a few hundred metres behind this

tent, and then follow it along the grass towards where the victim was found. We've not yet had a chance to do that, and we're looking for signs of egress – whoever did this left the park somehow.'

Gavin saw the desperation in her eyes. 'Except it hasn't rained, and the ground is dry so we won't be finding footprints.'

'Not footprints, no – but broken sapling branches, trodden down grass, anything like that. It's why we've cordoned it off so no one can go through that area. The clean-up volunteers hadn't walked across it yet, had they?'

He shook his head. 'No, they confirmed that in the initial statements they gave to the first responders. Okay, I'll relay that request.'

Harriet's eyes softened. 'Kay's given you a huge task here, hasn't she?'

'That she has.' He grimaced. 'But it isn't the first time.'

'And it won't be the last – she's been championing your work for a long time now, Gav. Between you and me, I think if she got half the chance, she'd be handing you a promotion but you didn't hear that from me.'

His cheeks burned, and then his eyes found the pile of evidence bags once more, the surface of the table all but hidden beneath the carefully organised cataloguing system that Harriet and her team were using. 'Can anything in that lot be pinpointed to our victim yet?'

Harriet gave a slight smile at the change in subject, then reached out for three bags off to the side of the rest. 'These were the knickers that were found this morning, so we'll be prioritising those first. Then, there's this macramé bracelet. It looks homemade, but having said that there are plenty of people who make this stuff in bulk to sell online so that might be more difficult to trace unless someone remembers her wearing it. Finally, we found this hair elastic caught in the branches close to where the victim was found – there are hairs caught in it that match her colouring but obviously until we can process DNA checks, I can't say for sure. If it *is* hers, then there might also be trace evidence from her killer.'

Gavin took one last look at the meagre contents of the bags. 'I'll find someone from uniform to organise the search team ASAP.'

Leaving the tent, he stalked across to the lip of the hill and stared down at the swelling number of people gathered at the foot of the winding path leading through the campsite.

As people started to wake up and hear the news from neighbouring festival-goers, he could sense a growing unease from where he stood. The silence from the stage was deafening, a muted malevolent undercurrent that underpinned the park.

Beyond the dirt track that led in and out of the site, he could see a large horse trailer, its rear doors open and the first of four enormous animals being led down the ramp. The tack glistened in the sunlight, and as he watched, a rider wearing Kent Police insignia and a bright yellow high visibility vest was given a leg up into the saddle of the nearest horse.

The process was repeated until all four riders were mounted and began walking towards the crowd, which parted as one to let the beasts through.

'About bloody time,' he said under his breath, noting a minibus drawing up to a standstill beside the horse trailer before ejecting a steady stream of uniformed officers into the park.

Tearing his gaze away from his colleagues for a moment, he looked back to the campsite, at the hundreds of colourful canvas tents covering the grass, and exhaled.

The place was so vast, so cluttered with people from all over the country and beyond, that it was overwhelming.

How the hell were they going to find a killer that had managed to dump a body in the middle of a park during a music festival without anyone seeing or hearing anything?

SIX

Kay could sense the energy changing amongst the people she passed as she weaved between the tents with Barnes, her eyes scoping the refreshments stalls on either side of the wide grass-covered aisle.

The tables were starting to fill with those seeking caffeinated hot drinks – or something stronger – to ease them into the day, with the conversations rising in volume as rumours began to spread.

Their surreptitious glances had changed from inquisitive to accusatory, and she knew if they didn't provide the crowd with some answers soon, the newest arrivals to the police cordon would have their hands full.

Her phone buzzed in her pocket, and she bit her lip after reading the text message on the screen.

'Ian, wait.' She waved him over to one of four empty barrel-shaped tables set out in front of one of the bar tents away from a crowd of early drinkers, ducked underneath the frill of a sun umbrella decorated with a local brewer's logo and pulled out her phone. 'Just give me a sec. I need to speak to Sharp.'

He nodded, resting his elbow on the table and turned his back on the open maw of the bar tent, studiously ignoring the hoppy aroma escaping from it.

Her call was answered immediately. 'Kay, what's the latest?'

'Thanks for the reinforcements, guv – they got here ten minutes ago.' She lowered her voice as two teenagers walked past arm-in-arm, their carefree giggles at odds with the news she was delivering. 'Gavin's advised that he's been on to the incident room to coordinate house-to-house enquiries for the properties bordering the park and CCTV for all egress points that might've been used by her killer. As soon as Barnes and I have spoken to the woman who organises the volunteers here, we're going to head back to the station to oversee the investigation from there. But, guv – it's getting fractious here. I think we need to make that announcement sooner rather than later.'

'Sounds like you want us to put out a press release with very little information,' Sharp said.

'I think it's going to be the wisest option in the circumstances, guv. There are already rumours circulating, and I'd rather those were contained as soon as possible. Better that we control the narrative, don't you think?'

He mulled over her words for a moment, then cleared his throat. 'Right, we'll have something basic sent out to all news outlets within the next fifteen minutes along the lines of a woman having lost her life at the festival. We'll say that our enquiries are continuing and ask anyone with information or concerns to call a hotline number that we've already set up here at headquarters. Does that suit you? I'll have the media relations team liaise with the festival organisers to get that broadcast across their social media too.'

'That'd be great, guv. Thanks. I'll phone you later when I have more to report.'

Lowering her phone, she noticed the notification alert displayed on her email app, her heart sinking at the number of unread messages, and then tucked it away. 'Okay, Ian – let's go.'

They found the administration tent within moments. A steady stream of volunteers trotted back and forth through the open side of it, the whole canvas wall rolled up and roped out of the way to provide easy access.

Kay held up her warrant card to an older man with white hair who hovered just inside to keep out of the sun while doling out water bottles to anyone who needed them.

He straightened when he realised who they were, and pointed to a woman with a long brunette ponytail who was dashing back and forth between the different volunteers, issuing orders in a clipped voice.

'Wait,' he said as they turned away. 'How are Andrew and Susie doing? Are they okay?'

'As well as they can be in the circumstances,' said Kay.

A baleful expression crossed his face. 'If I'd have known, I would've stayed with them. I used to be in the army y'know. As a medic.'

'Sorry, you are?'

'Lewis.' He jerked his thumb over his shoulder towards a large metal biohazard waste bin that took up a corner of the tent. 'I'm in charge of that, so they were sending me all over the park this morning to collect any needles and stuff the other volunteers found while they were clearing up. Susie found a needle just before...'

Kay eyed the bin. 'I suppose the one you found is already in there.'

'It is, yes. But she didn't find it anywhere near... It was about halfway up the hill, just off the path.'

'Okay. Thanks.' She turned to Barnes. 'We're going to need to ask Harriet to take that bin.'

'Already on it, guv,' he murmured, pulling out his phone. 'Hopefully she doesn't shoot the messenger.'

Kay wandered over to where the woman in charge of the volunteers was hefting a sizeable pile of paperwork over to a wooden trestle table, her bright orange top and turquoise skirt providing a blast of colour in the gloom of the canvas tent.

'Excuse me, are you Dana Schuldberg?' She introduced herself and Barnes as he joined them, and gave a sympathetic smile. 'I can see you're busy but we're going to need a word.'

'That's okay.' Dana shoved the pile of paperwork to one side and adjusted her ponytail with a practised twitch. Her brow furrowed as she watched Barnes pull out his notebook. 'I figured you would.'

'How long have you been working for the festival organisers?' said Kay.

'About four years. They don't just do music festivals – they hold all sorts of outdoors events during the year, so that's why I like it. I get to see all sorts of things.'

Kay looked around the tent, at the dozen or so people of varying ages who were moving back and forth with different equipment, clipboards, all in a hurry to be somewhere or do something. 'Do you actually get a chance to see anything?'

Dana smiled. 'Sometimes. At least here, I can hear it.' She lowered her voice. 'Is it true that a woman's been murdered?'

'The only thing I can confirm at the moment is that the body of a woman was found by two of your volunteers this morning. We can't venture a cause of death, not yet.' Kay shot the woman a conspiratorial smile. 'And I'd appreciate it if you could help us contain any rumours amongst the volunteers for the time being.'

'Of course. What else can I help with?'

'We're going to need a list of names for every volunteer you've got working here over the weekend, contact details too if you've got them.'

'No problem. Got an email address? That's probably easier, right?'

'Thanks.' Kay handed over a business card. 'Where do you get your volunteers from?'

'Some apply via the website, like Andrew and Susie did. Others we know from helping out at prior events – those people get first refusal because they're a known quantity,' said Dana. 'It means we have to spend less time training them if they've done this before. We probably only take on twenty to thirty new volunteers for an event this size, the rest – like Lewis over there – have been with us a while.'

'What sort of duties have the volunteers been doing here?'

'Pretty much anything you can think of. Checking

tickets at the gates alongside the specialised security personnel – checking bags and vehicles as well. There's a strict policy as part of the licensing rules so only on-premises alcohol is allowed.' Dana rolled her eyes. 'You wouldn't believe some of the places we find the stuff. Drug checks obviously, although this year there's a voluntary scheme so there are special bins around that people can dump anything they don't want to take in those. It's proved successful at other festivals around the country, and we've noticed a decrease in first aid cases in the past twenty-four hours already. Oh, and sunscreen – we've got volunteers walking around with complimentary sunscreen sachets. And then there's the admin work behind the scenes and helping the bands get to and from the stages…'

As Kay listened, she felt an overwhelming sense of admiration for the woman. 'Sounds like you've had your hands full. Have any of the volunteers caused you problems, or given you cause for concern?'

Dana shook her head. 'None of them, no. Not that anyone's reported it to me, anyway.'

'Okay, we'll let you get on.' Kay pointed at the business card in the woman's hand. 'Please send those details over as soon as you can though.'

She raised a hand to shield her eyes as she led Barnes out of the tent and into the late morning heat, and frowned as a steady stream of people hurried past them, heading for the main stage.

'They're not starting the live music, surely?' she murmured, taking a step back to let people pass while Barnes stopped in his tracks, his gaze lowered to his phone.

'I doubt it, guv. Look.' He turned the screen to face her. 'They've updated their social media to say there's going to be an announcement at twelve o'clock.'

Kay checked her watch. 'That's fifteen minutes away.'

'I think this lot are going to be disappointed.' Barnes watched a group of eight men in shorts and T-shirts stagger past clutching half-empty plastic pint glasses. 'And it might be worth closing the bars before they get the bad news.'

SEVEN

Detective Constable Laura Hanway paused at the door to the incident room, her heart racing as she clutched a pile of manila folders to her chest.

The Palace Avenue police station had morphed from its origins in the early 1900s and was now a hodgepodge of buildings added one onto the other over the intervening years.

The public-facing reception area gave way to a series of corridors that wove away from the busy street and up several floors, one side of which faced the town's magistrates' courts.

Over her shoulder, the sounds of a busy county town police station echoed off the walls and up the stairwell – somewhere downstairs, towards the cells, a metal door slammed into its housing, the noise ricocheting through the building.

In front of her, the sight of a murder investigation gearing up to full throttle confronted her – a murder investigation she was now managing until Kay and Barnes returned from Mote Park and took command.

She swallowed, heart racing.

Despite being an integral part of Kay's team for a few years now, despite having experience across a wide range of crimes during that time, she had – until now – never led the team herself.

And they were all depending on her to deliver a concise and clear way forward.

Right now.

The incident room had been created by opening a partition wall between two meeting rooms, after the normal office where she worked was deemed too small for the murder investigation now underway. Computers and screens were hurriedly being set up on desks that were fast disappearing under cables snaking across their surfaces, while boxes of equipment lay strewn about the threadbare carpet.

'Beep beep.' A uniformed constable elbowed her out of the way with a box of paper reams in her arms, on top of which she had balanced a takeout coffee cup and a plastic desktop tidy chock-full of different coloured pens. Placing the lot onto the nearest clear space, she turned and cocked an eyebrow at Laura. 'No good standing there. Come on, this lot need a ringleader and at the moment, that's you.'

Laura exhaled, then forced a smile. 'Thanks for the reminder, Debs.'

'We're missing three admin staff, but this is everyone you're getting.' PC Debbie West pointed to the tall officer who was wiping down a whiteboard in preparation for the initial briefing, his back turned to the room. 'And Kyle got back from the park just in time to update you.'

With that, the constable moved the coffee cup out of the way and hefted the box of paper over to an enormous printer and photocopying machine in the far corner, her voice carrying across the room as she issued instructions to junior members of personnel.

Laura bit back a grin, knowing full well that the investigation was in safe hands with Debbie as exhibits officer. The constable was well versed in major incidents and had been an integral part of Kay's team well before Laura had joined the police station from her home county of Lancashire.

Quickly surveying the layout of the desks, she hurried over to a group of four closest to the whiteboard and set the manila folders in the middle of one before joining Kyle.

'You made good time,' she said.

'I might have used the lights to get here.'

'Naughty naughty.' She picked up a whiteboard marker pen and handed it to him. 'Okay, tell me what you can. Let's get some actions on here to get us going before the boss gets back.'

'Right.' He started a bullet-point list, beginning with the known facts about the victim and her injuries. 'I've downloaded some photos and emailed them to Debbie. She'll have those in HOLMES2 within half an hour and we'll put one or two on here so everyone can see what we're dealing with. Barnes phoned and said the woman who's in charge of the volunteers will email us a list of those so we can start doing background checks, and once the festival organisers have calmed down enough, they'll do the same with all ticket holders.'

'The legal ones, at least.' Laura frowned. 'Not sure what we're going to do with second-hand sales that didn't go through one of the proper companies.'

'There'll be gaps, for sure.'

'What about house-to-house enquiries?'

'Underway.'

She turned at the familiar voice to see Gavin weaving his way between the desks towards them, a can of energy drink in his hand. 'How many officers have we got doing that?'

'Eight at the moment, with another four on the way. Aaron Stewart's coordinating on site – they've set up a command post off Willington Street, out the way of the media.' Gavin popped the can open and took a long swallow, suppressed a belch and then scowled. 'And two TV news crews from London turned up just as I was leaving. Kay didn't look happy.'

'I'll bet.'

'Social media's gone off on one,' said Kyle. 'There's a new hashtag trending and everything. Hope the organisers' insurance is up to date.'

'One of them was already talking to the insurers when I was leaving. He sounded more stressed about the logistics of closing down the festival early and getting everyone out of the park safely than the fact we've got a murder investigation underway. At least with the extra manpower over there it should go relatively smoothly.' Gavin drained the rest of the drink and tossed the can into the nearest waste bin before turning his attention to the board. 'I got a text message from Harriet when I pulled into the car park here – she's going to let us have a preliminary report by Tuesday afternoon at the earliest, so what's your plan of action for us this weekend, Hanway?'

Laura eyed the neat capitalised letters of Kyle's bullet-point notes, and took a few seconds to gather her thoughts. 'With the house-to-house enquiries underway, we won't be able to do anything there until we hear something back from uniform. I presume the house-to-house enquiries will include requests for doorbell and security camera footage from residents? At least then we can check to see if anyone was acting suspiciously around the perimeter.'

'It will, yes,' said Gavin. 'I've also asked Aaron to make sure his team speaks to any businesses along those roads as they work their way around too – there are a lot of small businesses run from home that might have additional footage or people who work nightshifts that might've seen something.'

'Great, okay so let's get another team focused on the larger premises and start as soon as possible.' Laura waited while Kyle added the action to the board. 'As soon as Debbie's got her computer set up, I'll ask her to add these tasks to HOLMES2 so we can track progress. Has anyone heard from Lucas or Simon yet about a post mortem date?'

'Monday, at eleven,' said Gavin. 'Simon phoned Kay just before I left. She said she'll go with Barnes after the briefing that morning.'

Laura chewed her lip for a moment. 'Did he say whether he's going to manage to find a forensic odontologist at short notice? If our victim's missing her fingertips and we don't find any ID, then we're going to be dependent on dental records, aren't we?'

'He didn't, but knowing Lucas he'll probably be phoning around as we speak to bully someone into being available.'

'True. Okay, well there's not much else we can do there until we have the results of the PM, so…'

'Just a thought, but what about the Specialist Search Team?' said Kyle. 'Has anyone called them yet? I mean, her killer might've thrown evidence into the lake or any of the streams that go through the park.'

Laura's stomach flipped. 'Shit, no…'

'It's all right, I'll give them a call and organise that,' Gavin said kindly. 'You can't think of everything. Remember, we're a team, right?'

He was already pulling out his phone and turning away before she could thank him, but she shot Kyle a grateful smile.

'I think you're going to pass your detective's exams with flying colours.'

EIGHT

Barnes jangled his keys from hand to hand before aiming the fob at the car, the ignition lights flaring once.

'Back to the incident room then, guv?'

Kay surveyed the lines of cars queuing to leave the park, each vehicle being stopped at the exit by a uniformed constable so that contact details could be taken and checked against ticket sales.

Tempers amongst some of the more inebriated festival-goers had frayed, their patience expiring once news of the cancellation of all further live music had spread, despite the circumstances. Others tried to offer stoical advice, attempting to defuse any conversations that turned accusatory while shuffling forwards in three snaking queues that had formed at the pedestrian exits.

All around her, tents were being dismantled and stowed away, backpacks were shoved full of clothing and souvenirs and whatever else attendees had got their hands on over the past twenty-four hours, while stall-holders stripped signboards and decorations from their pitches while ruminating how much the festival organiser's insurers would pay them.

And every single person had to be accounted for.

The resulting man-hours required to process the ensuing information would use all their resources.

She rubbed at her temple. 'No, let's have a drive round to the Willington Street exit to see how Aaron's getting on with those house-to-house enquiries. I want to get a feel for how we're progressing there before we head back.'

Opening the door, she climbed in, clipping on her seatbelt before realising Barnes hadn't joined her.

He was still standing outside, his back turned to the vehicle.

'Ian? Are we going or what?' she called.

A moment passed, and then he opened his door and peered across to her, his mobile phone in his hand. 'Change of plan, guv. The specialist search team just turned up.'

'Shit, the lake.'

Kay scrambled out to join him, their footsteps hurried as they trod the well-worn footpath up the hill and then taking the left fork to follow it down to the ornamental lake that hugged the northern fringes of the park.

The novelty swan-shaped pedaloes that normally filled the watercourse during the day were all moored against a long wooden jetty on the far side, and the shed that housed the hire company's ticket office had its metal shutter pulled down tight.

Two uniformed constables were walking along the bank beyond the jetty, pausing to speak with a pair of fishermen and sending them on their way before continuing their patrol.

And then she saw the familiar Kent Police-liveried Land Rover from the specialist search unit's fleet, with its bodywork covered in an array of aerials, roof racks and equipment boxes.

'Laura said on the phone that the team have a second crew available if they're needed,' Barnes said, loosening his tie as they began the short descent down the hill. 'Given all the streams that lead into this and border the park, it might be an idea…'

'True. Let's see what they say. I'll be guided by them rather than try and tell them how to do their job.'

Her colleague nodded in acquiescence as they drew closer, and Kay's gaze quickly singled out a broad man in his forties she recognised from a seminar about the search unit that had taken place at headquarters the previous year.

'Terry, thanks for coming out at such short notice,' she said by way of greeting.

He turned, zipping up a neoprene suit that clad his bulk from ankle to neck and gave a slight nod, then looked to Barnes.

'Ian, this is Sergeant Terry Clybourne from Gravesend,' she said. 'What's the plan here?'

The search unit leader jerked a thumb over his shoulder to where two colleagues were unloading a reinforced cube-shaped crate from the back of the Land Rover before setting it on the ground. 'We'll send up the drone first, to have a look around the shallower reaches of the water and see if we spot anything obvious. After that, it'll be a grid search I'm afraid.'

Kay's heart sank despite the knowledge that procedures had to be followed. There was no quick way to investigate such a large expanse of water, not without the risk of missing vital evidence. 'Okay, just so you know the only information we have from the Home Office pathologist so far is that our victim's fingertips were removed – by what isn't clear, so—'

'We'll keep our options open.' Terry nodded, gesturing to a second man who was wearing a dive suit and was now pulling on thick protective gloves. 'So we won't just be looking for knives, we'll consider any sharp objects. Did you hear that, Michael?'

The other man gave a thumbs up in response, then peered across the lake towards the incline of the path. 'Whereabouts up there was she found?'

'Further over to the left,' said Kay. 'See that tree line? There's a clump of brambles about four hundred metres away.'

Terry's attention shifted to his colleague. 'Best we start over that side then, and work our way around the same route that the path takes as it comes down the hill. If her killer panicked and left the park this way, he might've thrown whatever he used as he went past.'

'Sounds good.' Michael turned back to checking the diving equipment.

Kay watched for a moment as the drone lifted into the air, the operator thumbing the radio control unit to achieve the best altitude for the search, then glanced at Terry. 'You're going to hate me for asking this, but how—'

'Long?' He shot her a rueful smile. 'As long as it takes. We'll be here all day, that I have no doubt. Even if we do find something that might assist your investigation, we still have to continue searching the whole area to rule out any other objects.'

'I understand. We'll let you get on. Could you call me later with an update? I need to keep this moving.'

'Will do. I'll be in touch.'

Kay led the way back along the path, the beauty of the sunlight sparkling on the water lost on her as the enormity of the investigation seeped into her bones.

Heart heavy, knowing she would do all she could to provide answers for the victim's family and bring her killer to justice, she stomped up the hill back towards the car, jaw set.

'Are you going to give Sharp another update on the way?' Barnes said, climbing behind the wheel and easing the car into the snaking line of slow-moving traffic.

'Not yet, no.' She sighed. 'I'd like to be able to update him with more than the promise of a list of names before I have that conversation.'

NINE

Kay's adrenaline levels ratcheted up another notch when she walked into the incident room.

The team had grown exponentially in the hours that she had been at Mote Park, the usual faces joined by administrative and uniformed staff from around the area.

The noise levels were still that of a fledgling investigation as people introduced themselves, settled into smaller groups to focus on one part or another of the many enquiry threads that were forming, and dealt with the myriad of phone calls that were filtering through from headquarters.

Already, the smell of various hurried late lunches and sugary snacks filled the room, but no one looked up from their desks as she passed, their focus intent on their computer screens or phones.

'Guv, here you go.' Debbie West caught up with her mid-way and thrust a steaming mug of coffee at her before handing another to Barnes. 'There are cheese and pickle sandwiches on your desks from the deli up the road too. I figured neither of you would've had a chance to eat yet.'

'Debs, you're an angel,' said Barnes.

Kay took a tentative sip and closed her eyes as the caffeine ran across her tongue. 'Oh my god, I needed this. Thanks.'

The constable smiled, then swept her hand over the gathered officers. 'Everyone's up and running with access to HOLMES2, we've got additional phones set up on those four desks over there ready for when headquarters divert the hotline to us on Monday, and I'm waiting to hear from the IT department about getting the printer from our usual room brought in here. I think we're going to need it.'

Some of the tension began to ease from Kay's shoulders as she listened, the knowledge that the administrative side of the investigation was in safe hands meaning she had fewer tasks to manage.

Crossing to where Gavin and Laura sat with their phones to their ears, she took a moment to unwrap the sandwich and listened in to their conversations while she chewed.

The older of the two detective constables leaned an elbow on the desk as he worked, his notebook open while his pen scratched across the page, brow creased.

Laura's voice was little more than a murmur, but it seemed she was speaking to someone with knowledge of one of the local chains of petrol stations.

They finished simultaneously, and Kay threw the sandwich wrapper in the bin before wiping her hands. 'Okay you two, let's have a quick briefing with the rest of the team and you can give us an update at the same time to save repeating yourselves.'

She led the way over to the whiteboard, a steady stream of officers and administrative assistants in her wake. Turning to the assembled group, she cleared her throat.

'For those of you who haven't worked with me before, I'm Detective Inspector Kay Hunter. I'll be gold leader on this murder investigation, with DS Ian Barnes deputising for me. DCs Gavin Piper and Laura Hanway are also points of contact during this time.' She paused to take a sip of coffee, vowing to get a bottle of water from the vending machine downstairs before she dehydrated in the summer heat. 'PC Debbie West will be exhibits officer and her team are also responsible for ensuring the HOLMES2 database is kept up to date. If you have any technical queries or other issues, speak to Debbie in the first instance. Okay, moving on – latest updates please.'

'Ladies first,' said Gavin.

'We should have CCTV from three garages owned by that lot on the A20 heading towards Bearsted by Monday morning,' said Laura. 'They can't get it to us sooner because the feeds are sent through to head office and on a rolling system so anything from last night will have already been uploaded. I had more luck with the two smaller garages nearer the park – one of the managers will be in tomorrow so I can go and speak to him then, and the other's making their system available straight away, so I sent Kyle over there to take a look.'

'Good work.' Kay turned to Gavin. 'Next.'

'I was just talking with one of the business owners who

has a unit down on the Turkey Mill estate – some of those units back onto the park so I'm working my way through them to request security camera footage in case the killer escaped through there and out to the A20.'

'Anything yet?'

'No, but I'm going to head over there first thing Monday morning and speak to the other business owners as they turn up to ask the same thing.'

'Keep on top of that, Gav – it's a good theory. Who's looking into the missing persons database?'

'That's me, guv,' said Laura. 'I've kept it to the Kent area for now. If we don't find anyone resembling our victim, I'll widen the search.'

Kay updated the notes on the whiteboard, recapped the pen and faced her team once more. 'There isn't much more we're going to be able to do today given that we're waiting on so much information to come in from the house-to-house enquiries and our experts, so if your work is at a point where you can leave after this briefing, then do. But I want you all back in here by eight o'clock sharp tomorrow. We're going to be in for some long days in the coming weeks but we owe it to our victim and her friends and family to work as diligently as possible and bring her killer to justice. I won't rest until we do, is that understood?'

She eyed each member of her team in turn as murmured agreement filtered through the gathered officers. 'All right, that's enough for today. Dismissed.'

TEN

The horizon was tinged with blush pinks and orange by the time Kay's car crackled over the loose gravel driveway of her home.

She sat for a moment after turning off the ignition, listening to the engine ticking while it cooled and her thoughts settled.

An exhaustion seeped across her chest and shoulders, and she closed her eyes, rolled her neck and heard a satisfying *crick* as a muscle spasmed, and then climbed out, her stomach rumbling.

The sweet smell of jasmine carried across from a shrub that was quickly outgrowing the wooden barrel planter it was in beside the front door, the aroma creating a heady mix with the lavender that filled the flower borders.

A bumblebee buzzed past her, its focus on a large fuchsia that hung across the low fence of her neighbour's garden that it landed on with the gusto of a child on an inflatable bouncy castle.

Kay aimed the key fob over her shoulder at the car,

then stabbed a key in the front door lock and walked into a hallway that was cooled by a delicious breeze emanating through the house from the back door of the kitchen.

Somewhere in the distance, she could hear whistling, and seeing a pair of sandals discarded haphazardly next to the front door mat, she smiled.

Adam Turner, her partner, had taken the weekend off work – a rare occurrence, but one that he could afford now that his busy veterinary practice was fully staffed.

Closing the front door, she pulled the free local magazine from the letterbox flap and kicked off her shoes beside Adam's sandals, then wandered through to the kitchen.

Out of habit, her gaze scanned the worktop surfaces and the tiled floor, seeking out any hint that Adam had brought one of his patients home.

Seeing nothing, she sniffed the air, then narrowed her gaze as her eyes caught movement through the open back door and she heard the rhythmic sound of hammering.

'What are you up to, Turner?' she murmured.

Four months ago, the elderly woman who owned the property backing onto theirs had been moved by her family into a care home. The woman's son and daughter had elected to sell the property, but not before they had approached Kay and Adam to see if they would be interested in purchasing some of the land that abutted the house.

Kay had never taken much notice of the trees she could see over the back fence from her garden, assuming that the property owner simply had some old fruit trees that blossomed every year and provided a handy privacy screen between the two properties.

To her amazement, once she and Adam had taken the family's invitation and ventured around to have a look, they discovered that there was a quarter of an acre of established orchard beyond the fence – land that was prime for housing development if they didn't want to buy it.

A frantic few weeks followed, during which they met with accountants, mortgage advisors and conveyancing solicitors, but they were finally able to agree a price with the family and for the past two months had dedicated every spare moment to the parcel of land.

After removing the fence separating their garden from the orchard, she and Adam had spent back-breaking hours removing the rotten trees, digging out the stumps and tending to land that had been left to grow wild for nearly a decade.

Now they had a place that had quickly become a bolt-hole in the evenings, a place to relax and decompress after a day's work.

Kay slipped on a pair of flip-flops and fetched two bottles of beer from the refrigerator before walking out over the lawn and over a slim timber bridge that crossed a small stream dividing the original properties. She glanced down as she passed, grimacing at the lack of water, and making a mental note to top up the water bowls dotted around the garden nearer the house for the hedgehogs and other wildlife.

Reaching the orchard, she crossed to a wrought-iron table and two chairs set underneath the boughs of a thirty-year-old apple tree laden with the promise of autumnal fruit and set down the beers before seeking out the sound of Adam's whistling.

She found him beyond a thicket of clumping bamboo they had planted as a temporary screen between the orchard and their house while the new saplings they had planted took hold.

Wielding a mallet, he was driving in a fence post – one of eight that described a rectangular box taking up half of the land they had cleared.

'What's that for?' she said, waiting until he paused to wipe the hem of his T-shirt across his brow. 'Chickens?'

Adam grinned. 'No. I thought until we decide what to do with this bit, I could use it for a temporary overflow for the occasional patient. Not the really sick ones, just the ones that might need keeping an eye on or a special diet for a few days, that sort of thing. I might have a guest that needs a home for a few days this week – I'm just waiting to hear from Scott whether it's going ahead or not.'

He pulled her into a sweaty hug and kissed her, and she broke away laughing.

'You need a shower. Come on, I brought some beer – come and drink it before it gets warm.'

'Music to a man's ears.' He dropped the mallet to the ground beside a bag of cement mix and a spade. 'I'll wait until the morning to fix the rails and pickets.'

'Not too early, otherwise next door will have your guts for garters if they hear a nail gun before nine,' she said. 'You know what he can be like.'

'Kevin will be fine. He wants me to give him a hand next week with that broken fence panel on his side anyway.' He followed her back to the table and chairs, sinking into one and toeing off his work boots with a sigh. 'Dare I ask how your day went?'

Kay took a long sip of beer before answering. 'We don't know who she is, Adam. Whoever killed her removed her fingertips, and we've got so much information to sift through it's almost worse than having no information at all.'

'Jesus.' He reached out and clasped his hand over hers, running his thumb over the back of her fingers. 'I saw on social media they closed down the festival.'

'Had to really. Never mind the fact half the park is now an active crime scene, it would've been incredibly bad taste to continue in the circumstances.' She wrinkled her nose. 'Despite what the lead act's manager had to say about it.'

'Is Sharp getting involved?'

'Headquarters are staying clear at the moment, thank goodness – apart from providing the extra manpower we needed today and a hotline service for any leads we might get. Whether that remains the case in a few days will depend on whether Lucas or Harriet can give us some answers.'

Adam shuffled in his seat and extracted his mobile phone from the back pocket of his board shorts. 'You're looking done in. I'll order us a takeaway rather than cooking tonight. I have a feeling you'll be asleep before we dish up otherwise.'

'I'm not that bad, honest. I'll be okay—' Kay broke off as an enormous yawn took hold.

Adam laughed. 'Good job you're a detective and not a criminal, because you're a really crap liar.'

ELEVEN

Ian Barnes plucked his mobile phone from its magnetic holder on the dashboard air vent grille, tucked it into his shirt breast pocket and pushed open the car door into another searing summer morning.

It was only seven thirty, but already a humidity clung to the air, the stillness accentuated by the muted tones of a sleepy Sunday morning in the county town.

The last nightclub had ejected its patrons just over an hour ago, and for a moment he savoured the quiet that was only interrupted by a wailing gull that arced and wheeled overhead.

Taking a deep breath, he squared his shoulders and turned for the back door of the police station, swiping his security card and hearing a metallic *click* before pushing his way into a wide corridor.

It had been painted a corporate beige colour six years ago, and showed the scuffs and grazes of the intervening years as people were escorted along it to the custody suite or made their way to the locker rooms to his right before starting another shift.

On his left, the corridor angled away to the cells, the walls covered in various posters providing information about helplines, crisis centres and health and safety, while in front of him the passageway dog-legged past a staircase and through to the public-facing reception area.

He climbed the stairs, the bannister still reeking of chemical products from the cleaners' progress through the station the night before. Reaching the second floor, he stalked towards the incident room.

Someone had already switched on the coffee machine, and the smell of fresh caffeine carried on the air towards him as the door swished shut in his wake. The printer was whirring away in the corner, spitting out page after page of a report that appeared to be never-ending.

A smile formed as he spotted a familiar figure sitting in front of her computer, fingers stabbing away at the keyboard while she glared at the screen.

'Morning, guv,' he said, slinging his backpack under his desk and logging in. 'Putting the rest of us to shame as usual?'

Kay looked over her screen at him, shot him a sardonic smile, and turned her attention back to her work. 'Just trying to get a head start on some of these emails. I was winning the battle until we got the call yesterday when our victim was found.'

'I hear you.' He leaned his elbow on the desk and mulled over the list of new messages that had appeared overnight in his absence. 'How much of our caseload are we going to be able to delegate to concentrate on this one do you think?'

'The way things are going, probably none of it, which means we're going to have to make sure we split our work carefully to manage this team, Ian.' She glanced over her shoulder towards the closed door, then back to him. 'What's your feeling about Kyle? Are you happy with his progress so far?'

Barnes nodded. 'It was his call on getting Terry's search team to the lake yesterday. He's a good listener, and he knows the procedures inside out. It's just lack of frontline experience at the moment in relation to cases like this. As it is, we both know he's going to pass his detective's exams without a problem.'

'Yeah, my thoughts exactly.' She drummed her fingers on the desk for a moment. 'What about his overall health? Have you got any concerns there?'

'No. I had a quiet word with him a few weeks ago just to check in, but he assured me then that everything was okay and I haven't seen anything to give me cause for concern. Have you?'

'No, and I'm sure his psych evaluations ended a few months ago. The personnel department haven't raised any issues with me, either.'

Neither of them voiced it, but Barnes felt a tug in his chest at the memory of another young officer gunned down in the line of duty, his presence in the team sorely missed – especially now, in the midst of an active murder inquiry.

'Okay, good.' Kay's attention turned back to her screen. 'In that case, we'll get him to lead a small team on this one and see how he fares. If you spot anything that worries you though, you tell me straight away, got it?'

'Got it.' He looked past her shoulder as the door opened and a steady stream of officers entered the room, the noise level increasing as they quickly dispersed amongst the desks and the investigation gathered momentum once more. 'Here we go again.'

'Give me five minutes and we'll start the briefing,' she said.

Barnes raised a hand in greeting as Gavin and Laura joined them, the pair already bickering good-naturedly as they settled.

'Honestly, you two sound like an old married couple sometimes,' he chuckled.

Gavin grinned. 'That's what Leanne said last time we were all out together.'

'Any news from the lake search, guv?' said Laura, placing a takeaway coffee cup next to her computer and tying her hair back. 'They were still down there at nine o'clock last night – a friend of mine saw them when she was out for a run.'

Kay looked up. 'She was running in the park?'

'No – that was still closed off to the public. She was running along one of the side roads and saw them working.'

'Well, nothing's come in on the emails yet.' The DI pushed her chair back. 'Right, it looks like everyone's here so let's make a start, shall we?'

Barnes swung his chair around to face the whiteboard as Kay crossed to it, a polite stampede of officers and admin assistants in her wake forming a loose semi-circle that jostled for position.

'Guv, this is the latest out of HOLMES2,' said Debbie, handing her an agenda and then distributing copies amongst her colleagues. 'And I just had a call from Terry Clybourne. They completed the water search an hour ago and he says he'll call in on his way back to Gravesend.'

'Okay, thanks.' Kay ran her gaze down the page before putting it to one side. 'While we're waiting on that update from Terry, how did the house-to-house enquiries go yesterday, Aaron?'

The uniformed sergeant stepped to the front of the room and raised his voice so he could be heard. 'We completed the initial round of door-knocking at seven o'clock last night. That's not accounting for no-shows, and in some of those instances neighbours have informed us that residents are away for the weekend or longer. We've got a separate list of those to follow up with when they're back so we can ask them to check their gardens for any suspicious activity, particularly the properties that back directly onto the park. At the moment, we haven't received any information that could link to our victim, although we are reviewing all the statements over the course of the next day or so to double check.'

'Thanks, Aaron. Laura – how many have you got working through the missing persons database at the moment?'

'Three, guv, plus me. We've got a few hundred names to work through but I'll let you have an update as soon as I can.'

'Okay.' Kay looked around until she found Gavin. 'What about CCTV? What's the latest progress with that?'

'We won't be able to access local council cameras until they get back into work tomorrow, guv, but we have started receiving files from some of the residents that Aaron's lot spoke to yesterday.' The detective constable grimaced. 'I've put four officers onto it, but at that rate it's going to take a while to work through it all.'

'Understood. Do the best you can with what you've got, Gav, because we're not getting any more bums on seats for the foreseeable future, and—'

Barnes turned at the sound of heavy footsteps approaching the group to see Terry Clybourne advancing towards them, his arms cradling an archive box overflowing with evidence bags, then glanced over his shoulder to see Kay's eyes widening at the sight.

'Jesus, Terry,' she managed. 'Don't tell me you dragged all of that out of the lake?'

The search team leader gave a sheepish shrug as he dropped the box onto the desk beside Laura and took a step back. 'Fourteen knives, three pistols – I'll let the major crimes team at Gravesend know about those – and what looks like an early twentieth-century dress sword.'

'And everything will need to be tested for traces of our victim's blood,' Kay murmured, sifting through the bags.

Barnes sighed. 'We're going to be on Harriet's shit list for a long time after we send her that lot, aren't we?'

TWELVE

Kay dropped the desk phone back in its cradle and swore under her breath, her chest tight.

Peering over her computer screen, she saw Barnes's face puckered in concentration, his mouth downturned. Over his shoulder, the incident room was thrumming with activity, the briefing having concluded thirty minutes ago with Terry bidding them farewell and Debbie currently working with one of the admin assistants to log every evidence bag into HOLMES2 before they were despatched to Harriet's laboratory.

A mobile phone pinged off to her right, closely followed by another and then a cascade of beeps and pips filled the incident room, her colleagues pausing their work in response as one by one their heads lowered to their phone screens.

She glanced down as her own mobile emitted a dull buzz and saw a national newspaper's app alert displayed, and swiped it open to read.

Police at a loss to explain death of woman at Mote Park festival.

'Oh shit,' she groaned, scanning the article.

In it, the reporter had launched into a scathing attack on the festival organisers and the police, citing several so-called experts who ventured an opinion on the situation. Both the headline act's manager and lead singer had waded in with their opinions, expressing only a passing sorrow at the death of the young woman before bemoaning the cancellation of what they said would have been a "monumental return" for the band.

And then, right at the end of the piece, the reporter had included Kay's name as the senior investigating officer together with a snide remark that at present, the police had been unwilling to provide comment.

'Fucking great,' she murmured, shoving the phone aside. She rose to her feet. 'Everyone, back to work. Thanks to this lot and their compatriots, we're now under even more pressure to get a result for our victim, and fast. Don't let this distract you from what you're doing, so focus please.'

A muted response met her words, but after a few mutters and grumbles that carried over to where she stood, the gathered officers returned to work.

'Don't let the bastards get you down, right?' Barnes said as she retook her seat. 'It was sure to happen, guv. Especially after the TV reports that went out last night. Pia said one of the local ones was syndicated onto breakfast news this morning.'

'Marvellous.' Kay glared at her computer screen, her gaze shifting to her desk phone as it trilled. Not recognising the number, she took a deep breath and answered. 'DI Hunter.'

'Detective Hunter, it's Alistair Featheringham. I'm hoping you can give me some answers.'

Kay frowned. 'I'm sorry, your name's not—'

'I own Crusader Events, the organisers of this weekend's festival in the park. Dreadful business.' The man paused for breath. 'Given this morning's news coverage, I need to talk to you about damage limitation.'

'Damage limitation?' Kay raised an eyebrow in Barnes's direction. 'We're dealing with a murder inquiry, Mr Featheringham. Exactly what sort of damage limitation were you thinking?'

'Well, firstly there's the business of the way communications were handled yesterday. As you can imagine, we've got a lot of angry ticket holders demanding refunds, which we're not able to issue given that the festival was already well underway before being interrupted—'

'Interrupted? Mr Featheringham, a young woman was found murdered yesterday morning by two volunteers contracted by your company. At the present time, every person who attended the festival is a suspect. Does that give you an idea of the scale of what we're dealing with here?'

'I, er... the news—'

'I'm well aware of what various news outlets are reporting at the moment thank you, and none of it is helping me and my team to find a killer. Was there anything else you needed?'

'Could we perhaps speak tomorrow when you have something more concrete—'

'Perhaps,' Kay said, and dropped the phone in its cradle.

Barnes chuckled. 'And the insurers haven't started calling yet.'

'I thought headquarters was fielding these calls today to give us a head start?'

'Someone must've given him your direct number then.'

'The woman who was organising the volunteers, Dana Schuldberg. I gave her my card.' Kay groaned. 'Jesus, Ian – we're already twenty-four hours into this investigation, and we've got nothing to work on.'

Barnes swivelled in his chair and surveyed the room. 'We've got plenty to work on, guv, it's just that there's too *much* to work on. All those statements, lists of attendees – I've just been sent the suppliers' list on email and that's going to take a few days to work through to see who was in attendance and check against criminal records – and I can't even start that until tomorrow when half of these companies are open again for business. There's hardly anyone available today.'

'We'll just have to do the best we can. We still have a young woman lying in Lucas's mortuary.' Kay clenched her jaw. Pulling up the crime scene images on HOLMES2, she scrolled through them, absorbing every detail, committing them to memory. 'I'm not going to let her down. We'll find who did this to her.'

The phone at her elbow trilled once more, and she saw

a Gravesend number displayed on the screen with a familiar extension number.

'Guv?' she answered. 'It's still early days at this end, so I've got nothing new to report yet.'

'I have,' Sharp's familiar bark replied. 'The hotline here just took a call from a woman in Kingswood – Georgina Leneghan. She says her daughter, Tansy, was meant to come and stay with her last night, but after phoning to let her know she was planning to meet someone on Friday afternoon on the way, she hasn't been heard from since. Her mother was about to report her as missing, but then saw this morning's news.'

Dread filled Kay's stomach, and she closed her eyes. 'Has she provided a photograph?'

'She emailed it through a moment ago,' said Sharp. 'It's her.'

THIRTEEN

Barnes drove the pool car through a set of sandstone gate pillars and parked outside a characterful converted Victorian vicarage.

There was already a patrol car beside a low-slung sports car on the gravel driveway, its paintwork sparkling under the mid-morning sunlight.

'What've you managed to find, guv?' he said, his hand on the door catch.

Kay finished scrolling through a social media app and looked up from her phone screen, eyeing the solid oak front door that stood between her and a grieving mother.

A pale purple wisteria softened the harshness of the building's brick exterior, the twisting branches framing the windows and reaching upwards to the guttering. Colourful shrubs filled the borders under the windows, carefully tended and trimmed, and she spotted a paved path leading around the left of the house that she guessed led to the back garden.

'Tansy Leneghan was twenty-four years old,' she said

as she stared through the windscreen. 'She graduated from Reading University and had a few different jobs until she moved to Bristol to work with an advertising company earlier this year. She rents a house just outside the city, seems to have a close-knit group of friends there, and keeps in touch with her old university crowd on a regular basis – they've all scattered to the wind since graduating. Her dad doesn't appear on either her or Georgina's social media. She seemed to be close to her mother though – she was an only child.'

Barnes shook his head. 'Jesus. I hate this part.'

'Me too. Shall we?'

She didn't wait for his response.

Crossing the driveway and climbing the three steps to the front door, a shiver seized her shoulders despite the morning's heat.

She straightened her suit jacket, took a deep breath, and knocked softly.

The door opened, revealing a familiar face.

'Hazel, thanks for getting here at short notice,' Kay said. 'Especially when you weren't rostered today – you were the first person that came to mind in the circumstances.'

Hazel Aldridge gave a slight nod. 'It's okay. It was the right thing to do. Come in and I'll give you a quick update.'

The experienced Family Liaison Officer took a step back, showing them into a gloomy hallway that captured none of the outside light.

A silence filled the house, broken only by the occasional *drip drip* from a tap emanating from a doorway off to the right of the staircase that Kay assumed led to a downstairs bathroom. Then she heard the sound of a faint sobbing.

'Where's Georgina?'

'In the living room, just through there. I've got a colleague with me – Diane. I hope you don't mind, but she's one of my trainees and showing a lot of promise,' said Hazel. 'If I get called away in an emergency, Diane will take over so I wanted her to build a connection right from the start.'

'Understood. Has Georgina provided a statement?'

'Yes, mostly confirming what she told the hotline when she called. Tansy was never meant to be anywhere near that park, Kay. She left work in Bristol at one o'clock on Friday because she'd arranged with her boss to leave early to try to beat the worst of the traffic. She phoned Georgina on the way to say she had to divert into Maidstone and so she'd be here about ten o'clock yesterday morning.'

'And never arrived.'

'Any idea where she was going in Maidstone?' said Barnes. 'Or who she was meeting?'

'I haven't delved into the details yet,' Hazel replied. 'I thought I'd leave that for you – Georgina's been asking a lot of questions since we arrived, and she's obviously distraught.'

'That's understandable.' Kay eyed the closed door to their left. 'Through here?'

'Yes. Diane's in uniform because she was on duty in Sittingbourne when we were summoned.'

'Thanks.'

Steeling herself for a moment, Kay then opened the

door and entered a plush living room that, despite looking comfortable, still managed to shelter itself from the summer warmth outside.

A clean hearth filled half of the far wall, and she dreaded to think how cold the house could get during the winter months. The only window overlooked the driveway, and the plasterwork walls had been painted a dark green, accentuating the Victorian architecture.

Two sofas were set opposite each other beside the fireplace, and two women looked up from where they were sitting on one of them as she walked in.

The trainee family liaison officer was in her mid-forties with short brown hair that skimmed her collar, her eyes kindly as she waited for introductions to be made.

Kay's gaze met Georgina Leneghan's and in that moment she knew she would do everything possible to bring the monster that had killed the woman's only daughter to justice.

'I'm Detective Inspector Kay Hunter, and this is my colleague, DS Ian Barnes. We're so sorry for your loss,' she said, sitting on the opposite sofa.

Georgina nodded, dabbing at her nose with a crumpled paper tissue. 'I've heard of you. You found that little girl that went missing a few years ago, didn't you?'

'I did, yes.'

'Tell me, detective. Do you have children?'

Kay blinked, the question an obvious one from a grieving mother, but the answer to which was something very few people knew. She sensed Barnes stiffen next to her, and gave a slight shake of her head. 'I don't, no.'

The woman before her sniffed. 'Tansy is… was… oh…'

Giving Georgina a moment to grieve, Kay looked down at her hands, her fingernails driving into the soft flesh of her palms. When she looked up, Diane was murmuring to the woman, who nodded in response and wiped at her eyes.

'You need to ask me some questions, don't you?' she said, raising her chin a little.

'We do, yes.' Kay forced her shoulders to relax while Barnes flipped to a clean page in his notebook. 'And I'm sorry if these sound repetitive, but I need to understand Tansy's plans for Friday from every angle. You've told Hazel and Diane that she left work early Friday afternoon to come here. How long had you planned this weekend with her for?'

'It was a last-minute thing,' said Georgina. 'She phoned me last Monday in a bit of a rush, and asked if she could come and stay. Of course, I didn't hesitate and said yes. We chat on the phone at least once a week but what with her work and catching up with her friends over the summer and everything, she hadn't managed to get down here since late May.'

'What does she drive?'

Georgina told her, reciting the licence plate from memory, a slight smile crossing her lips. 'I have a knack for remembering things like that. She used to tease me about it.'

'What about Tansy's father?'

'He left when she was three years old. Neither of us

have any contact with him. I don't even know where he lives these days.'

'We'll need a name, just to eliminate him from our investigation – and he needs to be told what's happened. Would you mind?'

Georgina sighed. 'It's Joseph Throndsen. I don't have an address for him, and I have no idea what his phone number is. I don't really want anything to do with him. Neither did Tansy, which is why she uses my maiden name, not his.'

'That's okay, I understand. I can assure you we won't pass on your details to him. If he wants to get in touch, I'll let you know, and you can make that decision,' Kay said. 'Can you recall what time Tansy phoned you to say she was going to Maidstone before getting here?'

'It was just gone three fifteen. She got stuck in traffic at the Leatherhead junction she said, so originally I thought she was phoning to let me know she'd been delayed. Then she said something had cropped up and she had to go and see someone before coming here. When I asked her what time she'd be here, she said sorry, and that she might have to stay overnight and so she'd aim to get here for ten o'clock yesterday.'

'How did she seem to you when she called?'

Georgina leaned back, her gaze drifting to the swirls of colour in the thick carpet before speaking. 'I was going to say coy, like she did the last time she told me about a new boyfriend, but it was more than that... *evasive*, that's the word I'm looking for. And she changed the subject.'

'Did she sound worried, or raise any concerns with you?'

'Not worried, no. Maybe like she had something on her mind, because I asked if everything was okay and she insisted it was. Then she said she ought to go as the traffic was starting to speed up again and she knows I worry about her talking on the phone while driving, even if she is using the hands-free. I told her I loved her, and that I'd see her soon. I…'

Fresh tears ran down Georgina's face, and Kay's heart crumpled at the sight of a mother who had lost a child in such terrible circumstances.

After reassuring her that she would do everything she could to find the person responsible, she led Barnes from the room and out the front door.

Heat and light seized her as she walked down the steps, and she paused for a moment out of sight of the living room window to close her eyes and bathe under the sun's rays. The warmth seeped through her clothes, through her skin and into her bones, softening the chill from the house behind her and all its grief.

'You okay, guv?' Barnes said, his footsteps shuffling on the gravel a few metres away.

Opening her eyes, she sniffed, then nodded. 'Yeah. Thanks.'

'Want to go and get a coffee before we head back to the incident room?'

'No, that's okay.' She shot him a grateful look, then stalked towards the car. 'I want to find the bastard who did this.'

FOURTEEN

Laura glanced down at another text message from the incident room on her phone, then looked across the road at the 1950s semi-detached house sheltering behind a shrivelled privet hedge that had seen better days.

She and Kyle had parked on one of the older residential estates in this part of Maidstone, the houses once owned by the local council and similar in design to many post-war buildings across Kent.

The gardens were larger than those of later properties along the road and each backed onto Mote Park, making them a high priority for the investigating team.

Larger than most contemporary homes, the house in front of her had large bay windows either side of a front door sheltered by a porch and a wide sloping red tiled roof. Both it and the neighbouring property bore a beige render that had been recently repainted, unlike some of the others at the far end of the street.

The spacious driveway to the side of it had been given over to a motley collection of cars and a sign over the top of a separate single cinderblock garage proclaimed it to be "Torsney's Motors".

A set of double corrugated iron doors were chocked open with a pair of house bricks, and she could hear the sound of an angle grinder from somewhere within the darkened interior. An occasional shower of sparks accompanied the noise and she automatically checked her watch, wondering if the neighbours were receiving a rude awakening.

Tugging her sunglasses down, she swore under her breath as they caught in her hair, then dropped them onto her nose and glanced over her shoulder as the car door slammed.

'Reckon I'll let you lead this one,' she said.

Kyle Walker shrugged his jacket over his shoulders and joined her, shoving the keys into his pocket before staring at her, a bemused expression on his face. 'Your hair's still standing up on end.'

'Shit.' She smoothed it down, then took off her sunglasses and put them in her bag. 'Thanks.'

He grinned and jerked his chin towards the house. 'How long has this bloke been running a business from home?'

'Ever since he retired as a mechanic from one of the big dealerships off the Loose road eight years ago,' Laura said. 'Gareth does MOTs, servicing, that sort of thing. He was out yesterday when Aaron's team were doing the house-to-house enquiries but they spoke to his wife. She said they hadn't noticed anything untoward on Friday night or Saturday morning but she told them Gareth has security cameras around the place and that we could have copies of the recordings. He gets a better deal on his business insurance for having them, especially as a similar place a mile down the road from here got broken into two years ago.'

'This place backs onto the park, right?'

'Yes, one of the uniformed lot took a look while they were here yesterday – there's a panel fence that's six foot high between the garden and a huge bramble hedge, but no sign of anyone climbing over it.'

The angle grinder whirred to a standstill and she was suddenly aware of the cheerful cooing of a wood pigeon from within a cherry tree beside the front gate. Someone was whistling along with an old rock song on a radio that kept a steady beat before a hammer joined in, the steady *whack* of metal on metal escaping through the doors.

'What time is it?' said Kyle.

'Just gone half ten.' She grinned. 'Wonder what time he started?'

'I don't know, but what do you say we give the neighbours a bit of a respite?'

'Good idea.'

She followed her colleague up the driveway and past the cars lined up either side. Some were worse for wear – one looked like it had suffered a rear-end shunt that had merely served to knock the existing rust off the bodywork – but two were gleaming as if just off a used car forecourt.

A man in his late sixties emerged from the garage wiping greasy hands on a once-blue towel, then twitched a black baseball cap around to shield his eyes. 'The missus said to expect the police this morning. I take it that's you?'

'Detective Constable Laura Hanway, and this is my colleague, Kyle Walker. And you're—'

'Gareth Torsney. Want a cuppa?'

'No, but thanks for the offer. Are we interrupting you?'

'Yes.' A mischievous twitch at the corner of Torsney's left eye softened his words. 'But I charge double on weekends, and the customer can afford it, so…'

'We'll keep it brief.'

'Come on in out of the sun. It's cooler in here. Just watch your step – I've got the air pressure hose out, and I don't want to have to explain to my insurers how I managed to trip up a detective if you hurt yourself.'

'Do all of these cars belong to customers, Mr Torsney?' said Laura, blinking to counteract the sudden gloom as she followed the two men into the garage.

'All except the blue convertible over near the house. The two newer ones are just in for MOTs. Three are waiting for parts that should come in tomorrow if there isn't another hold-up across the Channel, and one's due to be picked up and paid for later today. That old hatchback is the one I'm working on at the moment.' Torsney reached a long workbench that stretched the width of the garage and then turned, reaching into the breast pocket of his oil-flecked overalls. 'Before I forget, I copied the security footage off my cameras for you onto a stick.'

'Thanks,' said Kyle taking the USB. 'How much is on here?'

'I figured you'd want a couple of days maybe before the girl was found, so you've got from Wednesday onwards there, which is when the festival started letting in campers anyway.'

'That's great.' Kyle pocketed the memory stick, provided a receipt for it and then frowned. 'How'd you fit all of the footage onto this?'

'It's not a live feed. It's motion sensor only, so it saves file space. I don't know if the missus told you, but we've got four cameras, one on each corner of the house so two facing the road and driveway, then another two facing the garden – and the fence separating us from the park.'

'We understand you were out when our colleagues spoke to your wife yesterday. Where were you?'

'In Dorset. Me and some mates went along to a big tank display at Bovington museum.'

'Tanks?'

'Yeah. Armoured vehicles, y'know? We drove down Wednesday night. I only came back yesterday afternoon 'cause her indoors said there'd been a murder in the park and I didn't like the idea of her being in the house on her own last night.' Torsney visibly shivered. 'Doesn't bear thinking about. D'you know who she is yet?'

'We can't comment on an active investigation. What time did you get back?'

'About half eight. Traffic was pretty bad along the motorway as usual.'

'We'll need a note of the people you were with.'

Torsney looked taken aback. 'Why? I just told you where I was.'

'It's standard protocol, that's all,' said Kyle smoothly, turning to a fresh page in his notebook.

Laura bit back the small smile that threatened to form, pleased that her colleague let the silence endure rather than give the man any further reassurance.

The garage owner sighed, then reeled off the names of three other men, all with local addresses. 'I doubt they'll be back until this afternoon though. The museum was promising to fire up the Tiger tank this morning and that's really all we went there for. You should hear them engines when they start it up. Fair shakes your ribs around it does.'

Kyle snapped shut the notebook and glanced at Laura. 'Did you have anything else?'

'No, I think that's all. Thanks for your time, Mr Torsney,' she said. 'And thanks for the memory stick too. We'll be in touch again if we have any questions about the security footage. Could you make sure you keep the original recordings until we tell you otherwise?'

''Course, no problem. Mind you don't trip over that air hose on your way out…'

FIFTEEN

By the time Kay crossed the room to her temporary desk, a late afternoon sun shone through the incident room windows, its golden light bathing the plain plasterwork walls and softening the harshness of the otherwise utilitarian decor.

A faint murmur of voices carried over to where she collapsed into her chair and spun it around to face the whiteboard, the conversations muted after the news of their victim's identity had spread.

Exhaustion seeped through the team, the hours spent in front of computer screens and reading reports from the previous day's house-to-house enquiries starting to take its toll as they sought answers to the questions on everyone's mind.

Who killed Tansy Leneghan?

And, why?

Kay and Sharp had chosen to withhold the update from the media until the morning, giving a bereaved mother a few precious hours to grieve in private. However, once

Tansy's details were released, she knew she and her team would become the target of their and the reading public's rage at the young woman's murder.

At least until they found the person responsible.

Barnes walked back from the printer on the far side of the room, and handed her a warm sheaf of documents. 'That's the agenda for the briefing, guv. Do you want me to round up everyone?'

'Please. We're going to have to work hard to stay ahead of the media on this one now.' She stiffened as he emitted a loud whistle that carried across the room. 'Jesus, Ian – that'll wake them up.'

He grinned. 'That was the idea.'

It didn't take long for Kay's team to assemble around the whiteboard with her, and when the last officer had joined them, she rapped her knuckles against the photograph pinned to the top of the board.

'As most of you have heard, we now have a name for our victim. Tansy Leneghan, twenty-four years old and a Bristol resident, although her mother lives locally. She was last heard from at three fifteen on Friday afternoon when she phoned her mother to say she had to make a diversion into Maidstone to meet with someone. She didn't tell her who that was, and she was never seen alive again.'

Kay let her words sink in, the soft hum of computers the only sound while her officers digested the information. 'Her mother has provided us with a note of Tansy's employer in Bristol, and we're going to have to get a list of her friends' names from her social media profiles so we can speak to them. Given time and budget restrictions, all of those interviews will need to be carried out via phone or video link rather than anyone travelling to Bristol – the Avon and Somerset force don't have the resources to help us either. Gavin, can you divide up the interviews between yourself, Laura and Kyle with as many other officers as you can corral and make a start on that this afternoon? I realise some of those people might not be available but we need to make some headway.'

'Will do, guv.'

'Ian, I'd like you to get someone to try and track down this Joseph Throndsen, Tansy's father. Don't forget we've got the post mortem to go to at eleven tomorrow morning.'

Her DS nodded. 'We should have Harriet's preliminary findings by Tuesday afternoon as well, so with any luck that'll help us piece together Tansy's final hours.'

'Exactly, that's what I'm hoping.' Kay turned to a map of Mote Park that had been pinned to the wall beside the whiteboard. 'Despite the manpower issues we've got, there's a team of uniformed officers still searching the park and its perimeter at the moment. They'll have a few more hours of daylight today, but the longer it takes, the less likely it is that they'll find anything. There's over four hundred and fifty acres of land here, and numerous ways to get out of the park without using one of the marked exits. If we don't get some results from the search they're doing or the CCTV footage we've obtained so far, we're going to be struggling for answers.'

A collective sigh filled the room, and she held up her hand in response. 'That doesn't mean we give up. Once we have that list of friends and colleagues from Tansy's social media profile, your priority will be to find out if Tansy told any of them who she was planning to meet on Friday afternoon – just because she didn't tell Georgina until she was nearly here, it doesn't mean her friends weren't aware of her arrangements. And on that note, Laura – can you phone around hotels and guesthouses to see if Tansy made a booking? She was obviously planning to stay overnight somewhere on the Friday night if she wasn't going to her mother's, so we need to eliminate those rather than assuming she was staying with someone locally.'

'Yes, guv.'

'Are there any other matters that need to be raised?' Kay ran her gaze across the assembled officers, then spotted a raised hand. 'Debbie?'

'Guv, just a quick update with regard to officers joining the team from tomorrow morning – they were rostered off over the weekend. PCs Nadine Fleming and Sean Gastrell, and Sergeant Tim Wallace.'

'That's great, thanks.' Kay checked her watch. 'Okay, there's only so much you're going to be able to get done today given the time, so I want you all in here by seven thirty tomorrow morning. We'll have a briefing early afternoon once the post mortem is complete, but if you find out anything in the meantime, make sure you let myself or DS Barnes know immediately. Let's get on with it.'

'That's good about the extra help,' Barnes said as the team moved back to their desks. 'Some good officers, too.'

'They are,' she said, eyeing the additional tasks now written on the whiteboard. 'And we're going to need them.'

SIXTEEN

The next morning, Gavin straightened his tie, then took a quick slurp from a can of energy drink before placing it beside a row of lever arch files lining the back of the desk.

The box-sized meeting room was one of three squashed into the western end of the police station, and by the mustiness of the air, he suspected that until two days ago, it had been used as a storage cupboard.

He ran a hand across his spiky hair and shuffled in the swivel chair which had half of its foam padding hanging out from a hole in the side of the cushion and one of its casters perilously close to falling off.

It squeaked as he settled in to wait for the video call to begin, the sound accompanied by the persistent *tick tick* of the wall clock above his head and the tapping of his pen on a fresh page of his notebook.

A red LED light shone above the screen-mounted camera, and an automated message below informed him that the person he was waiting to meet with was on another call.

'Come on,' he muttered. 'I've got another six of these to do this morning.'

There was a soft *ping* and the screen flickered before the connection was made, and a man in his mid-forties appeared at the other end, his shirt sleeves rolled up.

His face was pale, but Gavin wasn't sure whether that was the effect of the camera the man was using, the video conferencing software, or the news that had been delivered by phone to Tansy's employer that morning by one of the uniformed officers on the team.

'Detective Piper, sorry to keep you,' he began. 'Especially in the circumstances. I can't begin to describe how devastated we all are here. I've had to send two members of staff home, they're so distraught.'

'Thanks for making time for me, Mr Paget. If you wouldn't mind, I'll skip the pleasantries – as you can appreciate, we've got a lot of people to speak to this morning.'

'Absolutely. No problem.' Paget settled back in a plush leather-looking chair that looked several times more comfortable than Gavin's. He seemed at ease in front of the camera. 'What can I tell you? Tansy was a model employee. We were lucky to get her – she had three other job offers open to her at the time, but decided ours was the best long-term option for her career prospects.'

'I understand from Tansy's mother that you run an advertising agency. What sort of clients do you work for?'

'Mostly local high-end companies, then there are some large hotel chains with interests in the city and one or two charitable trusts. We're a small company – there are only twelve employees. We're privately owned, with myself being one of the shareholders, and we've been active for about fifteen years. Tansy joined us earlier this year and fitted in right away.' Paget paused, his face crestfallen. 'I can't believe we're having this conversation.'

'What did you know of her plans for this past weekend? We've been led to believe that she left work early on Friday.'

'That's right. She came to see me on Tuesday afternoon to ask if she could leave at lunchtime on Friday – it was a bit short notice, but her work was up to date and she had no meetings booked in for that afternoon, so I said yes. As it was, she came in early that day to make up some of the time, and then left at one o'clock.'

'Did she tell you where she was going, and why?'

'She told my wife, who manages the HR side of things here, that she was going to see her mum. We knew she was in Kent – she's listed on Tansy's personnel file as her next of kin – so we didn't enquire further.'

Gavin updated his notes, then looked up at the screen once more. 'Did she mention anything about a last-minute change to her plans to see her mother?'

'Not that I can recall, no.'

The door opened to Gavin's right, and he glanced over to see Laura peering in, excitement in her eyes. He held up a hand to her, then turned back to Paget. 'And how did she seem on Friday, before she left the office?'

'A bit concerned about what the traffic might be like around the M25,' said Paget. 'But I wouldn't say she seemed anxious or anything. I mean, you know what that road's like on a Friday anyway, which is why she was leaving early to beat the worst of it. I didn't get the impression she was worried about anything else though.'

Gavin could sense Laura's eyes boring into the back of his head as she shut the door and hovered just out of sight of the camera, and quickly scanned the answers Paget had provided.

'Is there anything else you can tell me that might help our investigation?' he said. 'Anything at all?'

Tansy's boss gave a sad shrug. 'Not that I can think of. I certainly can't imagine why anyone would want to murder her. She was such a sweet person to have around the office. Conscientious in her work, but also compassionate for her colleagues. Like I said, we're going to miss her.'

'Okay, thanks, Mr Paget. We'll be in touch if we have anything further.'

Gavin ended the call and swung round in his chair to face Laura, the damaged caster squeaking ominously. 'What is—'

'I've found where Tansy was meant to be staying on Friday night,' she said, her words escaping in a rush. 'And they've still got her belongings.'

SEVENTEEN

Kay shrugged off her jacket, tossed it onto the back seat of Barnes's car and slammed the door shut before glaring at the glass double doors a few metres away from the hospital car park.

Her colleague walked towards her, shaking his head. 'Honestly, guv – what they charge for parking here, I reckon we ought to get our own exclusive space. With complimentary car wash.'

She grinned. 'Stop moaning – it's not like you're really paying for it, not when you're going to add it to your expenses.'

'Which then take two months to process.' He placed the ticket stub on the dashboard and locked the car. 'So... what d'you reckon he's going to find?'

'I honestly don't know, Ian.' She led the way across a service road and into the hospital wing, following the signs to the X-ray department. 'I've learned to not make assumptions as to the why and how people kill each other. It can get too depressing sometimes.'

They stepped to one side to let an orderly with a patient in a wheelchair pass, and then Kay took one look at the elevators, both of which had indicator lights showing they were resolutely stuck at the top floor, and headed for the stairs instead.

'Whatever he finds, I hope it bloody helps,' she said, reaching the landing and pulling open a heavy fire door. 'Because we've got very little else at the moment.'

When they entered the box-like reception area the mortuary assistant, Simon Winter, was hunched over his computer, the sleeves of his protective coveralls rolled up to his elbows.

He peered over the screen and gestured to a room off to his right. 'Morning, detectives. Lucas is already in the examination room. I'm just double-checking some details on our system before I join him.'

'How many have you got today?' said Kay, signing the register before passing the pen to Barnes.

'We've already done two and there are another three after yours,' said Simon, pushing back his chair and gathering pages off a printer as they emerged. He shot her a tired smile. 'Not to mention the paperwork.'

'We'll be in as quickly as we can.'

Five minutes later and clad head to toe in protective coveralls, she followed Barnes through a set of thick double doors with no windows and entered the cool enclosed environment of Lucas's examination room.

A pair of large deep stainless-steel sinks took up the far side of the room, with two metal gurneys spaced evenly apart so that post mortems could be carried out in tandem if the need arose – and if the staff were available to do so.

The Home Office pathologist stood beside the gurney at the far end, bent at the waist while he used a wicked-looking blade to slice around their victim's internal organs.

Kay paused a moment, the stench seeping through her mask which had seemed robust enough when she first put it on, and now seemed flimsy and unable to prevent the remnant smell from someone's intestines overwhelming her senses.

She blinked, then caught up with Barnes as he circled the gurney, eventually standing at Tansy's feet in silence rather than interrupt Lucas's train of thought.

The pathologist kept a running commentary into a microphone hanging from the ceiling while he worked, glancing up once to acknowledge their presence with a cursory nod, then refocusing on the victim.

Simon tracked back and forth between the gurney and the equipment laid out on a highly polished steel workbench opposite the sinks, carrying bowls containing the organs as they were removed, weighing them and adding his findings to Lucas's commentary as they worked.

Kay craned her neck to see past him and spotted rows of glass vials containing various samples and swabs that had been taken prior to her arrival, and wondered which of them would provide the answers she needed – and whether any of them contained the evidence needed to apprehend a vicious killer.

Her fingers dug into her palms through her protective gloves, and she forced herself to relax when she realised how hard she was clenching her jaw.

Finally, Lucas stepped back from the gurney, placed

his scalpel on a tray of bloodied instruments beside him and pointed towards the sinks.

She and Barnes trailed after him, waiting while he stripped off his gloves and shoved them into a biohazard bin before thoroughly soaping his hands under the taps.

That done, he lowered his mask and turned back to the gurney, leaning against the sink. 'I'll obviously have my report to you as soon as we can get it done, but I can confirm Tansy was killed by strangulation. Based on my observations at the scene and clarifications I've made today, I'd say her death occurred between one and five o'clock on Saturday morning.'

Kay exhaled, closing her eyes for a moment.

'Did she die where she was found?' Barnes asked.

As Kay opened her eyes, she saw Lucas grimace. 'What?'

'If it weren't for the fact I've seen too many pass through here over the years, I might say yes,' the pathologist said, rubbing his chin. 'But the lividity isn't quite right – if she had been killed where she was found, I'd expect to see more discolouration in the skin on the lower side.'

'I sense a "however",' said Kay.

'Mmm, and you'd be right. There is trace lividity on other parts of her body, which to me suggests that she was on her side for a time, and then rolled onto her back.'

Barnes frowned. 'For that to happen, she'd have needed to be on her side for at least half an hour or so, wouldn't she?'

'We usually say between thirty minutes and four hours, so yes, that's entirely possible.'

'So, was she moved from one location to where she was found?'

Lucas shook his head. 'I don't think so. I believe she was killed where she was found. Check with Harriet, though – her final report might help corroborate that.'

'Why would someone kill her, then go back and move her onto her back?' Kay said, turning her attention back to the gurney where Simon was starting to carefully collect the discarded surgical instruments.

In reply, Lucas replaced his mask and beckoned to them. 'Come and have a look.'

Despite the sight of her victim's body torn apart in the need for answers, Kay's inquisitiveness got the better of her and she joined the pathologist beside Tansy as he plucked a fresh pair of gloves from Simon and used his little finger to point out a series of bruises on the woman's neck.

'D'you see here? These are fingerprints, left behind by whoever strangled her. Despite what some people think, it's not easy to strangle someone and she put up a fight – hence the bruising to the knuckles. She's got a nasty bruise on her cheekbone here, look, which suggests to me that at some point during the attack she was punched.'

'To stop her fighting back,' Kay murmured.

'Exactly.' Lucas then moved to Tansy's limbs, the small stab wounds raw under the bright spotlights in the ceiling. 'However, these – and I suspect the removal of her fingertips – is different.'

'In what way?'

In response, he lifted one of Tansy's hands by the wrist and slowly turned it over to reveal another bruise.

'Because whoever did that gripped her like this while he removed them.'

Kay stared at the thumb-sized bruise that stained the alabaster skin and then glanced up at Lucas. 'I don't understand.'

'Tansy was strangled by someone,' he said. 'But then these stab wounds were inflicted before her fingertips were sliced away.'

'Why would her killer do that?' said Barnes.

'You know me better than to ask me to hazard a guess, Ian.'

'But off the record?'

'Maybe whoever did this to her thought they'd killed her but then had doubts and went back to check. Maybe she was still alive, and they lost their temper, hence the rage behind these stab wounds.' He sighed. 'Or maybe you need to look for two suspects, not one.'

EIGHTEEN

Laura almost had her car door open by the time Gavin pulled the hastily arranged pool vehicle into a space beside the hotel entrance.

Her heart racing, excitement turned to impatience while her colleague reached onto the back seat for his suit jacket, then paused to check his phone for messages.

She turned away, eyeing the twin brick pillars and angled tiles that formed a portico above a set of glass reception doors that sparkled in the early afternoon light, the aluminium handles gleaming.

To either side of the doors were a pair of deep rustic-looking horse troughs that had been filled with different coloured grasses, the flowering ones attracting a myriad of small bees that ducked and dived amongst the foliage.

The hotel spread out to the left and right of the reception block, its red brickwork exuding warmth. The windows were coated with a darkened privacy tint that she was sure helped keep some of the heat from the rooms as well.

Somewhere above her, on the roof, she could hear the steady whirr of air-conditioning units battling the midday temperatures and wondered whether the architects had been chastised for the oversight in providing windows that could open and let in fresh air.

Then she heard the rumble and honk of a large articulated truck thunder along the motorway behind the building and changed her mind.

'Sorry, ready now.'

She turned at Gavin's voice and raised an eyebrow. 'Anything?'

'Barnes says they're on the way back from the post mortem, and that Kay wants to speak to us before the briefing when we get back.'

'Problem?' she said, leading the way towards the entrance.

'No, I don't think so. I think she just wants to run a few things past us before speaking to the whole team, especially given this breakthrough of yours.' He smiled, holding open the door for her. 'After you.'

Despite its close proximity to both a busy ring road and the motorway, an aura of calm enveloped Laura when the glass doors swished closed behind them, and she could hear soft music bubbling through concealed speakers as her heels clacked across the polished tile floor towards the reception desk.

Two men and a woman were on duty, their simple dark blue uniforms looking a little dull under the harsh spotlights above their computers, and Laura felt goosebumps rising on her arms under the brittle air being pumped into the open space through a series of large vents in the ceiling tiles.

She fished out her warrant card as she approached the shorter of the two men, introducing herself and Gavin.

'Ah, yes – I'm Warren,' he said. 'I spoke to you on the phone.'

'Has anyone checked into the room since Miss Leneghan was here?' she said.

'No, but that's only because we were able to accommodate guests elsewhere.' He shot a sideways glance at his colleagues. 'Apart from putting her belongings in a safe place, there isn't a procedure about what to do if a guest disappears so we've just left her stuff in her room and told housekeeping to hang fire cleaning it until she gets in touch. Is she okay?'

Laura paused a moment too long, and the man's colleagues let out a collective gasp.

'Is she... is she dead?' the other man stammered. 'I heard that a woman's body was found in the park during the festival. Was that her?'

'I'm afraid we can't comment about an ongoing investigation,' said Gavin stiffly. 'What time did Miss Leneghan check in?'

Warren's fingers tapped efficiently across his keyboard. 'I've got her booking here. She made it direct with us rather than through one of the travel apps on Thursday afternoon, and requested a late checkout for yesterday. She was lucky to get a room actually – with the festival on, and this being one of our busiest times of the year, we didn't have many available over the weekend.'

'The time?' Laura prompted.

'Oh, sorry. Five oh three on Friday afternoon.' He picked up a pair of reading glasses from beside his keyboard and peered at the screen again. 'She didn't book in to the restaurant that night though. We always insist on a table reservation at this time of year because it gets so busy.'

'Were any of you on duty on Friday?' She pulled out a photograph of Tansy that Georgina had provided. 'Do you remember seeing her?'

'I was,' said the woman. 'But sorry – it was busy, I don't recall her name and only vaguely remember her. I had a party of thirty pensioners on a coach tour to France to check in, and they were... particularly demanding.'

'Are the reception doors kept locked at any time?'

'From eleven o'clock onwards in the summer,' said Warren. 'Guests are provided with a pass card to access the hotel out of hours – those doors stay locked until four in the morning when we start receiving deliveries for the kitchen.' He pointed over her shoulder. 'There's an intercom just outside the doors for out of hours check-ins.'

'Are you able to tell which guests enter and exit the building with those pass cards?'

'We can, yes.'

'Can you look up on your system if Miss Leneghan went in or out of the hotel between eleven and four?'

'Of course. One moment.' He clicked to another screen. 'It says she went out at one in the morning.'

Laura's heart leapt. 'Do you have CCTV in your car park? We'd need to see the recordings from Friday to see which direction she went in when she left here.'

'Oh, she didn't drive,' said the other man. 'At least, I don't think so.'

'What makes you say that?'

'Because her car's still parked out there.'

NINETEEN

Kay craned her neck to see across the dual carriageway of the ring road to where a collection of Kent Police-liveried vehicles and plain-coloured vans were parked in front of the hotel.

Turning away while Barnes eased off the brake, she glared at the bumper stickers covering the SUV in front of them as he inched the car forward another few paces.

Her fist beat against the door armrest, the knowledge that one of her team had secured a valuable breakthrough tempered with the fact that they now had more questions than answers about Tansy Leneghan's final hours.

And the fact that she was currently sat next to Barnes, stuck in traffic that crawled tantalisingly close to where the rest of her team worked.

'Come on,' she muttered.

'If Traffic had let us borrow one of its four-by-fours I could've just driven across the central reservation and down the hill,' said Barnes.

Despite herself, Kay laughed. 'Yeah, I'd like to see you explain that manoeuvre to Sharp.'

'What about switching on the lights then?'

'Don't you dare. I've already had to have a quiet word with Kyle after someone from Jasper's team dobbed him in.'

Barnes grinned before swinging into the far lane for the roundabout, and then powered through a set of traffic lights as they turned red. 'You didn't see that.'

'Ian…' She rolled her eyes. 'I wouldn't mind but you're meant to be setting a good example to the rest of the team.'

'That was a fantastic example of—'

'Not what I meant.'

Her mood sobered when he parked behind one of the plain-coloured vans, the ones that Harriet's team always used that bore no insignia or telltale clues regarding the contents.

There was a second identical van parked a few metres away with its side panel door opened facing away from any onlookers along the main road while a CSI technician pulled on fresh coveralls and donned a mask. The figure closed the door once fully encased in their protective clothing and shuffled towards the hotel entrance, carrying a boxy metal suitcase that Kay guessed contained a myriad of delicate instruments that were crucial to the forensic team's work.

She climbed out and peered over the roof to see three patrol cars and Gavin's allocated pool car, a silver hatchback with a scuffed front bumper.

The detective constable was standing beside it, his

phone to his ear, and he raised his hand in greeting as she and Barnes walked towards him.

'I've let Debbie know the briefing will probably be delayed by an hour or so, guv,' he said, ending the call. 'Hope that's all right – I figured we might have more to share with the rest of the team along with your post mortem thoughts by then.'

She shot him a grateful smile. 'Good idea. Okay, what's been going on here?'

'Laura found out that Tansy booked into this place, and when we got here and spoke to the receptionist, he informed us that her belongings were still in her room. The hotel records show that she used her pass card to leave the building at one in the morning on Friday night, and they're inclined to think she didn't take her car, given that it's still here – look.'

He led them round the parked patrol cars, pointing to a late model hatchback that had been reversed into a space by a thick privet hedge. 'It hasn't moved since she got here, according to the reception team, but we're obtaining copies of their CCTV footage to corroborate that.'

'So maybe someone picked her up, then...' Kay watched while a group of three forensic technicians edged their way around the vehicle, their movements meticulous while they swabbed and photographed, the taller of the group crouching beside the open driver's door while he used a pair of tweezers to pluck fibres from the upholstery. 'Or she walked. Any sign of a struggle in her room?'

'Not at first glance, no. Although we didn't enter it – once reception gave us a master pass card we just opened the door to check what they said about her stuff being there, and then called Harriet. If you want to go and have a look, we've been allocated a meeting room to suit up in. Laura's currently taking statements from staff members who were here Friday afternoon and Saturday morning, as well as finding out which cleaning staff had access to the room.'

'Okay, thanks. If I don't catch you when I leave here, I'll see you back at the station for the briefing.'

Barnes fell into step beside her as they entered the reception area, turning towards a door to the left of the main desk when a familiar forensic technician emerged, his protective mask pulled down and a clutch of empty evidence bags in his hand.

'Patrick, is Harriet upstairs?' she said.

'Downstairs, actually.' The CSI pushed back the hood of his overalls for a moment. He lowered his voice as a couple in their sixties walked past, their eyes widening at the activity all around them. 'The victim was allocated a single room at the back of the complex – apparently it's all that was available at short notice.'

'Gavin said we could get changed somewhere and take a look.'

'Sure, you'll find all you need through there.' Patrick jabbed his thumb over his shoulder. 'Once you're ready, just follow this corridor along until you find us. We've blocked off access to other guests until we're finished. Luckily the hotel manager's been able to move them to temporary accommodation at the other end of the building so we can work in peace. They're happy, as most of them got an upgrade.'

'See you down there.'

After struggling into a set of protective coveralls and donning matching booties over her shoes, Kay padded back and forth outside the door until Barnes was ready, then shuffled along a wide corridor towards Tansy Leneghan's room.

The hotel decor was similar in style to many of the roadside motels she had stayed in over the years, except the fixtures and fittings were of a higher quality and the paintwork on the walls was evidently maintained on a regular basis, given the lack of scuff marks from wayward suitcases and housekeeping trolleys.

The corridor dog-legged to the right, past a sign tacked to an A-frame board advertising an indoor pool and weights room that was on the other side of the building for guests' use, and then Kay turned the corner and saw the forensic team's equipment laid out across the floor a few metres away.

Murmured voices carried through an open door on the left, and after tiptoeing their way past the various carry cases strewn over the carpet, she and Barnes peered inside.

Harriet, only recognisable due to her short stature compared with the other two members of her team, had her back turned to the door while she dusted the window sill, her concentration absolute.

Kay waited until the CSI lead paused in her work, then gave a polite cough, the sound muffled behind her mask. 'Gavin said we'd find you here.'

Harriet stepped away from her work, handing a fine brush to one of her colleagues. 'This is going to take us the rest of the afternoon to process given all the guests that have passed through here. I mean, don't get me wrong –

the cleaners do a good job here, but there's always residual evidence of occupation in places like this.'

Kay wrinkled her nose, then looked across to the window. 'Did anyone come in through that? Does it even open?'

'Oh, it opens all right. Just not enough for anyone to get in or out of – not unless they're under nine years old anyway.' Harriet's eyes crinkled above her mask. 'Anyone else would be too big to wriggle through the gap. There's a hinge preventing the window from fully opening. Safety, I would think – it stops anyone breaking in.'

'What about Tansy's bags? Anything of interest in those?' Barnes said, pointing to where a small black nylon suitcase lay on a wooden rack, a canvas tote bag on the floor beside it.

'So far, we've only photographed them in situ – we haven't processed the contents yet. Are you still looking for her mobile phone?'

'Yes – it wasn't found during the search of the park, and no one's handed one in. The team back at the incident room checked with the festival's lost property lot this morning too, and they haven't been able to help us.'

'Hang on.' Kay took a few paces away from the door, unzipping her coveralls when she was safely away from the team's equipment, then pulled out her phone from her trouser pocket and hit speed dial. 'Debbie? Can you dig out Tansy's mobile number that her mum gave us and call it? Uniform tried the same trick this morning with the lost property. Thanks.'

She raised her gaze to see Barnes looking at her.

His head swivelled back to the room as a soft trill emanated from one of the bags.

'Got it, thanks, Debbie.'

Kay ended the call, rezippered her suit and joined him, holding her breath while Harriet began to lift one item after the other from the canvas tote bag.

Part of her wanted to stride across the room, rip the bag from Harriet's grasp and empty the contents onto the floor but she held back, knowing that every single piece of Tansy's belongings had to be processed carefully to maintain a chain of evidence.

Finally, Harriet held up a smart phone encased in a glittery pink hard plastic shell. 'It's got about five per cent battery life left.'

'Is it password protected?' Kay almost took a step forward into the room, catching herself at the last second.

'Yes.'

'Bugger. All right, we'll get someone from Andy Grey's team at digital forensics to deal with that.' She watched while Harriet went through the rest of the contents of the bag. 'Anything else in there that might help us?'

'I don't think so, not first impressions anyway.' The CSI lead held up a small make-up bag and a pack of tissues. 'We'll carry on here and I'll give you a call if anything else needs your immediate attention though if you like?'

'Thanks – we'll let you get on.'

Kay turned away from the room and stepped over a carry case containing a selection of sealed glass vials, then headed back along the corridor. 'Right, back to the incident room – let's find out if—'

She stopped, realising that her colleague wasn't following her, and turned to see him still standing by the open door of Tansy's room. 'Ian?'

He started at her voice, then hurried to catch up, dragging the protective hood of his coveralls from his head and lowering his mask. A frown puckered his forehead.

'Are you all right?'

Barnes glanced over his shoulder, then back to her. 'If she was meeting someone, guv, why didn't she take her phone with her?'

TWENTY

A distinct change in atmosphere greeted Kay when she walked into the incident room twenty minutes later.

The discovery of Tansy's whereabouts prior to her murder created an excitement amongst the rest of the team that emanated from the voices clamouring over the noise of ringing phones, and even the sight of over fifty new emails since her absence from the station failed to dampen her spirits.

That was until she joined Barnes beside the whiteboard and watched while he updated the notes there about Lucas's findings from that morning's post mortem.

'Two killers,' she murmured. 'Or, one killer and someone else who... what? What on earth were they doing, Ian?'

'I don't know, guv,' he said, recapping the pen and dropping it to the aluminium tray fixed to the underside of the board. 'I've been thinking about that, and—'

'Hold that thought a sec. Let's get everyone else over

here and discuss that and the other agenda items in one go rather than repeat ourselves.'

He peered past her, and then emitted a piercing whistle that carried across the room, and probably down the stairs to the cell block as well.

She saw two of the newer administrative assistants jump in their seats, and then the entire team scrambled towards them, dragging chairs with them or choosing to stand at the fringes of the group. 'You've got to teach me how to do that.'

'It's easy, you just put your lips together and blow,' he said, winking.

Rolling her eyes, she turned her attention to the team. 'Okay, we'll run through the agenda items in a minute but briefly, Lucas confirmed at the post mortem that one person strangled Tansy Leneghan and then either that person – or someone else – returned to her body and inflicted the stab wounds to her, and removed her fingertips to prevent, or at least delay us, identifying her.' She gestured to Barnes. 'Let's have your thoughts.'

'Right,' he said. 'If we take the theory that there are two people involved in Tansy's murder and subsequent mutilation of her body, I'm wondering if whoever removed her fingertips knew her killer, and if so why wait to do so? Lucas suggested there was a time delay between the two acts, so what happened? Did the killer go and fetch someone, or was that second person already at the park when Tansy was murdered? Or did the killer return to her body to remove her fingertips? And of course, was her killer – or the person who mutilated her body – known to her?'

A flurry of murmurs carried through the assembled officers when he finished speaking, and Kay gave them a moment to note down his suggestions before continuing.

'We'll have Harriet's report from the Mote Park crime scene sometime tomorrow, and given that she's currently at the hotel where Tansy was staying, I'd guess that's going to be later in the day now. However, one thing we will need to find out from that is whether there's evidence to help us to ascertain whether that particular theory can be substantiated, or whether there was only one killer.'

'Jesus, guv,' said Gavin. 'That's not going to be easy given the two volunteers trampled down a lot of the grass and dirt around the murder scene, let alone anyone else who was nearby before she was found. That is, if Lucas agrees that she was murdered there?'

'He reckons so, based on lividity and other observations that he'll include in his report. The lack of blood from the stab wounds is due to the fact she was strangled sometime before those were inflicted,' Kay said. 'Stopping her heart prevented the blood flow. But I take your point about how hard it's going to be to find anything to corroborate that theory.'

She searched the group, saw Laura, and waved her over. 'Can you update us with the latest findings from the hotel?'

The detective constable opened her notebook and faced the room. 'Briefly, Tansy phoned the hotel on Thursday to make a booking for Friday night. That was two days after she asked her boss if she could leave early on the Friday. She checked in, then left the hotel – either on foot or with someone else – at one o'clock in the morning.' Laura's face fell as she glanced over her shoulder at the photographs on the whiteboard. 'And soon after, someone did that to her.'

Kay let her colleague's words sink in for a moment before she spoke. 'Something happened between Tuesday when Tansy spoke to her boss and Thursday when she made the hotel booking. Up until that point she was planning to stay at her mother's house through to the Sunday. So, why didn't she tell Georgina about the change in plan straight away? Why wait? Why leave it that late to tell her she was going to meet someone in Maidstone? And what happened – or who did she speak to in the interim – that made her change her mind? Gavin, where are we up to with CCTV footage from the hotel?'

'They provided a copy of all the recordings before we left there earlier, guv,' he said. 'And I'm going to get someone to make a start on that while I'm finishing off the footage from the businesses around the Turkey Mill area and from the southern end of the park.'

'Thanks. Any other business before I start allocating tasks for the next forty-eight hours?'

'Guv?' Debbie raised her hand and then gestured to three young police constables who stood beside her. 'We've been given some more help with the investigation this afternoon so can I reintroduce PCs Nadine Fenning and Sean Gastrell and Sergeant Tim Wallace? I was going to ask Nadine and Sean to help out with the CCTV footage. Tim's available for additional support if you want that for witness interviews.'

'That's brilliant, thanks. And welcome back, you three. Good to have you here.' Kay ran her gaze down the agenda. 'Okay, Tim, can you liaise with Laura about the statements she's taken from hotel staff so far and help her trace anyone who wasn't working today who might've seen Tansy on Friday? We'll need those before Wednesday morning if possible.'

'Will do, guv.'

'Right, finally – gaps in our knowledge also include tracking down Tansy's father, this Joseph Throndsen that Georgina Leneghan told us about. She's given Dave Morrison this old photograph but it's over twenty years old and she says she's had no contact with him since he walked out on her when Tansy was three years old. That's now—'

'That's Joey,' Nadine exclaimed, then blushed as everyone turned to stare at her. 'Isn't it? I mean, the hair's shorter in that photo, and he's probably dyeing it these days.'

'Do you know him?' said Kay, incredulous. 'How?'

'Well, I don't exactly *know* him, guv…'

'Go on.'

'It's just that… I mean, I think it's Joey Twist.'

'Who?'

'Joey Twist. I only recognise him because it's been all over social media last week. I think he's the bass player in that band that were meant to be headlining on Saturday night, isn't he?'

TWENTY-ONE

'Okay, Nadine – I want you to work with Kyle to put together a full history on Throndsen, Twist, whoever he is,' said Kay, pacing the carpet.

Her thoughts tumbled over each other at the young police officer's identification of Tansy's father, and she paused in front of the whiteboard for a moment, forcing herself to concentrate and take one step at a time, just like her mentor Detective Chief Inspector Devon Sharp had instilled in her years ago.

'Ian, I need you to find out how we get in touch with him. Did that manager of theirs, Kasprak, give you a card when he saw us at the park on Saturday?'

'No, guv.'

'Me neither, but I'm sure he'll have a website for his company. Try there first, and if not it'll have to be an open source search – liaise with Nadine and Kyle if you need to do that, just to make sure you're not doubling up on what they've managed to find out.' Kay checked her watch. 'And I'd best give Sharp an update while you make a start on that. The rest of you, check your rosters for the rest of the week with Debbie. You'll find the latest task allocations in HOLMES2 but if you've got any questions come and speak to myself or DS Barnes.'

She waited while her officers and administrative staff returned to their desks, then picked up her purse and phone from beside her computer keyboard and headed for the door.

Once outside, she paused to inhale the fresher air at the side of the police station, then hurried round the corner to Palace Avenue and struck out towards the River Medway.

The shove and shunt of buses loaded with schoolchildren of all ages clogged the road, while cars and delivery vans zig-zagged between them along the dual lanes that curved around the town centre. The pavements were equally crowded, and she found herself dodging pushchairs and prams while fraught parents called to older siblings to stop running so close to the traffic.

Opting to dash through the stationary traffic at the junction rather than wait for the pedestrian crossing lights, she walked through the centuries-old graveyard of All Saints Church, its gothic design curving around a crooked path that wound its way beside ancient yew trees.

Moments later, she sank onto a wooden bench seat that was set in the crook of a sandstone wall beside the old college and breathed a sigh of relief as the traffic noise abated a little.

Here, she could hear herself think.

A loud quacking began upstream from her position, and her mouth quirked.

'That'll give the game away,' she murmured, pulling

out her phone and pressing the number for a familiar name.

'Kay? How's it going?' Sharp barked by way of greeting.

'Slowly, but I owe you a progress report,' she said, watching as four ducks drifted past on the current. 'We've had a couple of good breakthroughs today though.'

There was a pause at the other end of the phone after another loud quack, and then Sharp chuckled. 'Hiding in the usual spot?'

'Just for a bit. I'd never have been able to speak to you in peace otherwise.'

'Eaten anything today?'

Despite the strain she was under, Kay laughed. 'No, but—'

'I'll tell Rebecca.'

'No, don't, for goodness' sakes, guv.'

'All right, as long as you promise me you'll get something on the way back to the station. You're no good to the team if—'

Kay rolled her eyes. 'Guv, do you want to hear about the breakthroughs?'

It was his turn to laugh. 'Stop changing the subject, and yes – go on.'

She updated him about Laura's work finding where Tansy had been staying, and then the insight from Nadine as to who Tansy's father was.

Sharp gave a low whistle when she finished, one that was thankfully several decibels quieter than Barnes's. 'That's good going. So you're trying to pin him down for an interview I take it?'

'Yes, hopefully we can get him in for a formal one tomorrow morning. I presume they're still in the area because that concert on Saturday was meant to be kicking off their tour.'

'Hmm. Be interesting to hear what he's got to say for himself. You haven't told the media yet that you've identified Tansy, have you?'

'Not yet, and just as well if we're right about this bass player being her dad. Hell of a way for him to find out otherwise.'

'True.' Sharp paused. 'That name sounds familiar.'

'Well, they were quite a well-known band in certain circles for a time, guv.' She smiled.

'I don't mean musically. Throndsen, I mean. Who've you got doing the background checks on him?'

'Kyle, and Nadine, given she's the one who gave us the breakthrough. Barnes is currently tracking down the manager so we can arrange this interview. Why?'

She heard the shuffle of paperwork at the other end of the line, then a chair squeaked as if its occupant had leaned back in it before he replied.

'Have a look at arrests from twenty years ago, close to when the mother says he walked out on them,' he said. 'Might be nothing... I might've got my wires crossed, but just check to see if anything comes up.'

Kay's heart missed a beat. 'Do you think he's got previous?'

'Maybe. Worth a look, anyway. Like I said, I could be wrong but it's an unusual name.' Sharp paused and spoke to someone in the background before returning to her. 'I'm going to have to go. The Assistant Commissioner's requested my presence in a management meeting, and I'd hate to disappoint her.'

Kay heard the irony in his voice. 'We'll have to get you back here, guv, so you can teach the youngsters a thing or two.'

'Cheeky bugger.' He laughed. 'Call me if you need me, Kay.'

'Thanks.'

Ending the call, she stared at the screen for a moment, then saw the number of notifications on her email app, gave a last longing look at the tranquil waters of the river, and headed back to the incident room.

Via a café, just in case she bumped into Sharp's wife on the way.

TWENTY-TWO

Barnes was at his desk having an animated discussion with Nadine and Kyle when Kay walked back into the incident room.

She smiled at their expressions when she approached.

'I take it you've got some information for me,' she said, putting her half-finished can of soft drink beside her computer screen and leaning against her desk. 'Let's have it, and then I'll tell you what I've heard from Sharp.'

'Got him,' said Barnes, turning around his screen to face her. 'Joseph Throndsen, no middle name, born in Chatham, currently in his early fifties. He popped up on a website search in a story that was four years before Tansy was born.'

'What's the story?' Kay dropped to a crouch beside his chair and peered at the screen.

'Just an award that had been given to a local business he worked for – he was quoted as saying that the boss there was a good employer. There are a few quotes in the article like that,' Barnes said, scrolling down the page.

'Looks like this used to be an annual initiative for about six years up that way. The awards concentrated on North Kent small businesses, just to give them a bit of extra exposure I suspect. Nadine's checked the Companies House register and Throndsen's employer went tits up three years later.'

'So much for helping local business then.'

'Yeah.' Barnes chuckled. 'After that though, we lose him.'

'Lose him?'

'Throndsen. He must've changed his name by deed poll sometime around when Tansy was born.'

'Interesting.' Kay straightened as Kyle thrust a piece of paper at her. 'What's this?'

'A copy of an application to request more information from the National Archives about that name change, guv. They hold all the records up to 2003 so we can verify it that way. I put it in online just before you got back. The website says it can take up to ten days for a response, but I figured it'd be a good cross-check in case Joey Twist denies it.'

'Okay, thanks. When I spoke to Sharp, he said he recognised the name Joseph Throndsen. Have any of you checked our records for past convictions?'

'No convictions, guv,' said Nadine. 'But I can go through arrest records next.'

'Do it. I've never known Sharp to be wrong about something like this. Look a few years either side of that business award being handed out – Sharp said he thinks something happened around the time he walked out on Georgina and Tansy.'

'I'll do a search for companies around that time who were employing ex-offenders,' said Barnes. 'If this one that won the award shows up on the list, there might be someone around from that time who remembers Throndsen. We've already completed a social media search for the names on the Companies House register but some of the old networking contacts might still be around if we can cross-reference them somehow.'

'Good idea. How did you get on sorting out an interview with him – did you track down a phone number for his manager?'

'I did.' Barnes waved a pink sticky note at her. 'Kasprak and the band are currently holed up in a hotel in Brighton so he says he'll drive up with Throndsen – or Twist, as he's now known – tomorrow morning. I don't think they want us anywhere near the hotel. Too many fans around apparently.'

'Yeah, that'd put a dampener on the reunion tour, wouldn't it?' Kay eyed the whiteboard, all the threads in her mind slowly twisting into a tight knot that clenched her stomach. 'Do we know their planned movements while they're in Brighton?'

'Kasprak said they're playing an open-air festival down there over the weekend.' Barnes's lip curled. 'He said they're in "damage limitation mode" after their big comeback gig was cancelled.'

'Jesus.'

'We're going through the band's social media at the moment to try and see whether Tansy was following them,' said Kyle. 'That turned up nothing under her own profiles, but—'

'—She might've set up an alternative account just to follow him,' Kay finished. 'How many followers are there to go through?'

Her latest protégé's face fell. 'There're over fifteen thousand on one of the accounts.'

'Bloody hell. All right, it is what it is. Ian, when we interview Throndsen – I mean Twist – we'll have to find out if Tansy was communicating with him through one of those social media apps. She might've avoided text and email.'

'Good point, guv. I'll start writing up the interview plan now and email it over to you once I'm done, sound good?'

'Perfect. If you're going to stay late to do that, I'll do the driving for the rest of the week.'

'Sounds like a deal. But I'm choosing the music.'

TWENTY-THREE

Kay pulled the key from the ignition, closed her eyes and rested her head against the car seat while the engine ticked and cooled.

The drive back home from the incident room had been uneventful, but her mind continued to return to the decisions she had made since Tansy Leneghan's body had been discovered on Saturday morning, and the doubts were threatening, despite her considerable experience.

Yes, they had a breakthrough with regard to the young woman's father being in the vicinity of her murder, but was that sheer coincidence or indicative of something much darker?

'There's no such thing as a coincidence,' she muttered, climbing out.

Crossing the churned-up gravel that lined her driveway, she eyed the dust-covered four-by-four parked outside the garage. A narrow path led down the side of the left-hand corner of the house, and guessing that Adam would probably be working in the orchard finishing the fencing, she pushed her way past an overgrown buddleia that draped over the fence from the neighbouring property and made her way towards the back gate.

They usually kept the latch locked, but she had guessed correctly and found her partner whistling under his breath while he hosed down the patio pavers, the gentle hiss of pressure from the water tank casting rainbows in the air as the moisture met the warm summer evening.

'Thought I heard a car pull in,' said Adam, turning the tap off and enveloping her in a sweaty hug. 'I was just thinking it was time for a cold beer too.'

'I'll get them. I want to change into a pair of shorts anyway.' Kay's gaze fell to the remaining concrete pavers, spotting a set of mucky cloven hoof prints leading across to the lawn. 'Oh – your visitor's already here? I wondered what the extra tyre marks in the driveway were from.'

'Scott's dad loaned me his livestock trailer. It took a couple of goes to reverse it in at that tight angle from the road, but it was safer than trying to unload him in the middle of the lane.'

'Him?'

He winked. 'Get the beers and I'll see you down in the orchard. I'll introduce you.'

'Okay.'

Kay wandered through the back door into the kitchen, setting her bag on the central worktop and draping her suit jacket over the back of one of the bar stools before jogging upstairs to change.

As she threw her trousers and blouse into the laundry basket and pulled on shorts and a T-shirt, she recalled the last time Adam had brought home a large animal.

It had been a goat that time, one that had insisted on eating most of the ornamental roses planted by the previous owner of the house, as well as a number of vegetables that Kay had been trying to grow. The goat had eventually been returned to its owner after a few traumatic days for the garden, and she had sworn never to repeat the exercise.

'At least it's not in the garden, whatever it is,' she muttered, then tugged an old pair of running shoes on and made her way back downstairs.

After fetching two cold bottles of beer from the back of the refrigerator, she hurried outside, weaving her way between a privet hedge and over the stream.

A deep *baa* greeted her, and her jaw dropped.

'A sheep?'

Adam looked up from his phone and grinned, then pointed at the sheep that was staring at her from a shady spot beside a new galvanised water trough, its pale eyes narrowing. 'Meet Hovis.'

'Hovis?'

'Apparently he likes bread.'

Kay laughed. 'That's a new one. Is he friendly?'

'Yes, although a bit cantankerous after being shoved into that trailer earlier. He's not eating much at the moment but give him a few hours to settle in and he'll be all right I suspect.'

Placing her phone and the two beer bottles on the ornate wrought-iron table beside Adam, Kay wandered over to the sheep and held out her hand. 'Hey, you. Are you going to help keep the grass under control, huh?'

The sheep blinked, then stretched up its nose and sniffed before turning back to the water.

'Will he be all right in here on his own?'

'I finished building the shed for him this morning so he's got shelter overnight while he's getting settled in. He was on his own at the last place but we'll see how he gets on.' Adam reached into his pocket, pulling out a bottle opener on a keyring and opened the beer, handing one to her as she took a seat. 'There's enough room here for another one if he looks like he's getting lonely.'

'Cheers,' said Kay, clinking her bottle against his. 'Here's to Hovis, then.'

'And to not having to mow the grass around here anymore.'

She took a long swig, then groaned as her phone vibrated across the metal surface. 'I'm going to have to get this, sorry... Hello?'

'Guv? It's Nadine. Got a minute?'

'I have, yes.'

'It's just that DS Barnes asked me to look into DCI Sharp's comment about Joey Twist's past, I mean Throndsen. He left ten minutes ago, but I think I might have something.'

'Go on.'

'It happened twenty years ago, while he was working as a welder at that business in Chatham. He was arrested after making threats against his wife. The records are a bit sketchy because they were scanned into the new system a decade or so ago.'

Kay pushed the beer away and leaned an elbow on the table. 'Was he charged?'

'No, guv. I've double-checked and Georgina never pursued the matter. He was released within twenty-four hours with a verbal warning about staying off the alcohol – apparently he'd been down the pub and arguing with someone prior to one of the neighbours calling the police round to the house.'

'So he's got a temper on him. Interesting.'

'I also gave Diane, the FLO at Georgina's place, a call before phoning you, guv. I wanted to check when Georgina filed for divorce from Throndsen. Turns out it was six months after this incident – she told Diane that she moved in with her parents until she had an injunction in place to keep him away from her and Tansy before putting the house on the market and moving to where she is now in Kingswood. Her parents helped her out with the purchase.'

'Did you tell Diane we were interviewing Throndsen in the morning?'

There was a slight pause, and then, 'I didn't, guv. I didn't think that prudent in the circumstances in case you wanted to corroborate anything with Georgina after you spoke to him.'

Kay smiled. 'Good thinking. Was there anything else?'

'No guv, that's it.'

'That's great work. Get yourself home, and I'll see you tomorrow.'

Ending the call, she leaned back in her seat and took another sip of beer, her gaze unfocused on the grass at her feet.

'Progress?' Adam's voice broke through her thoughts.

'Maybe.' She blinked, breaking her reverie and then looked across the table at her other half. 'I hope so.'

'Good.' He drained his beer, stood and stretched. 'I'm going to have a quick shower before we eat. Do you want another one of these when I come back?'

'Please, and then I'll fire up the barbecue – I bought some fish and salad on the way home.'

'Sounds good.'

She watched him traipse back to the house, then snatched up her phone and opened a website search app, her thumbs quickly typing in the video she sought.

It was grainy, dating back well before the high-definition days of smart phones, but whoever had filmed it had been to the left of the stage when Joey Twist's band played what was to be their last gig.

The commentary below the video explained that the concert had been at a German location in a 2,500-capacity venue that had once been the town hall.

Sure enough, halfway through the second set, and in what looked to be a case of drunken antics, Thomas "Thommo" Smith, the guitarist, strolled across to where Twist was stalking the right-hand side of the stage and headbanging along to a raucous chorus with the crowd in front of him, then stuck out his leather-booted foot.

Twist stumbled, nearly tripping over the monitor speaker in front of him. He narrowly avoided disappearing head first into the trench between the stage and the security barrier, then glared at Smith. In one fluid motion, he crossed to where Smith stood grinning from ear to ear and punched his bandmate squarely in the nose before throwing his bass guitar at the drum riser and leaving the stage.

The video ended shortly after, the photographer

emitting a string of curses as it became evident Twist wasn't returning, and the concert was over.

Kay lowered her phone and drained her beer, eyeing Hovis as he wandered back and forth tentatively nibbling at the grass tussocks around the base of the apple trees, her mind already focused on the next day's interview with Twist.

Given the threats against Georgina and then the attack on Smith, albeit heightened by adrenaline and perhaps whatever substances the band were taking back then, it seemed that the man had a temper on him.

But was that temper enough to murder his own daughter?

And, why?

TWENTY-FOUR

Ian Barnes paced the tiles lining the corridor that led from the police station's reception area and the interview rooms, tapping a manila folder against his leg in time with his steps.

He knew the contents of the folder by heart, having spent most of the previous evening sifting through the collated facts about Joey Twist and familiarising himself with the bass player's history – both that of his musical endeavours and what Kyle and Nadine had gleaned about the man's previous work.

The early years were sketchy at best, little more than breadcrumbs dotted here and there like the newspaper article about the business award.

The man featured in social media posts under the band name, but there was nothing to suggest he kept a personal profile on any of the platforms.

Not publicly anyway.

The notes about the arrest in Chatham prior to his

musical career taking off had been requested, but Barnes held out little hope of anyone finding them given the years that had passed. They were lucky Nadine had found the scant information she had, and he had little doubt that Kay's interest had been piqued by the revelation.

She had seemed preoccupied when she picked him up from his house forty minutes ago to make the trip into town to attend the interview, confessing in confidence to him that she was concerned about how to approach it given the fact the man's manager would be present rather than any legal representation.

However, Barnes remained stoical.

Time would tell, and he was keen to start.

Glancing at the clock above the door frame leading out to reception, his top lip curled at the minute hand showing five minutes past the allotted hour.

By now, Twist and Kasprak should have been signed in and seated at the table in interview room two, the one to his left, and yet here he was, still waiting.

A shadow fell across the carpet at the far end of the corridor, accompanied by the sound of footsteps and then Kay rounded the corner, her expression determined.

'Is he here?'

'Not yet.' Barnes jerked his chin towards the reception area as she joined him. 'But speak of the devil.'

He watched through the toughened glass window in the partition door as two men walked up to the main desk, Kasprak wearing a similar black jacket to the one he wore at Saturday's festival over a plain white T-shirt and jeans, his grey collar-length hair swept back from his face by a pair of aviator glasses that glinted under the ceiling lights.

Twist followed in his wake, taller by a couple of inches, thin arms and legs offset by a slight paunch and shaggy blond hair.

'Definitely out of a bottle,' Kay murmured.

'Meow.'

She laughed under her breath and turned away from the two men as they were signed in. 'I'll let you lead this one given you probably know that folder inside out. Any highlights I should be aware of other than the historical arrest?'

'Nothing untoward, guv. Anyway, it's time to go digging.' He shot her a malicious smile as the reception door opened and a surly constable led the two men towards them. 'Mr Kasprak, Mr Twist. Nice of you to join us.'

Barnes ushered them into the interview room, started the recording equipment and recited the formal caution, eyeing both of them as he read out the words.

Kasprak fidgeted with the buttons of his jacket, a perpetual frown creasing his brow while Twist looked agitated, leaning away from his manager and keeping his gaze firmly on the table, his hands in his lap. In contrast to his manager, he wore a branded T-shirt depicting what Barnes supposed was the band's latest album and torn blue jeans. Faded tattoos covered his left arm in a design that swirled and curled up under his sleeve.

The citation complete, Barnes opened the folder and took a moment to skim-read the documents inside. His colleague was right, he did know the contents by rote but the action was born of habit, a way to pace the interview and ensure that the right tone was used given he was dealing with an as yet unknowing grieving father.

'First of all, can you confirm, Mr Twist, that until you changed your name by deed poll, you were in fact known as Joseph Throndsen?'

The man in front of him jerked his head up, piercing blue eyes clouding. 'I was. Why?'

'In a moment. Can you also confirm that the man in this photograph is in fact you? At this welding firm in Chatham?'

'Yeah, that's me.' Twist snorted. 'A lifetime ago.'

'How long were you there for?'

'I started as an apprentice for the owner's dad when I was sixteen, so I guess almost ten years.'

'Why did you leave?'

Twist's eyes narrowed further. 'If you're asking me that question, then you know the answer.'

'I'd like to hear it from you.'

'I had an... altercation with my ex-wife at the time.' The man shrugged. 'I liked a drink back then.'

Kasprak guffawed and clapped a hand on Twist's shoulder. 'You still do.'

'Carry on,' said Barnes, shooting a warning glance at Kasprak. 'What happened?'

'I... I felt that she'd trapped me,' said Twist. 'We were only seeing each other for four months when she told me she was pregnant. I thought she was on the pill or something. I was only twenty-three. It knocked me for six, I can tell you. I wasn't ready to be a dad for fuck's sake. I was focused on me music, y'know? Last thing I wanted was to get tied down to a wife and kid. I reckoned she did it on purpose, to make me get all sensible like. That's what her mum wanted her to do. But before I knew it, the whole nine months shot past and there I was with a baby daughter. Me and the ex got married two weeks before she was born.' He shrugged. 'I didn't want to be a dad, but I wanted to do the right thing by her too.'

'So you got drunk after work one afternoon, and…?'

A faint flush crept up Twist's neck. 'I'm not proud of what I did, understand? I managed to balance everything the first three years but when I got the chance to move to London, I had to take it. It was a case of now or never, y'know? We were arguing all the time by then anyway. So I had a few drinks to kill the nerves, headed home to tell her I wasn't having any of it anymore. I wanted a divorce.' He blinked, lowering his gaze while he ran his hand up and down his tattooed forearm. 'She told me I could forget having anything to do with me daughter. That was the last time I saw Tansy.'

'Look, detective – what's this all about?' Kasprak said impatiently. He gestured to Twist. 'Joey here's got a soundcheck back in Brighton at three o'clock and traffic's shit out there. You could've asked him all this over the phone.'

'One more question.' Barnes pulled a photograph of an evidence bag from the folder, turning it around so that Twist could see the pale blue scarf encased within. 'Do you recognise this?'

The man paled, his fingers trembling as he reached out to touch the photograph. 'I do, but I don't understand…'

Barnes clasped his hands together, took a deep breath and uttered the words that he had been dreading since the interview began.

'Mr Twist, I'm very sorry to have to tell you, and

there's no easy way to do this, but your daughter Tansy was found dead on Saturday morning.'

TWENTY-FIVE

'Here. Coffee, two sugars.'

Kay handed Brian Kasprak one of the takeout cups and watched as her colleague walked back into interview room two, leaving the door open.

Twist now sat slumped in his chair, red-rimmed eyes staring blankly at the table while Barnes slipped quietly into the seat opposite and pushed across an identical cup to the other man.

They had agreed a break and so Barnes was keeping quiet, waiting until the recording equipment would start once more and the interview continued.

For now, she watched and waited.

'So, that's why you didn't want to talk to him over the phone.' Kasprak wandered a few paces away, leaned against the plasterwork wall of the corridor and briefly pinched the bridge of his nose. He dropped his hand with a sigh. 'Christ, what a mess.'

'Did you know he had a daughter?'

'No idea. He's never mentioned her. I suppose like he

said, once he moved to London he concentrated on the band.'

Kay popped off the lid of her coffee and blew across the surface before joining him. 'How long have you known Joey?'

'I approached the band at a showcase gig in London way back when they were just establishing themselves on the scene there. I'd managed bands for years and saw a lot of potential. They were good musicians, they had a certain look about them – I reckoned at the time there was a gap in the market for what they were doing – and they had good songs. Joey was one of the founding members, and integral to the negotiations for me to take over their management.' Kasprak gave a sad smile before taking a sip of coffee. 'Even if they didn't make it big over here, there was a huge market on the continent for the sort of music they were playing, so that became our focus for the first year or two, until we had a summer Top 30 single breakout in the UK. The rest is history.'

'Until fifteen years ago.'

Kasprak snorted. 'Yeah. Until that.'

'Tell me what happened.'

'Uh, I don't know... maybe I'd been pushing them too hard booking back-to-back gigs but like I said, Europe was our playground. We made good money over there on album sales, concert bookings, merch... everything. They had a really solid fan base that supported them, unlike what it was like here. I'll be honest, Detective Hunter, their star faded a long time ago here in the UK, but Europe just couldn't get enough of them. We were lucky if we got played on commercial radio at all here at the time. After that Top 30 hit, we probably got two or three good years in the UK before it started to go quiet. We went from headlining gigs to scraping through as support acts for the younger bands.' He winced. 'Embarrassing really, given the talent in the band.'

'Tell me about the break-up.'

Kasprak rolled his eyes. 'The pair of them always did have short tempers, but Joey was the worst. Nothing major, more like a tantrum that would build up over time – y'know, classic straw that breaks the camel's back sort of thing. He'd sail through some of the bigger issues but the smaller ones... and Thommo knew how to wind him up. So he did. Once too often.'

'But on *stage*?'

'That had been brewing a while. They had an argument backstage before the gig, something minor that grew simply because we were all under stress about a German music press article that insinuated that year's new album was a last-ditch attempt to avoid obscurity. Joey thought Thommo wasn't taking it seriously enough... I dunno. I thought it was funny when Thommo stuck his foot out to be honest. I mean, it was the typical childish thing he'd do from time to time. Only Joey took it the wrong way – and punched him.'

'I've seen the video online. What happened after the rest of the band left the stage?'

'It was bedlam. Thommo went straight to the dressing room to have it out with Joey. Me and one of the security blokes had to drag 'em apart again. They were scrapping like a pair of teenagers in a playground was how Danny, the singer, described it and he wasn't far off. Then Joey walked out, got in a taxi back to the hotel, packed his things and fucked off to the airport. That was that.' Kasprak raised his gaze to the ceiling for a moment. 'Bear in mind I had the patience of a saint – still do. That's why I'm still able to do this job without having a cardiac arrest. But the bastards left me to deal with the aftermath on my own. Press releases, interviews, fielding calls from Melanie, the fan club president back in the UK – and she's a formidable woman when she needs to be.'

Kay shot him a sympathetic smile. 'She must be very efficient.'

Kasprak's eyes softened. 'Yeah, she is. And stayed true to them all this time. She's been integral to getting this comeback tour promoted. It's people like that we do it for. And couldn't do it without them.'

'Part of the family, then?'

'Exactly, detective,' he said, waving his coffee cup at her. 'Exactly.'

'So, this reunion tour – how did that happen given the past acrimony between Joey and Thommo?'

He grinned. 'It was easy. They're the same as all the other old rock dinosaurs out there. Their savings and pensions are worth next to nothing because the record companies had first dibs on all the royalties ages ago, but if you've got your copyright back for your songs – and this lot have, because I negotiated their contract with the record company back then and made damn sure they did – you can go independent and start again. Especially if you've got the quality of their songs. There's a market for this stuff now, people our age reminiscing about their youth, kids are grown up so they don't have to worry about babysitters so they can go to a gig. And of course, their fans have a disposable income these days. Easy money.'

'What are your plans for them?'

Kasprak's smile turned predatory. 'Off the record?'

Kay mimed zipping her lips closed, and he continued.

'They've been writing new material. The plan is to go into the studio in September, record a new album and release a new single before Christmas. To be precise, a *Christmas* single. We'll rake it in, especially as it'll be released independently.'

'Clever.'

'Bands have been doing it for years. Look at that bloke who wrote that rock hit in the early seventies. Killing it, he is…' Kasprak's voice stuttered at his last words, and he flushed. 'I mean, poor choice of words, but…'

'Guv?'

Kay glanced over her shoulder to see Barnes beckoning.

'He's ready, guv. Shall we continue?'

TWENTY-SIX

Laura paused, her hand on a battered white wooden gate hanging onto its hinges with a grim determination, then glanced over her shoulder at the tall uniformed officer who accompanied her and grinned.

'About time they let you out for good behaviour, Sarge.'

Tim Wallace smirked. 'Apparently they reckoned you needed keeping an eye on. Come on, get on with it – we've got two more to speak to after Ms Lightfoot.'

He removed his cap and turned down his radio while she eased the gate open, its metalwork groaning ominously.

The path leading up to the late 1950s semi-detached house had fared little better. Cracks had formed in the concrete with tufts of pale grass poking up through the gaps, the edges of the path overgrown with groundsel and dandelions, and roots from an enormous magnolia tree created fractures that zigzagged towards the front step.

Laura deftly stepped around those and a neat pile of cat

shit before rapping her knuckles on a frosted glass pane set into the middle of the door, eyeing the yellowed net curtains at the front windows.

A waft of nicotine-laden smoke preceded the resident's greeting when the door was opened, a foul stench that was deliberately puffed into her eyes and made them water.

'Whaddya want?'

Resisting the urge to cough, Laura turned away for a moment and blinked, then looked at the surly man in his early twenties who glared at her through the gap.

'Good morning,' she said. 'We wondered if we could have a word with Zena Lightfoot?'

'Wassit 'bout?'

'Work stuff. Is she in?'

''Ang on.' He pushed the door to, then hollered to someone in the house that there were two plods on the doorstep wanting a word, his blurry form disappearing into the gloom beyond the frosted glass.

A few minutes passed, and then the door opened to reveal a woman of around the same age dressed in a cornflower blue vest top and tight jeans, her hair and make-up immaculate.

She wasn't smoking a cigarette, either.

'Oh.' Her eyebrows shot upwards in surprise as she took in Laura's outstretched warrant card. 'What's going on?'

'Zena Lightfoot?'

'Yes…'

Laura smiled. 'Nothing to worry about. I'm DC Laura Hanway, this is my colleague PS Wallace. We wanted a quick word about one of the guests who was staying at the hotel on Friday night.'

'But I wasn't working then.' Zena's eyes darted between the two officers. 'Why do you need to speak to me?'

'You took a direct booking over the phone from someone called Tansy Leneghan on Thursday. One of your colleagues said it would've been unusual because most of your bookings are made through online third-party agencies. Can you remember the phone call?'

Zena folded her arms and leaned against the door frame, intrigue crossing her face. 'I can, yes – and that must've been Warren you were talking to, right? I mentioned it to him when he came on shift.'

Glancing through her notebook, Laura tried to stop the excitement bubbling. 'The hotel system said the booking was made just after half two on Thursday afternoon. Was there any delay between you getting the call from Tansy and putting the booking in the system?'

'No, I did it there and then while she was on the phone – otherwise one of those third parties you mentioned might've got the room instead if there was a sudden rush. There was that festival on, so we only had a few left as it was.' The woman's brow furrowed. 'That's right, I had to give her one of the rooms down the far end of the hotel, away from the spa. She didn't mind though. Said she had other plans.'

'Do you get much of a chance to speak to guests when they phone up?'

'Not always. But like Warren told you, we don't get many guests phoning up to make a booking. It's mostly done online. I think she'd tried a few of them, but they were all showing as full. She was just trying her luck I think, and as it happened we always keep a few rooms back for emergencies like that, or in case there's a problem with a booked room and we need to move someone at short notice.' Zena rubbed her hand down her arms. 'Look, what's going on? Why all the questions about her? Has something happened?'

'Has anyone from work been in contact with you?'

'No, I block their number when I'm not on shift in case they try to get me to come in at short notice.' Her nose wrinkled. 'They can be a bit cheeky like that, expecting me to drop everything because they're understaffed.'

'Can you—'

The door was wrenched open wider, and the man who'd answered it pushed past Zena and Laura before stomping down the path.

Laura watched with bemusement. 'Who's he?'

'My idiot brother. Take no notice of him. He's a pain in the arse.' Zena narrowed her eyes as he shoved his way through the gate and climbed into a rust-covered hatchback car that might have once been green in a past life. 'And lazy.'

The car coughed to life with an agonising groan, the exhaust pipe rattling and belching blue smoke as her sibling drove away.

'Tosser,' she muttered, then aimed a sweet smile at Laura. 'Sorry, you were saying?'

'Look, there's no easy way to tell you this and I'm going to ask that you keep this to yourself until a formal announcement is made on the news tonight because we're still speaking to family members, but the woman you spoke to – Tansy – was found dead in Mote Park on Saturday morning.'

'My god.' Zena brought a shaking hand to her lips. 'I heard someone was found... I thought it was a drug overdose or something.'

'Our investigation is ongoing, but you can appreciate why we're trying to understand her last movements before her death. What did you chat about with her when she phoned to make the booking?'

'God, I can't remember. I think... she mentioned something about her mum living locally, that's right. I wondered why – if that's the case – she didn't stay with her, but you can't ask questions like that, can you? I mean... you can, but I can't.'

'Did you enquire about what plans she had while visiting Maidstone?'

'No, but I did have to ask her whether it was business or leisure 'cos that's a standard thing. If she'd said leisure I might've bumped a late check-in to a different room to give her the option of one nearer the spa, y'know? But she said business. That's why I put her at the far end – our business clients often prefer to be tucked out of the way somewhere quieter at night, especially when the bar and restaurant empty out later in the evening.'

'She definitely said she was travelling for business?'

'Yeah. It'll be on the booking sheet anyway.'

Laura's hand automatically dived to her handbag, pulling out a well-folded photocopy and angled it towards the other woman. 'Here. Where does it say that on there? Can you show me?'

'Sure.' Zena's manicured forefinger traced the faint print at the top of the page, down to the line items that showed Tansy purchased a room and breakfast, then stabbed her nail at an abbreviation in tiny text near the footer of the page. 'There you go. That's the code we use for a business booking.'

'And how did she pay?'

'She didn't. We don't ask business guests to pay until they check out, and anyway she said she was on hands-free and couldn't get her debit card out while she was driving.' Zena watched as Laura tucked the paperwork back in her bag, and then wagged her finger. 'Hang on. She did say something as I was typing in the last details for the booking.'

'What was that?'

'She said that if anyone came into the hotel or phoned up asking if she was there that we had to tell them she wasn't. Which I thought was kind of weird given she'd just made a business booking. I mean, if you're here on business wouldn't you want whoever you were meeting with to know where you were so you could arrange a time to see them?'

Laura frowned. 'You're right, I would.'

TWENTY-SEVEN

Once everyone was reseated in the interview room, Barnes restarted the recording equipment, confirmed who was present, and launched into his next question, his voice soft.

'Joey, when we spoke to your wife she said that you'd walked out on her when Tansy was three, and yet you've confirmed that as per the arrest notes, you were drunk and threatening her. Why do you think Georgina lied after all these years?'

The man shrugged. 'I don't know. Maybe that's what she was used to telling Tansy. To protect her, y'know?'

'What happened after the neighbours called the police?'

'You've got it in that file haven't you?'

'I'd like to hear it from you.'

'I was arrested, and told to stay away from her. Then I found out through a mutual friend she wasn't going to press charges so I went round to the house to apologise. I still didn't want to be tied down to raising a kid but I wanted to try to make things right somehow.' Twist sighed, picking at a loose bit of fingernail. 'I didn't get a chance – the moment she opened the door, she started throwing my clothes out onto the step and told me she didn't want anything to do with me, and that as far as she was concerned, I wasn't going to get any contact with our daughter either. I was already playing in what evolved into the current line-up of the band, so me and the guys packed up and moved to London. We figured we'd give it a year to write and pull together enough money to record our first album, targeting a niche market that harked back to the glam rock and blues rock bands of the 80s. Thommo joined us that year and co-wrote most of the songs with me.'

'That's Thomas Smith, right?'

'Yeah. Thommo.'

'The bloke you punched on stage fifteen years ago.'

'I suppose you could call ours a "love-hate relationship",' said Twist, and shrugged. 'We spent so much time together we were bound to rub each other up the wrong way now and again.'

'They're like an old married couple most of the time,' said Kasprak.

Barnes shot him a glare. 'If you could keep your thoughts to yourself at this time, please.'

The manager held up his hands and leaned back in his chair, suitably chastened, and Barnes turned his attention to Twist once more.

'When did you change your name by deed poll from Joseph Throndsen?'

'Just before we started recording the first album.'

'Why?'

'I guess I wanted to sever all ties with my past. Make a clean start. I had a good feeling about the band, and the songs, and I didn't want anything to hold me back.'

'Was your daughter present when you had that argument with your wife?'

'She was... she was in the living room.' Twist's mouth downturned. 'She didn't see anything, but she must've heard us. Whether she worked out what was going on at that age, I don't know.'

'Did you ever see your daughter again?'

'N-no. Not until she got in touch.'

Kay held her breath as Barnes glanced down at his notes.

'When was that?' he said.

'About two weeks ago. She said she'd employed a private investigator to track me down.' Twist gave a sad smile. 'I always reckoned she was clever, like her mum.'

'Did she say why?'

'Yeah. She said one of her friends had done the same, reconnecting with her dad after he'd walked out, and she got curious about what happened to me I guess. She had no idea I'd changed my name or what I'd been doing since she was three.' Twist scowled. 'Georgina never said a word to her, even though she must've known. I mean when we had that hit single, we were all over the place. Couldn't escape us. She must've seen photos online and stuff. I suppose that's why Tansy had to get a private investigator involved. She hit a brick wall because I changed my name. I just disappeared off the face of the earth as far as she was concerned, and she was determined to find some answers.'

'How did the private investigator trace you?'

'Same as you I expect. Might've recognised me and put two and two together. I dunno – she never said.' He gulped. 'And I never got to ask her. Never will.'

Barnes gave the man a moment to compose himself, passing across a box of tissues. 'Tell me what happened after Tansy got in touch two weeks ago. How did she do that?'

'Via an email account she set up just for us to talk to each other. She set up a new social media profile too so we could message back and forth. I think she was still a bit shy about coming forward, and she certainly didn't want her mum finding out. After she said who she was and how she'd tracked me down, she said she wanted to meet. We were snowed under with last-minute rehearsals in Surrey at the time, but I told her our first gig was scheduled for that festival here. She said she could come and see me, but I… I suppose I was nervous. I mean, what if the press got hold of the story? What if Georgina found out? Tansy said she wouldn't tell her mother, not until we'd spoken first, but I needed to be sure. I… like I said, I guess I was scared. I didn't want to fuck it up. I hadn't seen her in over twenty years.'

He smiled through fresh tears. 'She's the spitting image of her mother at that age. I mean, was…'

'Where did you meet?'

'Brian here had booked the whole band into a pub on one of the quieter roads leading out of Maidstone to keep us away from the festival itself. All the major hotels were booked out by ticket holders anyway, save for a few single rooms here and there. The pub had rooms, and separate accommodation to the bar and restaurant, so we were tucked out of sight.'

'We'll need the full details of the booking from you.'

Twist glanced at Kasprak before answering. 'Yeah, won't be a problem. I couldn't tell Tansy where I was until late last week because Brian had to keep the whole thing quiet in case the fans found out—'

'The place is usually booked out for weddings so we paid a premium for our privacy,' Kasprak added, then clamped his mouth shut again as Barnes raised his hand to silence him.

'How did she get there?' he said to Twist.

'Taxi. We were paranoid about fans finding out about us, so she walked up the road from the hotel about half a mile and arranged for the driver to meet her there.'

'Did she plan to do the same on the way back?'

Twist nodded. 'I offered to pay though. She'd forked out enough to track me down as it was.'

'What time did she get to the pub?'

'About one thirty that night. It was all closed up of course, but the door to the banquet room at the back that they use for weddings and stuff was open so we found a table in there. I had a bottle of wine from the bar, so we just sat and talked for an hour or so.' Twist smiled through fresh tears. 'It was great, it really was. We just *connected*, y'know? I loved hearing about what she'd been up to, all about her studies and what her plans were for this year. She was going travelling in a couple of months, she said, so I convinced her to join us out on tour in Europe for a week or two, and she leapt at the chance.'

'What time did she leave?' Barnes said gently.

'The taxi turned up just after three – we were taking a hell of a risk meeting as it was, what with the fans and press and everything focused on the band's reunion, and I didn't want anyone spotting her. Not until we'd chatted some more and sorted out how we were going to tell Georgina before the media caught wind of it.'

'And you saw her into the taxi?'

'I watched her from the window, yeah. He was parked in the road outside the pub – I suppose he didn't want to risk driving into the car park and waking anyone up. Before Tansy left, we made plans to catch up Sunday morning but when she didn't show up I wondered if she'd mentioned our meeting to Georgina and changed her mind.' He sniffed, blew his nose loudly and then raised his hands to his eyes. 'Oh god.'

'We found Tansy's mobile phone in her hotel room. Why didn't she take it with her to your meeting?'

'Simple. I didn't want our first meeting in twenty years recorded. You have no idea what the press can be like when they want to be. I wanted to protect her from all that for as long as possible.'

Barnes leaned back in his seat, drummed his fingers on top of his notes for a minute, then eyed the man across the table.

'Mr Twist, can you tell us where you were between three and six o'clock Saturday morning?'

The musician looked down at his clasped hands. 'I was with Melanie.'

'You were what?' Kasprak's head swivelled towards his client, his jaw falling open. 'You're fucking kidding me.'

'Hold up, who's Melanie?' said Barnes.

Kasprak's attention snapped back to him. 'Melanie Cranwick. The woman who runs their bloody fan club, that's who.'

TWENTY-EIGHT

Gavin bit back a yawn, rubbed at tired eyes and refocused on the large computer screen in front of him.

Above his head, an air conditioning vent fanned a feeble attempt at a cooling breeze towards his scalp, the resulting effort doing little more than tickle the fine hairs on the back of his neck.

At least this side of the incident room was a little quieter, even if it meant he had to squeeze his frame into a chair that abutted a filing cabinet that should have been taken away for recycling three years ago. Every time he used the mouse, his elbow clanged against the metalwork, issuing a dull thud that died almost as soon as it was emitted.

The desk had been pushed against another that had somehow been manoeuvred into a gap between a stack of archive boxes from a recently closed case and an upended pair of office chairs, both with castors missing.

PC Sean Gastrell peered over his computer screen at him for a brief moment, then returned his gaze to the recorded images each of them was viewing. 'I reckon eating at our desks was a mistake. We should've gone outside and grabbed some fresh air.'

'Maybe.' Gavin blinked, his hand automatically reaching out for the can of energy drink next to the computer keyboard. 'But we'd have lost half an hour getting through these, and god knows there's enough of them.'

'Been a while since I've viewed surveillance footage this good,' Sean mused. 'The quality of the CCTV footage we get from the council is horrendous sometimes. Some of these home devices are light years ahead of what they're using.'

'Did you do much of this in the Marines?'

The constable shrugged. 'Only occasionally if we were recce'ing a location. Not often. I did a lot when I was on probation after joining here though. Thought it was punishment for cocking something up at college.'

Gavin glanced up to see Sean's gaze firmly glued to his screen. 'It usually is.'

'Bloody knew it.'

They both chuckled, and then Gavin sat back in his chair with a sigh as the recording ended. 'Well, there was bugger all from the last place we've got footage from at the Turkey Mill business units. What's the next one from the houses along Willington Street?'

'I'm currently watching the file ending in 345-8, and I'm nearly done.'

'Okay, I'll start the one after that and we'll take alternatives.' Gavin moused over the system folder and selected the file he needed. 'Only another forty-five to go. Might be done by the end of the day.'

'Depending on what time you wanted your day to end.'

'Quite.'

Checking Debbie's accompanying notes against the file he opened, Gavin saw that it had been obtained from Gareth Torsney, the man Laura and Kyle had interviewed on Sunday afternoon who ran his car servicing business from his home.

Impressed with the man's systematic way of cataloguing the files that had been provided, Gavin took another sip of soft drink and pressed the play button, settling in for another hour of reviewing files.

'We'll give it until three and then go outside for a breather,' he said. 'That should keep us going until six at least.'

'Sounds like a plan,' came the reply.

Resting his chin in his hand, Gavin toggled the controls so the footage played at three times normal speed, the film showing the Torsneys' driveway facing the street, and the angle of the camera capturing the back end of one of the cars parked outside the garage and the front gate, which had been closed overnight. Something dangled between the gate and a post, and he realised Torsney had probably looped a thick chain around it to prevent anyone stealing a vehicle.

The time in the bottom right-hand corner of the screen was a little after one in the morning on Saturday, and once two licensed taxis had passed by, the road fell silent save for the occasional car that shot past without stopping.

Just before two o'clock in the morning, a fox squeezed

under the gate and trotted across to the small patch of lawn off to the left of the camera before disappearing around the side of the house, and then the footage ended.

Gavin sighed, saw that Kyle had started the next file in the list, and so selected the one below that and repeated the exercise.

This time, the camera angle showed the back of the house, the time now three thirty.

In the ambient light from the street cutting along the side of the property, he could just see the wooden fence separating the garden from Mote Park, a pale strip of colour broken up by the darker shapes of the shrubs that lined it.

There was no wildlife in sight, no movement at all, and his gaze wandered to the current time at the top of the screen.

Another ten minutes, and he would take that break he and Sean were due. Otherwise—

Something flickered across the screen, and his attention snapped back to the recording.

He squinted, tweaked the controls to increase the contrast and hit the pause button.

There was something there, he was sure of it.

Right next to the taller of the plants in the far left corner of the garden where the neighbour's hedging smothered the fence and created a dark hollow that the street lighting couldn't penetrate.

'Dammit,' he muttered, ruing his distraction. He pressed the rewind button and stared at the screen.

Just as he felt the urge to blink, a figure emerged from the side of the house, their movements furtive as they skirted the border of the lawn farthest from the street light and scurried to the back fence.

'Fucking hell,' he breathed.

Sean's head jerked up, the sound of him stabbing his finger on the keyboard to pause the video he was watching barely registering in Gavin's mind before the constable moved round to his side of the desks.

'Found something?'

He tapped the screen in response. 'There. Someone just sneaked down the side of the house and over to the back fence. Whoever it is, they're in that darkened patch at the moment, and—'

'He's off.' Sean leaned forward. 'Is he going to try and climb over?'

They watched in silence as the figure scrambled up and used their arms to haul themselves over, disappearing from sight.

The recording ended a few seconds later, and Gavin sat back in his seat, stunned.

'So was that Tansy's murderer, or whoever went back and cut off her fingertips?'

TWENTY-NINE

Kay batted down the sun visor, glared at the traffic lights beyond the windscreen and willed them to change to green, her shoulders tense.

Beside her, Barnes stabbed at the car's radio settings, flicking from station to station before settling on a mid-seventies disco number.

Despite her frustration at the congested traffic, she laughed. 'Trust you to pick that.'

'Better than that eighties glam rock stuff you were playing last week.' He settled back into his seat. 'So... Joey Twist.'

'Yeah.' Kay shoved the car into gear and accelerated away, cutting past a bus that was waiting to pull out from the kerb before taking a left turn that led out of town. 'God, you can't imagine can you? Hearing from your daughter after twenty-odd years, only to find out she's been murdered hours after you saw her.'

'Where was Kasprak while Joey was meeting Tansy? Did he tell you?'

'I had a quiet word while you were showing Joey where the men's toilets were after the interview. Apparently he was on the phone with a German radio station promoting the tour and new album on one of their late-night rock shows. Did you manage to track down that woman, Melanie, he told you he was with after Tansy left the pub?'

'I did, but she wasn't answering her phone so I've left her a message.'

'Okay. What about the transcripts from Joey's phone? Did he send you those?'

'Yeah, Kasprak emailed over some screenshots and Debbie's saving them to the system before she leaves today. They corroborate what he said about Tansy contacting him through a different social media account to her usual ones, which is why we couldn't find them. I'll be chasing up Andy Grey about accessing her phone as quickly as possible to see who else she might've been talking to using that account.'

'Let me know if you need me to escalate that,' Kay said, flicking the indicator as she approached the turning for Georgina Leneghan's street. 'And ask Debbie to get someone to speak to Tansy's friends today to see if they knew about her getting in touch with her father.'

'On it.'

She listened while her colleague phoned the incident room and relayed her instructions while she slowed to overtake a horse and its rider, then pulled in to Georgina's driveway and parked beside a ten-year-old green hatchback that she hadn't seen before.

Diane, the new FLO, answered the front door. 'Guv?'

'Sorry I didn't phone ahead. Is that your car?'

'Yes. I came with Hazel last time but she's been recalled to Chatham.'

'Okay.' Kay glanced over her shoulder as Barnes slammed shut his car door and hurried towards her, tucking his phone into his jacket pocket. 'We need a word with Georgina.'

'Of course.' Diane stepped aside, closing the door behind them. 'I'll just nip upstairs and see if she's awake. She went for a lie down about an hour ago.'

'How's she doing in the circumstances?'

'Not too good. Her GP managed to get here late yesterday afternoon after surgery hours and prescribed something for her so I went out this morning to pick it up. Whatever it was made her drowsy very quickly.'

Kay bit her lip, a pang of guilt seizing her. 'All right. See if she's awake and if she'll mind speaking to us. Let her know it's urgent, will you? We can come back later but I'd rather not.'

'No problem, guv.'

Barnes circled the room after the FLO disappeared, his shoulders slumped as he took in the photographs arranged on the window sill and shelves. 'I can't imagine what she's going through. When I thought I was going to lose Emma to that killer…'

He broke off, shaking his head.

'I know.' Kay joined him, picking up one of the silver-framed photographs and eyed the young woman in the graduation gown who smiled back at her. She glanced around the room. 'And these are new, aren't they? There are more photos in here than there were last time.'

Barnes wrinkled his nose, scowling at the flowers that filled vases wherever they looked. 'I hate the smell of lilies.'

'Me too.'

She fell silent at the sound of voices from the room above, the floorboards creaking before the rush of running water reached her.

Moments later, Diane reappeared and began tidying away crunched up tissues that were scattered around the sofa cushions. 'She's just having a quick shower.'

'How're you getting on? This is your first assignment as a solo FLO isn't it?'

'Second. It doesn't get any easier though.' The constable paused, eyeing the row of photographs. 'Not that it should. I mean, if we didn't care we wouldn't catch the bastards that do this to families, would we?'

They fell silent at the sound of footsteps on the stairs, and then the door eased open and Georgina Leneghan shuffled in, her face wan.

'Sorry to keep you waiting,' she murmured, crossing to the sofa and sinking into the soft fabric. She reached out and tugged a cushion towards her, clutching it over her chest.

'I'm sorry we had to disturb you,' said Kay.

The woman shrugged. 'Believe me, I'd rather be helping you than lying there thinking I'm helpless to do anything. Have you found whoever did this to my daughter?'

'We've a number of leads we're pursuing at this time—'

Georgina's shoulders sagged. 'So that's a no then. What did you want from me?'

'We spoke to Joey Twist this morning.' Kay softened her voice as she took in the look of shock that crossed the other woman's face. 'He told us about the events leading up to the divorce, and that you stated at the time that he couldn't have anything else to do with Tansy. Is that correct?'

'It is, yes.' Georgina bit her lip. 'I only wanted the best for her, understand? Joseph – Joey – and I, we tried, we really did, but I don't think we were meant to be together in a long-term relationship. I know he felt trapped when I fell pregnant. I didn't mean to, but I couldn't bear to get… I just… When she was born, she was the most beautiful little thing I'd ever seen. I knew I'd do anything to protect her… and I failed.'

Fresh tears spilled over her cheeks, and she sniffed while Diane crossed to an oak lamp table and plucked a handful of paper tissues from a colourful box that was at odds with the sombre atmosphere.

Kay waited while the two women conferred in low tones, then took a deep breath. 'Did you know that Tansy had been in touch with her father?'

'I didn't, no…' Georgina's eyes widened as she looked to Diane and then back to Kay. 'Why wouldn't she tell me something like that?'

Kay remained still, letting the silence spin out while Tansy's mother nibbled at a hangnail and stared at the carpet.

'Unless…' She dropped her hand. 'When she turned eighteen, she said that she wanted to know more about him. Of course, by then the band had split up after that fight between Joey and Thommo years before, and I had no idea how to contact him... and even if I did, I didn't want her to have anything to do with him.'

'Why not?'

'Because he's a selfish bastard.' The woman sniffed, her spine straightening a little as she lifted her gaze to Kay. 'And I knew if she did meet him, he'd charm her and tell her all sorts of lies about me, and that she'd get all caught up in the glamour of what he used to do... the band, I mean. She'd forget that I was the one who brought her up single-handed, that *I* was the one who worked so fucking hard to give her the best childhood ever despite not having him around. I didn't want to lose her. And now I have...'

Kay sighed, the woman's pain and grief stabbing at her own heart. 'Tansy used a private detective to trace Joey, and made contact with him last week. She checked into a hotel in Maidstone rather than coming straight here because she and her father had arranged to meet late Friday night. He's confirmed that she left the pub where the band were staying in the lead-up to the festival just after three in the morning when she left there in a taxi. We're currently trying to trace the driver.'

'Jesus.' Georgina's hands shook as she dabbed the tissue at her cheeks. 'That means her father was one of the last people to see her alive, doesn't it?'

'It does, yes.'

'And what happens if you can't trace this taxi driver?'

Kay pursed her lips. 'Then we'll be taking another look at your ex-husband's movements that night.'

THIRTY

Kay sipped at a bottle of cold beer and shaded her eyes with her hand as the sun began to dip below the ridge line of her neighbour's house.

A slight breeze rippled at the long grass around her feet, and she shuffled sideways as a large black beetle ambled between the blades, glistening as the light caught its armoured body.

She looked up at a guttural bleat to see Hovis trotting towards her, before he stopped and ducked his head to a fresh patch of hay that Adam had placed in a makeshift manger under one of the trees.

The sheep studiously ignored the turquoise dragonfly that hovered across the galvanised steel water trough beside his food, but glanced over his shoulder every now and again to where Kay sat.

'I haven't got anything better than that, so there's no good giving me that look,' she said.

Disgruntled, Hovis turned his attention back to the manger.

Adam placed a laden tray on the table beside her, taking the seat opposite before clinking his beer against hers. 'You're a bit reticent tonight. I take it that was a difficult day.'

'Yeah.' She swung around to face him as he handed her a small plate, and eyed the array of food that he had doled out into different bowls. Olives, hummus, savoury crackers and smoked salmon jostled for space amongst freshly sliced sourdough bread and more. 'This looks good.'

'I could hear your stomach rumbling from the kitchen.'

She laughed. 'I did eat today you know.'

'I can phone Barnes to check.'

'He'll back me up.' Grinning, she dived in, piling a bit of everything onto her plate before settling back in her chair. She stabbed an olive. 'I didn't get a chance to ask last night – did you hear back from that journal about the paper you submitted?'

Adam winked in reply, then got up and walked around the tree to a pile of chopped wood they were saving to mulch for the garden.

Kay frowned, then a smile formed as he emerged from behind the pile with a stainless-steel bucket.

The dark green neck and golden foil of a champagne bottle protruded from it, and he held two crystal glasses in his other hand, grinning as he set them in front of her.

'I did, and I got the contract through this afternoon,' he said, expertly opening the bottle with a soft *plop*. 'And they've asked me to write the feature article for the same edition.'

'That's fantastic.' Kay pushed her plate away and

raised her face to kiss him, taking one of the glasses. 'Congratulations.'

'Thank you.' He clinked his glass against hers, took a sip and sat once more. 'Hopefully once that's published in the winter edition, I might see more offers on the lecture circuit on that subject. It'll be good for the networking anyway. It's hard to tell who might read it – the journal's got an international audience.'

'So does that mean you might get the opportunity to speak at conferences, things like that?'

'Perhaps, yes And if you can tear yourself away from work now and again, we could make a break of it from time to time if you like?'

'That'd be good.' She jerked her chin towards Hovis. 'I take it then that he's got a clean bill of health the way he's tucking into that hay.'

'And he hasn't managed to work out how to cross the bridge into the garden yet,' Adam said between mouthfuls. 'Maybe he doesn't like the sound of running water.'

'There *is* no running water. That stream bed's been dry for six weeks now, apart from the odd puddle here and there. I think it's only a matter of time before he susses out the lawn. Never mind those roses – they've never recovered from having that goat rip through them.'

'Don't worry, I was planning on building a gate this side of the stream, just in case. I reckon the bank's too steep for him to climb down so I don't think he'll try that in the meantime.'

Kay narrowed her eyes at him. 'Are you sure?'

'Positive. He might've tried it when he was younger, but not now.'

A FATAL SILENCE

'A gate would be good though. The way he's been looking at me, I have a sneaking suspicion he's already making plans.'

THIRTY-ONE

A pale golden glow bathed the walls of the incident room when Kay walked in a little after seven o'clock the next morning.

The muted sounds of the lower levels of the police station filtered up the stairs and through the door in her wake, a cell door slamming shut and laughter reaching her as she placed her bag under her desk and wandered across to the whiteboard.

The rest of the team would be arriving shortly but she needed this space, this time to herself to take a moment to reflect on the investigation to date.

Clenching her jaw, she ran her gaze over the notes she and Barnes had added since they returned from the crime scene on Saturday morning, the knowledge that the golden hour for gathering evidence and gaining momentum on the case had long passed adding to the desperation that consumed her.

Her eyes fell on the photographs of Joey Twist that Gavin had pinned to the board, one showing the man in his early twenties when he was still called Joseph Throndsen, and the other from that fateful night when he'd punched his bandmate on stage, resulting in a fifteen-year hiatus.

A fifteen-year break that had led to a reunion tour, and a meeting with his long-lost daughter before she was brutally murdered.

'Why?' she whispered, her attention moving to the photograph of Tansy that Georgina had provided. 'Why did someone kill you? And why did they kill you there?'

She swallowed, taking in the young woman's open smile, sparkling eyes and glowing skin. A whole life ahead of her, cut short by a violent and terrifying death.

'Morning, guv.'

Kay turned at the sound of Gavin's voice, raising an eyebrow as the detective constable expertly tossed an empty energy drink can into the recycling bin by the door as he entered the room. 'I take it that was breakfast?'

He grinned. 'Breakfast number one. I'll get something to eat later. And you're starting to sound like Sharp, guv.'

'Perish the thought. Can you imagine?' She jerked her chin towards the whiteboard. 'Any thoughts about motive yet?'

'Nope.' Taking out his mobile phone from his pocket and sliding it onto his desk, he joined her and stared at Tansy's photograph. 'I was lying awake thinking about it at two o'clock this morning, and I... I mean, *would* her own father kill her?'

Kay chewed her lip before answering. 'I don't know. Why would he? When we spoke to him yesterday, he said they'd been making all sorts of plans to spend more time together.'

'But we've only got his word for it that he saw her get into that taxi.'

'So far.' She glanced past him as the incident room began to fill with more officers and administrative staff, then spotted Laura and Barnes heading her way. 'I'm going to grab a coffee, and then we'll make a start on the briefing. There's a ton of information to go through so we might as well do it all together.'

'I saved you a trip to the kettle,' said Barnes, handing her a takeout cup. 'Thought you'd want to get started as soon as possible this morning.'

'Thanks, you're a mind reader. Okay, round 'em up.'

Within moments, a small crowd was gathered around the whiteboard facing her, their faces attentive.

Kay took a moment to eye each of them in turn, gave a reassuring nod to a pair of newer administrative assistants who had joined the team from another investigation, then turned to Laura. 'Let's start with the hotel staff interviews.'

'A couple of interesting points, guv,' said the detective constable. 'Zena Lightfoot was the staff member working on Thursday afternoon who took Tansy's booking. She stated that Tansy said she was travelling for business so Zena put her in that room – they're quieter that side of the hotel apparently. Also, Tansy told Zena to put a note on the booking that if anyone asked if she was staying there, they were to say no.'

Kay frowned. 'Any idea why?'

'Not from Zena, no, but we tracked down the staff member who was working the night-shift, Chris Brandle. He said Tansy asked him to order a taxi for her just after one o'clock but when he explained to her that it would pick her up outside the reception doors, she asked that it meet her further up the road. There's a bus stop on the other side of the dual carriageway before you get to the roundabout, and that's where she asked him to tell the driver to meet her. He confirms he phoned the taxi company to make those arrangements.'

'Please tell me you got the driver's name.'

'Tim got a message back from them late yesterday afternoon passing on his details,' said Laura, smiling. 'And I'm speaking to him this morning.'

'Great work, both of you. Keep me up to date on that. Twist told us that Tansy arrived at the pub where he was staying at half past one so see if what the driver tells you tallies with that. Gav, on to you and Sean.'

'Guv, we've had a bit of a breakthrough we think.' Gavin consulted the notes in his hand, then walked over to the map of Mote Park and the surrounding streets that had been pinned to the side of the whiteboard. 'We've finished going through the home security footage provided by the residents around here, but it's the footage Gareth Torsney gave us that's proved the most interesting. Someone *did* access his garden at three thirty on Saturday morning and one of his security cameras shows that person going over the fence into the park.'

Kay's heart punched her ribs. 'Any idea where they went?'

'Not yet,' said Sean. 'I'm working back through the footage from the other properties again to see if I can spot anyone matching this person's description moving along that street – although we can only see they're wearing dark clothing, so...'

'Anyone helping you with that?'

'No, but—'

Kay held up her hand and turned to Debbie. 'This is a priority. Who can we spare?'

The uniformed constable jogged back to her desk, returning with a three-page document that she quickly thumbed through. 'If we take two probationers off the phones, they can help Sean.'

'Do it. Like I said, this is a priority. Kyle – anything of interest regarding Joey's bandmates?'

'Nothing untoward, guv. A few misdemeanours here and there in their younger days, but nothing on our files.' The probationary detective shrugged. 'Most of the research I did into them was via online fan sites, which I then corroborated with Kasprak. It certainly seems like the fifteen-year hiatus softened any animosity that was between them the last time they toured.'

'I'd imagine the promise of more money helped, too,' said Kay, before allowing the subsequent smatter of sardonic laughter to die away and directing her attention towards Barnes. 'Any news about the woman who runs the fan club?'

'Nothing from her yet,' replied her colleague, waggling his mobile phone in the air. 'I'll give her another call after this to chase her up.'

'Please. The sooner we can corroborate Joey's statement about who he was with either side of that meeting with his daughter in the early hours of Saturday morning, the better. Especially if Laura can track down the taxi driver to support that too.' Her eyes found Gavin again. 'Has anyone looked into whether we've had any similar attacks like this in our area? Or any recent reports of assaults that might have led to an escalation in violence?'

'I ran a report on Monday, guv,' he said. 'There were half a dozen that I thought might be relevant but after uniform interviewed the people involved, all their alibis checked out. No unsolved murders cropped up with similar trends to Tansy's, and there was nothing in the system recently for attacks in or around the park either.'

'Okay, do me a favour and widen your search to a county level. Have a chat with Paul Solomon over in Northfleet to see if he's heard of anything like this on his patch before, and if he doesn't come up with anything let me know and I'll take it up with Sharp to get us some help over there to do a dive into the archives.' She rolled up the agenda and tapped it against her leg while her gaze roamed the whiteboard once more. 'Maybe there's something from Joey's past we've missed. Debs, anything from speaking with Tansy's friends?'

'We've finished collating statements from those she went to university with and her Bristol-based colleagues,' said the uniformed constable. 'But I've got a friend of hers from her schooldays here in Kent I thought you might want to have a word with yourself – they kept in touch all these years, and Natasha says that often when Tansy came to visit her mum, they'd meet up for a drink. I thought maybe Tansy might have confided in her about her search for her father, but I didn't want to discuss it over the phone with her. She lives near Tenterden and works from home.'

'Perfect. Thanks, Debs. Let me have her number and

I'll go and speak with her today. Did we get Harriet's final report?'

'We did, guv – I've had a read through but you're not going to like it.'

'Why not?'

Debbie pursed her lips before answering. 'Because the forensic evidence she and her team gathered is inconclusive about Lucas's theory that there might've been two people involved in Tansy's murder and mutilation.'

'Shit.' Kay's heart sank as she took in the same dejected expressions in her colleagues' faces that she was sure she wore. 'So we don't know whether we need to look for one suspect or two. Christ, that casts a wide net.'

'Harriet asked me to let you know that she's now got her team processing all the other evidence collected from around the periphery of the crime scene – they've been focused on where Tansy was discovered and following up Lucas's theory. She also confirms they found more than thirty samples in the hotel room,' Debbie added. 'Partials, mostly. I mean, once we do have a suspect we can run those against fingerprints, but it's a hell of a lot of information to sift through, guv, and...'

'First we need a suspect.' Kay ran a hand through her hair, then scrunched up the agenda and tossed it onto her desk. 'Or two.'

THIRTY-TWO

'Natasha Berrington? I'm Detective Inspector Kay Hunter, and this is Detective Sergeant Ian Barnes. My colleague, PC West, spoke to you yesterday. Could I have a word?'

The twenty-something on the doorstep of the tiny terraced house looked as if she had spent the past twenty-four hours in the clothes she was wearing, her face bearing no traces of make-up.

Or sleep, for that matter.

She blinked, huffed a strand of dark brown hair from her eyes and leaned against the doorframe, crossing her arms over her ample chest. 'Couldn't you have called first? I'm in the middle of a software upgrade and the client's been on the phone all night. I'm knackered.'

'This won't take a minute.' Kay flashed her most endearing smile and took a step forward. 'We were hoping you could tell us more about your friend, Tansy.'

Sadness rippled across Natasha's features, and she blinked back tears. 'Sorry. I'm tired, that's all. Of course, come in.'

Kay let Barnes go on ahead of her, then closed the front door as an articulated truck roared past, the uPVC doing little to counteract the noise.

A narrow hallway had once been papered in a light and airy floral design, no doubt in an attempt to offset the lack of natural light in the gloomy space. Most of the wall to her left was obscured by boxes of various shapes and sizes, some overflowing with books and various knick-knacks, one with half a dozen different computer keyboards poking out through a gap in the top.

'I'm about to move out,' Natasha explained over her shoulder, leading the way into a kitchen at the back of the property. 'I don't normally live in a shithole, but there's only so much room for that stuff and the storage unit I've booked isn't vacant until Tuesday.'

'Staying local?'

'Nah, heading north. Sort of, anyway. My boyfriend's accepted a job in Milton Keynes so we've bought a place on the outskirts there.'

Kay ran her gaze over the cluttered crockery and open kitchen drawers, noting the flat-packed cardboard boxes that had been stacked against the oven door. 'When do you leave?'

'A week on Wednesday.' Natasha leaned against the lip of the sink and resumed crossing her arms over her chest. 'What did you want to know? I told the woman I spoke to yesterday everything I know.'

'When did you last speak to Tansy?'

'Um, probably a week ago. She was coming over to see her mum and we usually catch up for a drink. I don't get out much because of work at the moment, so I hadn't had a chance to go to Bristol to see her for a while.'

'How did she seem to you?'

Natasha's shoulders lifted, then sank before a sigh escaped her lips. 'I can't believe we're talking about her like this. I don't even know what to say to her mum. She's probably wondering why I haven't called. But... Tansy seemed fine when we spoke. Busy – she was at work when she phoned. So it was a bit of a rushed call.'

'Did she seem anxious, or happy?'

'Just... busy. A bit frazzled maybe, but I put that down to work. Like I said, I'm working all hours at the moment so I probably wasn't taking much notice to be honest, except for noting down what time to meet her Saturday night.'

'That was Saturday just gone?'

'Yeah.'

'Did she make any changes to that plan?'

'No. Why?'

'Did Tansy tell you anything else about her trip here, perhaps anything about any meetings she might be planning to have?'

'No.' Natasha frowned. 'Why? What's going on?'

'Did she tell you she was hoping to meet her father while she was here?'

'What?' The woman's eyebrows shot up. 'You're kidding me? That piece of shit? When did he contact her?'

'He didn't. She did. Tansy employed a private investigator to track him down.' Kay watched as Natasha dropped her hands to the sink, gripping the surface as if to try and stop herself falling. 'You had no idea?'

'No... why... wow.'

'Did Tansy often keep secrets from you?'

'I... never. Well, I guess not. I mean, she didn't tell me about her dad, so who knows, right?' Natasha's gaze fell to the cheap tiled floor. 'Shit.'

'How long had you known Tansy?' said Barnes.

'Since primary school. I started three months into the first term there because my mum and dad moved over from Spain. My mum had been working as a translator in the diplomatic service but wanted to be closer to her parents. She got a job in London when we moved back here, and dad was often away – he used to work on oil rigs – so my grandparents used to look after me and stuff.'

'So you were close?'

Natasha nodded, a fat tear rolling over her cheek before she swiped it away and sniffed. 'Really close. Which is why it hurts that she didn't tell me about her dad.'

'Maybe she wanted to wait and see how the meeting with him went,' said Kay. 'After all, you said you'd arranged to meet with her for a drink on Saturday night, yes?'

'I suppose so.'

'How did you and Tansy communicate? By call? Text?'

'A messaging app. Sometimes through social media if we were sharing a post we'd seen, y'know?'

'And what was her account name on those apps?'

Kay waited while Barnes jotted down the details, then turned her attention back to Natasha. 'Were those the only accounts she used with you?'

'What do you mean?'

'Did she ever use a different social media account when she contacted you?'

'No. Why would she do that?'

'Tansy was using a different account to set up the meeting with her father,' Kay explained. 'We think they were worried the media would find out otherwise.'

Natasha's lip curled. 'You mean, *he* would've been worried about the media. Bet they're all in damage limitation or whatever they call it now, aren't they? Or is that manager of his working out how to make the most out of Tansy being murdered?'

'Do you know Brian Kasprak?'

'No. Just what I've read online today. That tour of theirs, it's all about the money isn't it?'

Kay ignored the question. 'Is there anyone else Tansy might've contacted prior to coming back here? Anyone else from your schooldays, or an old job perhaps?'

'I don't think so.' Natasha threw up her hands in frustration. 'Believe me, if I knew anything about why she was killed, and who might've done it, I'd tell you. I'd do anything to get her back, and if I can't have that, then I want to help you find the bastard who killed her.'

Kay's gaze flickered to Barnes as his phone vibrated. His eyes widened at the number on the screen before he shot her an apologetic look and dashed for the door, his voice a low murmur. Turning back to Natasha, she fished out a business card from her bag and handed it over.

'Thanks for your time, and I'm so sorry for your loss. If you think of anything, anything at all that might help us, don't hesitate to call my direct number. It doesn't matter what time it is, I'll try to answer and if I can't, I'll call you back as soon as possible, all right?'

'Okay.'

Five minutes later, Kay joined her colleague, who had already got in the car and started the engine.

'What's going on?' she said, clipping her seatbelt into place as he accelerated away from the kerb.

'The woman from the fan club – Melanie Cranwick – just called. She's due to go into work in an hour but says she can speak to us now if we hurry.'

Kay wrapped her fingers around the arm rest set into the door. 'Right, well, let's see how quickly you can get us there, shall we?'

THIRTY-THREE

Laura switched her phone to silent mode, then peered up at the scratched and peeling metal sign that hung precariously from a wrought-iron bracket above a dirty off-white wooden door.

It proclaimed that the taxi company had been operating since 1976, and she wondered whether anyone had taken a paintbrush to the façade in the intervening years, or whether the low-slung corrugated industrial unit was simply an afterthought for what otherwise appeared to be a thriving business.

The large double-glazed pane set into the upper half of the door looked as if it hadn't been wiped in the last decade, and what glass she could see was peppered with stickers suggesting that there might be CCTV cameras in operation but that there was definitely no cash kept on the premises.

She frowned, trying to recall when she had ever used cash to pay for a taxi – or even *used* a taxi instead of her preferred rideshare app, then shrugged away the thought as

Kyle locked the pool car they'd been allocated that morning and strolled over.

'Let's go and find this Toby McKinnon then,' she said. 'Hopefully he's here.'

'Was he working today?'

'Not until ten, which is why we're here now.' Laura checked her watch as they crossed the pockmarked asphalt. 'It gives us half an hour to do the interview before his shift starts.'

She was half tempted to pull down the sleeve of her jacket to push open the door, such was the grime that smeared the handle's surface, and instead shouldered herself against it. Resisting the urge to wrinkle her nose at the pungent stench of body odour that filled the box-shaped office, she approached the withered man sitting behind a raised counter, a look of perpetual weariness etched into his features.

A modicum of interest flickered across his face as she withdrew her warrant card, and then he leaned back and bellowed over his shoulder.

'Toby? That copper's here to speak with you.'

That done, he ignored the pair of them and turned back to an ancient-looking computer monitor as the black console in front of him lit up and a phone ring blared out.

Laura winced at the volume that filled the room, then turned as a polite cough filtered through the noise.

'I'm Toby,' said a stocky forty-something who stood next to a scratched and dented grey filing cabinet with his thumbs jabbed into his jeans pockets. 'D'you want to come on through to the garage? Believe it or not, it's a bit quieter in there.'

He gave a cheeky smile, then spun on his heel and led the way, past two wooden desks covered in lever arch files and scrunched up paperwork.

Laura's lip curled as the soles of her shoes stuck to the cheap linoleum flooring, forcing away her disgust at what she might be walking on, and followed him to the back of the office and through a fire door that might or might not have passed the last health and safety inspection.

She bit back a gasp when they entered the garage.

In contrast to the state of the reception office, the place was immaculate and resembled a larger version of Gareth Torsney's slick operation.

Oil splats covered the concrete floor here and there, and dust gathered in the corners but the workbenches that bordered the space were tidy and organised. A cork board similar to the one used by the investigation team back at the incident room stretched above it with a collection of work orders and job sheets tacked in neat rows for ease of reference.

McKinnon crossed to a radio playing on the far corner of the workbench and turned it down before beckoning them over to a metal fold-out table and four chairs beside it. 'Will this do? We just use it for the occasional tea break, that's all. It's better than trying to hear ourselves over Maurice in there, and it stops him ear-wigging.'

Laura smiled as she took a seat while Kyle extracted his notebook from his utility vest. 'I take it he'll be disappointed.'

'He'll live. Right, I'm due to clock on in about twenty minutes if I don't want to lose money. You wanted to ask me about a job on Friday night, yeah?'

'That's right. We're going to make this formal in the circumstances though, so I'll begin by cautioning you and then if you've got any questions about that before we start, you can do so. Okay?'

McKinnon sat up straighter in his seat. 'Yeah, okay. Doesn't mean I'm under suspicion or anything, does it?'

Laura ignored the question, and instead read out the caution before launching into the interview. 'Can you confirm you received a request on Friday night to collect a woman from a bus stop along the road from the hotel where she was staying?'

'Yeah. It came through from the despatcher here. Janie was working that night. I think you spoke to her to arrange this meeting, right?' He reached into his shirt pocket and took out a well-thumbed notebook. 'I keep a note of all me jobs in here, just as a back-up so when they pay me I can check I've got everything, know what I mean?'

Laura waited while he thumbed back through the pages.

'Here you go. I'd just dropped off a fare at that hotel near Leeds Castle so I picked her up at one fifteen.'

'How did she seem when you saw her?'

'Not drunk,' he grinned, then sobered when Laura's face remained passive. 'I think that's why I remember her so well. She wasn't dressed for a night out, although she was wearing a summer dress. She had on a grey cardigan that she was hugging around herself when I pulled in to the bus stop. Wasn't that cold though, so maybe she was nervous or something?'

'Did she say anything during the journey?'

'Not really.' He gave a slight shrug. 'I tried talking to

her, you know, just asking how her day had been. She sort of mumbled "okay" and then I confirmed where she wanted me to take her, and that was that until we got to the pub. Then she told me I needed to keep it quiet because she didn't want to wake anyone up, and could I drop her off round the back near the kitchen door.'

'Did you find that strange?'

'A bit, I suppose. But she's the customer, right? And the customer's always right.'

'How did she pay?'

'She didn't. A bloke came out the door and handed me twenty quid. Cash, I mean.'

'What did he say to you?'

'Not much. Asked what the fare was, paid me, told me to keep the change, and said could I pick her up at three.' McKinnon leaned forward, resting his elbows on his knees. 'Course, by then I'd figured out what she was up to.'

'What do you mean?'

McKinnon gave her a leery smile. 'Pub in the middle of nowhere? Older bloke, younger woman and in and out in an hour. Come on, you're the detective.'

'She was his daughter,' Laura snarled. 'And she was murdered within a few hours of you last seeing her alive.'

The taxi driver paled. 'His... his daughter? What d'you mean, murdered?'

'Tell me what happened when you picked her up. You said this man told you to go back at three o'clock—'

'—But that's the thing. I didn't.'

'What?'

'Yeah. I got a call, like, at ten to three. I was already on me way when my phone rang and some bloke – I'm presuming it was him, her father you said – told me she'd made other arrangements and not to worry. Then he hung up.'

Laura's throat dried. 'So, wait a minute – are you telling me that you never went back to the pub after dropping her off?'

'That's right. Once that job got cancelled I phoned Janie and told her I was available. I got another job within about five minutes, picking up a couple of blokes from a nightclub in town and taking them back to Kemsing because the trains weren't running. Look, it's in me book here.'

'I'm going to need to take a copy of that.'

'Be my guest. There's a photocopier in the office.'

Laura rose to her feet, then paused. 'Can you show me the recent calls in your phone? I'll need the number you took that call from.'

Waiting while McKinnon dabbed at his phone screen, Laura tried to ignore the pounding of her heart as a sickness enveloped her.

Eventually the taxi driver turned the screen to face her. 'Here you go. It came through at two fifty-three.'

'Shit,' Laura whispered. 'It's a different number.'

THIRTY-FOUR

'Seventeen minutes. Not bad, detective sergeant,' Kay said, checking her watch. 'Are you sure you haven't got Finnish ancestry somewhere along the line?'

Barnes aimed the key fob over his shoulder, then frowned as the detective inspector's cheeks dimpled. 'No. Why?'

'I've heard they make the best rally drivers,' she said. 'I thought I was meant to be doing all the driving this week anyway?'

Tossing the keys to her in response, he bit back a smile and headed towards a freshly varnished wooden gate set into a thick laurel hedge. 'I forgot.'

'Must be an age thing.'

He laughed, knowing full well his driving skills were legendary within the investigation team, and that Gavin was fast becoming a serious contender for the title of who could get to a crime scene the quickest. 'You youngsters have a long way to go before you'll catch me.'

Hearing a chuckle over his shoulder, he pushed open

the gate, held it open for Kay and then followed her along a tidy paved path that was bordered on each side by lush grass.

Colourful flowerbeds framed the property, and matching wooden tubs were set either side of an open front door through which he could hear a local radio station playing the latest Top 10 hit.

He rapped his knuckles against the wood panel work and heard an airy "Come in!" from somewhere within the depths of the house.

Instead of entering a hallway, he found himself in a living room with a high ceiling and a window overlooking the front garden. A wood-burning stove sat dormant within a stone hearth to the far side of the room, in front of which a vase containing dried flowers had been placed.

Black and white photographs adorned the wall to the left of the hearth, and as he and Kay paused to look at them, he recognised a lot of members from seventies and eighties rock acts, all posing with the same woman, her smile wide and eyes sparkling.

'Found my rogues gallery then.'

He turned at the voice to see a slightly older version of the same woman placing a full laundry basket on the colourful rug in front of the sofa, her hair swept up in a messy ponytail.

'Melanie Cranwick?'

'That's me. You must be DS Barnes.'

'And this is my inspector, Kay Hunter.'

Melanie paused with her hands on her hips. 'Right, so what do you need from me? They usually offer cups of tea at this point on the telly.'

Barnes smiled, raising his hand. 'No tea required, thanks. Shall we sit?'

'If you want to.' She sank onto the cushions while Kay removed her notebook and Barnes cited the formal caution.

She gave no indication of panic about their presence, and in fact, he thought she looked bored by the whole affair.

'How long have you and Joey Twist been seeing each other?' he began.

A sly smile crossed her lips. 'Unofficially, for about twenty-five years. I suppose the wider fan base knew about us by the time the band split up fifteen years ago though.'

'Do you argue much?'

'Why?'

'Answer the question please.'

'Now and again I suppose. Nothing major, just sometimes we both get frustrated I suppose, same as any relationship that's been around the block a few times.'

'Has he ever been violent towards you?'

'No,' she said emphatically. 'Definitely not.'

'Did you keep seeing each other during the band's hiatus?'

'On and off.' She reached out and plucked at a loose thread in her fashionably torn jeans. 'I mean, neither of us is after anything serious. I see another bloke now and again. Before you ask, Joey knows we're not exclusive, and I know he's seen other women over the years.'

'You don't mind?'

She shrugged. 'No. I married young – eighteen – and that was a disaster. I was divorced just after my twenty-first birthday, and vowed never to walk down the aisle again after that. What me and Joey have suits me fine.'

'Got any kids?'

'No, thank god.' She laughed, a raucous bark that lit up her face. 'I have three nieces and a nephew and trust me, a few hours with them knocks any broodiness out of my system for a few months.'

'Did you know Joey had a daughter?'

'Tansy? Yeah. He hasn't seen her since his ex kicked him out years ago though. I think he said she was about three the last time he saw her.'

Barnes watched her face carefully. 'So he didn't tell you that he met with her in the early hours of Saturday morning?'

'What?' Melanie sat upright, her jaw dropping.

'Tansy made contact with him a little while ago,' Barnes continued. 'She wanted to see him, so they arranged for her to go to the pub where the band were staying on Friday night.'

'But I was with him Friday night. I….' She sank back into the cushions, her gaze falling to the carpet. 'Son of a bitch… Just after one o'clock he got out of bed and started pulling on his clothes. I asked him where he was going, thinking he was heading down to the bar to nick a drink or something, and he said he'd remembered Brian had organised a video interview with a US music programme. I couldn't believe Brian could be such a dickhead pulling a stunt like that the night before their comeback gig, but Joey seemed happy about it. Now I know why…'

'Did he mention Tansy at all?'

'No. Not even when he came back to the room. I

thought he sounded more upbeat than usual. Normally if they do an interview that late, he can be bloody grumpy. He – and the others – they get fed up answering the same questions over and over.' She shook her head in wonder. 'He was... *happy*. Couldn't stop talking about the gig and how it was going to be the start of a new phrase in his life and all that.' Melanie sighed. 'So, when do the rest of us meet her?'

Barnes looked over his shoulder to where Kay sat, stoical, her gaze fixed firmly on her notebook, then turned his attention back to Melanie and took a deep breath. 'He hasn't told you?'

'Now what?' The woman gave a sardonic smile. 'More secrets?'

'His daughter was killed shortly after leaving the pub on Saturday morning.'

Melanie paled. 'Killed? You mean in an accident?'

'No, she was murdered. Her body was found at the park by two of the clean-up volunteers. Has no one told you about this?'

'No... I... I haven't spoken to Joey since Monday. I mean, I heard a woman died at the festival but I thought that was a drug overdose or something.'

'We only spoke to him ourselves on Tuesday. I have to ask you, Melanie – what time did Joey get back to your room that night?'

'Three thirteen.' She held up her hand as he opened his mouth. 'I know that for sure because I couldn't get back to sleep so I was scrolling through social media on my phone. The band's pages were going off with comments from the fans excited about Saturday night's show so I was trying to get a head start on replying to some of them and sharing the rest.'

'Did he stay with you for the rest of the night?'

'Yeah. We only got up at eight because he had another....' She broke off with a bitter snort. 'Interview. And this time, it really was an interview because I listened in on it. It was with a radio station over in Cardiff where they're due to play next week. I take it they're still playing that one?'

'You'd have to check with Joey,' Barnes said smoothly.

THIRTY-FIVE

'I figured this was better than a phone call,' said Gavin, pointing to a table in the far corner of the franchised café.

The place was doing a brisk trade via the drive-through window but inside it was less than half full, the nearest customers being two women and a small child that was screeching at the top of its lungs.

He winced at the escalating crescendo then shot DC Paul Solomon a resigned smile. 'At least we won't be overheard.'

The Northfleet-based detective grinned. 'I take it you and Leanne aren't going down that route yet.'

'Perish the thought.'

They fell to silence while each demolished a pastry that had been reheated in a microwave moments before, and after he finished, Gavin pulled out his notebook and a pen before taking a slurp of coffee.

'Thanks for seeing me at short notice.'

'No problem. How's things in Maidstone?'

'Busy, as you can imagine with this festival death.'

'I'll bet. Progress?'

Gavin wrinkled his nose. 'Not yet.'

'Okay.' Paul dabbed his mouth with a paper napkin before tossing it onto his empty plate and pushing it away. 'How can I help?'

Lowering his voice despite the distance between them and the other customers, and the noise from the toddler who was now chortling as one of the women jiggled him on her knee, Gavin flipped to a new page of his notebook. 'The victim was strangled, and then either her killer – or someone else, because the post mortem results are ambiguous – removed her fingertips. Have you ever come across something like that before around here?'

Paul's gaze turned to the window as one of the takeaway customers drove past, and remained silent for a moment before answering. 'I can't think of anything, no – and I've been here a while. Strangulations, yes. But the fingertip removal... maybe, I don't know. About seven or eight years ago, there was a... What are you thinking anyway? That it was done to delay identification?'

'Exactly. And it did for a few days.' Gavin paused while a waitress came over to clean the table beside them. 'Turns out it was the daughter of one of the band members who was due to play on Saturday night.'

Paul's face turned to face him once more, his eyebrow cocked. 'Coincidence?'

'We don't know.' He sighed, dropping his pen to the table. 'I mean, we've got nothing. Absolutely nothing. I was hoping if something similar had happened this way, we'd have another angle to pursue, but...'

'Tell you what, I'll make a few phone calls – just in

case there is something in the records I don't know about. I mean, so many records got consolidated and moved up to HQ over the past few years that there could well be something buried in there from either Division, right?' He gave a malicious smile. 'I'm sure there are a couple of probationers I can coerce into a few hours' work.'

'True.' Gavin tried to inject some enthusiasm into his voice, but his mind was already turning to how he was going to deliver the news to Kay.

'And I'll phone a mate who works for the Essex lot. Maybe there's something like this over the Estuary we don't know about.'

'Yeah, okay – thanks. I like that idea.'

'All right then.' Paul's phone buzzed, and he swiped the screen before reaching out and draining the rest of his coffee. 'Sorry, that's the boss. Got a meeting back at the office about a raid that's taking place later tonight.'

'No worries. Thanks for the help.'

'Any time.'

'Stay safe.'

'Will do.'

Paul threw a wave over his shoulder as he hurried past the other customers and out the door, his car shooting out from the car park moments later.

After watching the older detective go, Gavin sipped his coffee and flicked through his notes, his frustration deepening.

If Paul – or the two unlucky probationary constables who were about to be corralled into helping – were unable to find anything linking Tansy's murder to another case, then what next?

Working with Kay had instilled a thirst for justice in him and the other members of the team, and when he recalled the sight of Tansy's mutilated body amongst the summer grasses of the park, an anger surged within him.

Updating his notebook with what Paul had told him and making a bullet-point list of what the other DC was going to do next, he forced his shoulders to relax, and then gave a slight jump as his phone vibrated.

Sean Gaskell's mobile number filled the top of the screen, and he answered it, keeping his voice low.

'Piper.'

'Gav? How far away are you from the station at the moment?'

'About half an hour if I push it.'

'I've been working through the CCTV footage again,' said the constable. 'I think you need to see this.'

Gavin was already pushing back his chair and hurrying towards the door. 'What have you found?'

'That person we saw on the security camera in Gareth Torsney's garden. I think it's Tansy Leneghan.'

THIRTY-SIX

'How long does it take to fetch a bloody pizza?'

Kay looked up from her computer screen and grinned while Gavin paced the carpet in front of the whiteboard, his stomach rumbling loudly.

The rest of the incident room was deserted save for her tight-knit team of detectives, the last constable disappearing twenty minutes earlier and the ebb and flow of late afternoon commuter traffic now reduced to a steady purr beyond the windows.

The sun was dropping in the sky now, lending a soft yellowish-purple stain to the gathering clouds while, every now and again, a flash of lightning reflected off her screen.

It seemed there would finally be a respite to the blistering heat that had gripped the south-east part of the country this past week, and she relished the thought of lying in bed listening to the rain patter on the roof later that night.

Pushing away her computer mouse, she tucked her hair back into a loose ponytail and eyed the detective constable as he paused with his hands on his hips, glaring at the door.

'You were the one who ordered the extra garlic bread,' she said. 'That's what's probably taking so long.'

Gavin aimed a glare at her, then laughed. 'Don't forget the garlic mayo too, guv. Got to have that.'

'There you go, then.' She frowned. 'Anyway, I thought it was your turn to go and get it?'

'I figured as Kyle's the newbie I'd take advantage of my superiority within the team.' He was still smiling as he turned away to eye the updated notes she'd scrawled across the whiteboard. 'And reread these.'

'I'm not sure that's the sort of leadership I try to advocate around here,' she said, smiling. 'Mind you, I'll remember that superiority thing next time I'm handing out tasks. Might have to get you to do some running around for me more often to try it out.'

Barnes wandered over with a half-used roll of kitchen towel, placing it on his desk before shaking his head. 'Honestly, anyone would think it was a kindergarten around here listening to you two.'

'You should've heard him and Kyle earlier,' Laura added, following in his wake with a six pack of lager that dripped with condensation. 'I nipped out to get these. That all right, guv?'

'Anyone see you?'

'No, I used that massive tote bag from the bookshop you gave me.'

'Okay. Good work.' Kay took one of the beers from her and cracked it open as her stomach rumbled. 'Okay, Gav – you're right. That pizza's taking too long.'

They were still laughing when Kyle walked in, his arms laden with four pizza boxes that he proceeded to lay out on the table beside the whiteboard.

'Before you start moaning, they were understaffed and someone placed an order for eight pizzas before ours,' he said, then stood to one side as Gavin and Laura launched themselves at the food. 'And one of you bastards ordered extra garlic bread.'

'Thanks, Kyle,' Kay said, handing him a beer. 'Right, let's eat.'

The conversation turned to office gossip before she shared the news regarding the new addition to her home, and Barnes choked on a mouthful of garlic bread before beating his chest with his fist.

'Bloody hell, guv – I thought you said never again after that goat.'

'I know, I know. Adam assures me Hovis won't cross the stream into the garden though.' She glanced over her shoulder as a rumble of approaching thunder shook the windows. 'Especially if we get a decent downpour tonight. There'll be more water in it, and I know we call it a bridge, but it's really just a plank of wood. It's not very stable so I doubt Hovis will risk it.'

She turned back to see four incredulous faces staring at her. 'What?'

'I reckon we need to start a sweepstake,' said Gavin.

Kyle thumbed through his wallet and then fished out a five-pound note. 'I'm in.'

'Me too.' Laura dashed over to her bag and returned with her purse. 'This is a slam-dunk. What do you reckon? Pick a day, or a time?'

'Both,' said Barnes, handing over his contribution. 'And I'm getting first dibs. Tomorrow afternoon, between twelve and five. I don't reckon he'll be able to contain himself once he works out that so-called bridge will hold his weight.'

'Oh come on. Seriously?' Kay watched while Gavin collected the pot of cash and then waved it at her. 'What? You want me to join in?'

'Churlish not to, guv.'

'No. No way.' She wiped her hands on a page of paper towel, then pointed at the whiteboard. 'Back to work.'

Ignoring their muffled sniggers, she stalked over to the board and gathered her thoughts.

'Okay, Gav. Get over here – tell me about Sean's theory that this is Tansy in these CCTV pictures.'

The detective constable finished sealing an envelope with the sweepstake pot inside, then joined her. 'I think he's got a fair point, guv. I mean, obviously the photos pixelated the more we tried to enlarge them, but he did the same with a couple of photos from her normal social media account – not the hidden one Joey alerted us to – and look, the same figure is seen on this council-managed camera walking down New Cut Road towards the park. The body build is strikingly similar.'

'Yeah, but she's not wearing a dress, Gav.' Kay tapped the photograph from the crime scene. 'And she was when those volunteers found her. And Joey confirmed this was the same dress she was wearing when they met. Sean's lurker is wearing what looks like jogging bottoms. And a sweatshirt. How d'you explain that?'

'I don't know. But on the video footage they've got the

same sort of gait to their walk and I mean, who wears those sorts of clothes at that time of night? And, look – they're wearing their hair tied back in the photo from Torsney's garden, and here in the other photo.' He pointed to the social media photos again. 'Tansy tended to wear her ponytail pulled a little to the left each time, look. Leanne does the same thing – it's just a natural habit. It's the side she ties her hair so when she finishes, it's got that same slant to it.'

'It's a long shot.' Kay gave her colleague a sideways look, hearing the desperation in his voice. 'But, all right. Say it is Tansy, then. What was she doing sneaking around Torsney's garden?'

'More to the point, guv, whoever picked her up from the pub after her meeting with Joey didn't kill her,' said Barnes. 'So who cancelled the taxi, who picked her up, and—'

'Who gave her a sweatshirt and jogging bottoms?' Laura finished. 'And where are they now?'

Kay turned to her. 'How did you get on tracing the number that was used to cancel her taxi ride back to the hotel?'

'No luck.' Laura bit back a belch, then put down her can of lager. 'Sorry. I went through the mobile numbers we've got for people we've spoken to so far like Georgina, Joey, Brian Kasprak and Melanie Cranwick's and it doesn't match theirs. I've widened the search too, and it's coming up a blank. Whoever called the taxi firm isn't someone we've come across yet.'

'Or it is, but they were using a different SIM card. Any idea whether it's a contract number or pay-as-you-go?'

'Not until the communications company comes back to me, and that could be—'

'Sometime in this century or the next.' Kay sighed. 'Dammit, we just can't catch a tangible break, can we? Kyle – how's Harriet getting on with the rest of the material gathered from the festival site on Saturday?'

The newest member of the detective team put down the pizza slice he had been contemplating and shot a warning glance at Laura. 'Mine. Guv, I spoke to Patrick at the forensics lab before they clocked off this afternoon and he said they're hopeful they'll finish the preliminaries by the weekend. It's just that because of the nature of some of the stuff – such as the biohazard bins that were used to collect spent needles in – it's taking longer than usual. Not to mention the sheer volume of evidence they collected. They only finished yesterday afternoon.'

'Yesterday?'

'Yeah. Patrick said they had to work with the festival organisers while the camping village and refreshments tents were dismantled and then process all that too…'

'Jesus.'

'And they've got three of their team on holiday this week and aren't allowed to bring in contractors to cover them.' Kyle picked up his pizza slice. 'I won't repeat what Patrick said about that.'

Kay let his words sink in for a moment while she sipped her beer. 'So we're days away from getting any findings from that. No wonder Harriet's report was inconclusive about Lucas's theory that two people might be involved in Tansy's murder.'

'Do you think there'll be anything to help us amongst that peripheral search?' said Barnes.

'I don't know what to think anymore. Gav, what happened with Paul Solomon over at Northfleet? Anything to help us?'

'He said he's going to get a couple of probationers to do an archive search, but he couldn't recall anything like this in his time there. He's going to have a word with an acquaintance in Essex Police too, just in case.'

'Sounds good. What about Sean? Is he going to continue with the CCTV footage tomorrow?'

'There's no more to review, guv. He finished earlier this afternoon but Tansy – or whoever that is – doesn't appear on any other recordings.' He jerked his chin at the whiteboard. 'That's all we've got. Unless…'

'What are you thinking?'

'It's just something I thought of while I was speaking to Paul earlier. When he said about checking with Essex regarding any potential similarities to cases they've had. I got distracted when Sean phoned with the news about the CCTV footage, but I was going to see if I could find someone in Sussex and Surrey to run the same checks. Just in case. I mean, we've got nothing else, have we?'

'Not yet, Gav. Not yet.' Kay ran her gaze one more time over the whiteboard, her shoulders tensing. 'But we will. I won't let Tansy's murderer get away with what they did to her.'

THIRTY-SEVEN

Thick droplets of rain lashed the windows an hour later, and purple-white streaks of lightning angled across the darkening sky and illuminated the walls of the incident room in a ghostly glow.

Now and again, one of the phones on the far side of the room trilled in a soft monotone before being automatically diverted to the Northfleet call centre, while Kay sat at her desk staring at her computer screen, chin in hand.

The rest of her team had left as one, each offering words of encouragement as they walked out the door, and she smiled as she recalled their determination and resolve.

Leaning back in her chair, she wrapped her fingers around the tepid can of beer and checked the clock on the wall behind Barnes's desk.

Adam would be here in half an hour, his evening surgery appointments finishing before he picked her up, and she had taken advantage of not having to drive home, snatching the spare can from the pack before tossing the cardboard into the recycling bin beside the photocopier.

Rather than watch the incoming storm, she had chosen instead to reread the statements from the interviews conducted to date, sifting through the ones collated from neighbouring properties around the park and focusing on Joey Twist and his entourage.

'There's got to be *something* in here,' she muttered, turning the pages of the neatly typed-up statement from Laura and Kyle's conversation with the taxi driver, before shoving it aside in frustration.

The grey cardigan that Toby McKinnon had mentioned Tansy wearing on that journey was still missing, and so far they had no leads on who might have been responsible for cancelling her booking for him to take her back to the hotel.

And then there was Sean and Gavin's theory about the young woman attempting to get into the park without being noticed by the festival security guards. There were plenty of other incidents over the opening days of the music festival where the security contractors had ejected people trying to get in for free, and Kay was sure there were plenty of others who evaded capture.

Could they be certain the person they had seen was Tansy, or would they waste valuable time chasing a lead that went nowhere?

Her gaze fell to Brian Kasprak's statement, and she wondered what sort of damage control the manager was concocting following the revelation that Joey's daughter had been murdered.

The band had released a statement three hours ago, just in time to hit the six o'clock news cycle, and she wondered with a cynical twist of her lips whether Kasprak had done so in order to ensure maximum coverage for the now delayed reunion tour – and subsequent new album.

There was a ruthless edge to the man, that was for sure.

When she picked up the statement, the stapled pages fell open to the last one, with Kasprak's signature embossed below the neatly typed lines and dated yesterday.

Both he and Joey Twist had opted to wait while the interview was transcribed, and Kay had added her own conversation with Kasprak to a formal addendum to his original statement, the photocopier darkening the effect of the black biro she had handed to the man before he had added his name with a flourish.

'Anyone would think you were signing bloody autographs,' she murmured, flicking back through his words.

She recalled the statements taken from the other band members, each echoing the other, that despite the well-earned reputation of their younger years they were taking advantage of the pub's remote location and having relatively quiet nights prior to headlining the festival on Saturday.

Two of them were able to show social media posts they'd sent out telling fans how much they were looking forward to seeing them soon, one was having a video call with his daughter who lived in Portland, Oregon and Thommo – Joey Twist's erstwhile nemesis and now bandmate once more – was alibied by his wife who had joined the band for the UK stretch of their comeback tour.

Kay frowned, her attention refocusing on the statement in her hand as an idea nibbled at the fringes of her thoughts. Turning the pages, she found the part where she and Kasprak had been talking in the corridor outside the interview room.

She tapped the text with her forefinger, mind racing.

'If you were doing a radio interview to promote the comeback, why weren't any of the other band members with you? Wouldn't the host want to speak to one of them?'

Leaving the statement to one side, she smacked the computer keyboard once to wake up the screen, entered her password and quickly opened a new window. After typing in the band's name together with Friday and Saturday's dates, she added the words "radio interview" and "Germany", then watched as the search engine started displaying its results.

She ignored the first few listings, noting that they were all sponsored links of one form or another, and scrolled down the page.

Right there, on the seventh line, was what she was looking for.

'Got you.'

Clicking the link, she found an embedded audio file under the title of the page. Ignoring the text underneath the video as her German was next to useless apart from working out she was indeed listening to the interview Kasprak had mentioned to her, she hit the "play" button.

The announcer's voice began proceedings with a short introduction lifted from one of Kasprak's press releases no doubt, and then the band manager's distinctive chuckle filled the speakers and the interview began in earnest.

Thankfully, it was in English and as she listened Kay

realised that there was nothing new to be learned from the conversation – the announcer was merely sticking to a script he had no doubt used for countless interviews with bands before, and Kasprak was hell-bent on selling the album and tour as the biggest rock music event of the year.

As the interview drew to a close, her attention wandered once more to the text underneath the video, and she scrolled a little further down.

'Huh.' She paused as the text ran out after just two paragraphs. 'That's not a transcript. And why's there a different date?'

Finding the translate option at the top of the screen, her gaze returned to the text.

'Shit.' She pushed away the rest of the can of lager as her brain caught up with what she was reading. 'It wasn't a live interview.'

THIRTY-EIGHT

'What do you mean it wasn't a live interview?'

Barnes clipped his seatbelt across his chest before gripping the armrest in the door as Kay accelerated from the kerb, narrowly missing his neighbour's black and white cat that shot out from under a parked car.

'It was recorded two days before Tansy was murdered,' she said, braking hard and swearing under her breath while a school bus idled at the junction. 'It was broadcast in the early hours of Saturday morning, but it wasn't live.'

'Fuck. So Kasprak's lying.'

'Yes.'

'Shit. Where is he now? Do we know?'

'I got our colleagues in Sussex to inform him in person last night that he's expected here at nine o'clock this morning and he might want to bring a solicitor.'

'Spoil his beauty sleep, did they?'

'Probably.'

'Good.' Barnes settled into his seat a little more as she

eased into the traffic queue heading towards the town centre. 'Means he'll have spent most of the night organising that legal representation then.'

'And working out what he's going to say to us.'

'How d'you want to approach it?'

'I'd like you to lead it. He's seen how you operate when you interviewed Joey, and after the way he was chatting to me on Tuesday he might view me more as a confidant. We might be able to use that to our advantage.' She sighed. 'Maybe.'

'Hell of a breakthrough though, guv,' he said admiringly.

'I got lucky, that's all.' Drumming her fingers on the steering wheel, she watched as a group of kindergarten-aged children were led across a zebra crossing in front of her like a line of bedraggled ducklings, their colourful waterproof coats providing a bright contrast to the grey skies and drizzle that cloaked the town. 'We need more though, Ian. Motive, for a start. And if Sean and Gavin are right about Tansy getting into the park somehow... I mean, why... Oh, I don't know. For fuck's sake, come on, people – the lights are green. Sorry.'

'That's okay. It's getting to us all.'

She looked across at her colleague, fully expecting to see a telltale smirk forming on his lips but he wore the same look of consternation she was sure etched her forehead. Turning her attention to the rear-view mirror, she caught sight of herself and groaned. 'I'm going to have frown lines by the end of this one, that's for sure.'

'Maybe switch some of that caffeine you're drinking for water, guv. Hydration, that's the key, I hear.'

'Piss off.' She laughed. 'Oh, thank god. Knightrider Street is clear. Let's go.'

Five minutes later, she pulled into the police station car park and hurried after Barnes, nodding her thanks as he swiped his security card across the door and led the way up the stairs to the incident room.

'Okay, so I'll run through everything with you before they get here,' she said, eyeing the clock. Flipping open the manila folder on her desk, she turned it to face him and started sifting through the documentation she had gathered the previous evening before Adam arrived. 'This is a copy of Kasprak's original statement together with the additional one he signed after he and I spoke out in the corridor – I wanted him to sign this in case anything came back to Joey, particularly given how much information Kasprak shared about how he got involved in the band in the first place. And then here's a run-down of his personal and business history that I've gleaned from OSINT – you know, social media, Companies House information, business-related interviews he's done over the years. I just made a bullet-point list for ease of reference, but the URLs for the original articles are saved to the system in case you want to refer to them afterwards.'

'This is good, guv,' Barnes murmured, taking the crib sheet from her. 'What about specific questions?'

'I think start off with getting him settled in, nice and friendly – and then hit him with the outright lie about the radio interview being his alibi for his whereabouts.' She huffed her fringe from her face and raised an eyebrow as her desk phone rang and she recognised the front desk's extension number. 'Ready to do battle?'

He gathered up the paperwork and squared his shoulders. 'More than ever.'

THIRTY-NINE

Despite her anticipation at the interview, and despite her desperation to see Tansy's killer arrested, Kay made sure that she carried herself with an air of confident authority when she walked up to the front desk.

She nodded to the uniformed constable behind the perspex security screen, then crossed to where Brian Kasprak was sitting beside a broad man in a sombre grey suit, a pale blue tie around his collar being the only concession to colour.

Kasprak himself wore his trademark jeans and black jacket over a white T-shirt, although she noted with a fleeting sense of satisfaction that he had bags under his bloodshot eyes, and had nicked himself shaving earlier that morning by the look of the make-up concealer dabbed on his neck.

'Mr Kasprak, thank you for being prompt,' she said. 'And you're…'

'Steven Javernick,' said the solicitor, handing over a business card. 'I can't tell you how much I regret…'

'Then don't.' Kay turned and led the way to the reinforced security door before swiping her card and holding it open for them. 'Through here, please.'

Barnes stood at the far end of the corridor, and beckoned to the two men. He had chosen the interview room farthest away, deliberately giving Kasprak plenty of time to contemplate the seriousness of the situation he was in as he passed by each closed door.

Kay watched as the man slowed the closer he got to her colleague, delaying the inevitable confrontation that was about to unfold.

He paused briefly before following Javernick into the room, then again as he turned a full circle, taking in the plain beige plasterwork walls and the four chairs around a laminate-covered metal table.

'Mr Kasprak, if you could take a seat and we'll begin,' said Barnes, unbuttoning his jacket and pulling out a chair for Kay opposite the solicitor.

She listened while her colleague recited the formal caution, and watched while Kasprak's Adam's apple bobbed in his throat, his gaze locked to the table surface.

He cleared his throat before confirming his name and occupation, went to clasp his hands, then seemed to think better of it and dropped them to his lap out of sight, affecting a relaxed gesture that fooled no one.

Barnes began the interview with a recap for the recording. 'Mr Kasprak, when you spoke to my colleague DI Hunter on Tuesday, you stated that you've known Joey Twist since the early 2000s, and have consistently represented him and the band since that time, including during their fifteen-year hiatus. You further stated that at the time Tansy Leneghan was meeting with her father at the pub in the early hours of Saturday morning, you were being interviewed by a German radio station. Do you wish to change anything in that statement?'

The band manager shook his head. 'No.'

'When was the interview organised?'

'A few weeks back. Germany's one of the band's biggest markets and the whole reunion has hit the rock music press over there. There's a lot of anticipation for the new album, so anything like that interview helps get the promoters on board with the tour later this year.' Some of Kasprak's confidence returned as he settled into familiar territory, his voice steady and his shoulders relaxing. 'It means some long hours talking to people like that, but it'll be worth it.'

'Right, okay.' Barnes opened the manila folder and shoved across two pages. 'For the purposes of the recording, I'm showing Mr Kasprak a print-out from the German radio station's website showing a screenshot of an audio clip and some text underneath. The second page is the English translation of the same page. The URLs for each appear in the footer of the print-out. Tell me about this, Mr Kasprak. What does it say?'

The man reached into an inner pocket of his jacket and pulled out glasses, a bashful expression flitting across his features. 'Confession time. I need these to read anything under fourteen point these days.'

Kay watched while he put on the glasses before leaning forward to read the text, and noted with some satisfaction that the colour drained from his face.

'Um… I… erm.' Kasprak removed his glasses. 'I'm

sure there's a reasonable explanation, I…'

'I would certainly hope so,' said Barnes, then waited, his gaze never leaving the man's face.

The seconds dragged by, and then the band manager cleared his throat. 'Oh, that's right. Yes. It was *Thursday* night I recorded the interview with them, not Friday. With everything going on leading up to the festival, I must've got my days mixed up. Sorry.'

Barnes slammed his hand on the table, making Kasprak and his solicitor jump. 'Not good enough, Mr Kasprak. We're dealing with the brutal murder of a twenty-four-year-old young woman, specifically the daughter of one of your clients. Unless that isn't enough to get your attention and focus, then let me tell you this. You are currently our only suspect in her death.'

The man's eyes widened, his lip trembling. 'But… but I didn't kill her.'

'But you *did* know she was meeting her father that night, didn't you?'

'Y-yes.'

'How did you find out?'

Kasprak appeared to recover some of his bluster and a sly smile formed. 'She employed a private investigator to poke around and find her father, did you know that?'

Barnes remained silent, and the only sound filling the room came from the faint scratch of the solicitor's pen across his legal pad as he furiously took notes.

Kay wondered how much he had been told prior to the interview, and whether it was progressing as he hoped – or whether her colleague's questioning had raised concerns about what else his client might be keeping from him.

'I don't know where she found him. He was about as subtle as the proverbial bull in a china shop,' Kasprak continued, shaking his head in disbelief. He patted his hands against his chest, his eyes darting between the two detectives. 'I mean, look at me. I've been in the music business for over thirty years. I'm used to spotting crazed fans from a mile off. Did he honestly think that someone following my car from the office wouldn't get my attention? Let alone phoning my admin assistant when I'm not there so he could poke about and find out where Joey was these days? For fuck's sake…'

Javernick raised a warning finger from his legal pad and gave a slight shake of his head before lowering his gaze once more, and his client leaned back in his seat.

'All I'm saying is that whoever she got to help her, he wasn't as discreet as she thought. I mean, what did he think, that sticking his nose in Joey's business wouldn't get my attention?'

'How did you find out about the meeting?' said Barnes.

'By accident. Like I said, you need eyes in the back of your head to do this job, especially when it comes to all the different ways fans will try to get to their favourite band members. Honestly, it's like herding cats sometimes. If they knew how much…' He broke off, then sighed. 'Look, I was worried, all right? There's a lot riding on this album and tour. A *lot*. I didn't want Joey to lose focus. I needed him to—'

He broke off as a sharp knock on the door resonated off the walls, and Kay's head swivelled as it opened and Kyle peered in.

'Guv, apologies for interrupting but I need an urgent word.'

FORTY

'This had better be good, constable.'

Kay eyed her newest probationary detective as he shuffled from foot to foot, then realised it wasn't from nerves. A tangible energy was emanating from him, and her heartbeat quickened.

Kyle chewed his lip while Barnes closed the interview room door, then walked a few paces away and beckoned to them, lowering his voice.

'We've just taken a call from Andy Grey in digital forensics,' he said. 'He finally managed to access Tansy's mobile phone, and he's got into the social media account she created to message her dad.'

'Thank Christ for that,' Barnes hissed. 'And about bloody time.'

'What did he find?' Kay fought down the urge to reach out and shake Kyle to hurry him along, realising that he was no doubt learning how to deliver his news in bite-sized chunks from Gavin. 'Anything that can help us?'

'Yeah, yeah. He thinks so, anyway.' Kyle paused again, wetting his lips. 'He's going to send through all the screenshots and transcripts so Debbie can get them into HOLMES2 and distributed to the team straight away, but he said there was one person who contacted *her* from a separate account and sent her a couple of threatening messages about keeping her distance from Joey and the band.'

'What? Who? When? I mean, timeframe-wise, when did she open that account, and when did those messages start coming through?'

'The account was opened at the beginning of last month, so about six weeks ago. The first message, saying something along the lines of "I know what you're up to, and you need to stop" was sent two weeks after that, so mid-May.'

'But you said there were a couple of messages,' said Barnes. 'When was the other one sent?'

Kyle grinned. 'Last Wednesday.'

'Jesus.' Kay spun away from him, covering her mouth to stop herself from yelling at the top of her voice in relief. She walked away a few paces, glared at the closed interview room door, then turned and stalked back to her colleagues and took a deep breath. 'What did that one say?'

'It was to the point, guv. It just said "Back off". Tansy didn't reply to either of them, but they were definitely delivered and seen. As far as Andy can tell, and as far as we know from the statements, Tansy was the only person with access to that account.'

'All right – has Andy got any idea who sent those messages?'

'Only a hunch, and only based on cross-referencing that person's activity on another account that's more official because both messages were sent from a private account like Tansy's. I mean, based on that person's *normal* account on that site. It looks like the message was sent to Tansy in between activity on the official account, and they were *really* active on that in the same time period because of the festival.' He gave a slight shake of his head at Barnes, who'd taken a sharp inhalation. 'And before you ask, he cross-checked everyone else we've spoken to in relation to Tansy's meeting with her father too.'

'Dammit, Kyle,' said Kay impatiently. '*Who?*'

The probationary detective jerked his thumb towards the interview room. 'Kasprak.'

'Fuck me,' Barnes breathed, smacking the manila folder against his leg. 'We've got him.'

'Not yet,' said Kay. 'But it's a bloody good start. Kyle, let Andy know I appreciate his help will you? And get those transcripts into HOLMES2 and a print-out of the whole lot on my desk so I can take a look after this interview.'

'Will do, guv.'

She watched him go, and then looked at Barnes, seeing the wolfish smile he wore. 'I take it you want to get back in there?'

'Let's go, guv.'

The door hit the plasterwork wall when her colleague pushed it open, and she winced at the loud smack that resonated around the room before closing it behind her and following him over to the table.

His posture remained business-like as he restarted the recording and recited a formal introduction, then lay the manila folder open in front of him and eyed Brian Kasprak.

'Which social media accounts do you have, Mr Kasprak?'

The man frowned. 'Um, the usual ones.'

He rattled off some familiar names, confirmed what his accounts were called on those, and then frowned. 'Why?'

'Tell us about the two messages you sent to Tansy Leneghan telling her to avoid her father,' said Barnes. 'Specifically, the second one that reads "Back off".'

'I don't know anything about that.' Kasprak jutted out his chin, colour rising to his cheeks.

'Are you sure?'

The man swallowed, but said nothing.

'Okay,' said Barnes unperturbed, 'what about the first message telling her "I know what you're up to, and you need to stop"?'

The solicitor leaned over and whispered in the band manager's ear, his words inaudible from where Kay sat. She scowled at the pair of them until Kasprak lowered his gaze to the table and gave a slight nod.

'Okay, I erm…' He paused to clear his throat. 'I did send that one, yes.'

'Why?'

'It's like I said. I was worried Joey would lose focus if she came sniffing around. Besides, my first interest is in each member of that band, and their welfare. Tansy could've been after his money, right? I mean, I've got nothing against her trying to get in touch, but she needed to wait. At least until the tour was over. She'd have ruined everything.'

'In what way?'

'Wanting to tag along with them or something. Distracting him. I mean, Christ, they had twenty years to catch up on, right? Do you really think Joey would've gone into a studio to record an album rather than spend time with his daughter?'

'Did you ask him?'

'No. I didn't get the chance, did I?'

Barnes leaned closer, ignoring the warning glare from Steven Javernick. 'So, Mr Kasprak, where exactly were you when Tansy Leneghan was at the pub early on Saturday morning? Because you weren't talking to a German radio station, were you?'

Kasprak ran his hands down his face before sighing. 'I was hiding in the storeroom just off the kitchen. I heard Joey moving about in his room and could hear voices, then heard him leave the room and go downstairs. You've got to understand, it's my job to make sure that lot deliver on the promises we've made to promoters so if he was up to something that could've jeopardised that day's event, I was damn well going to put a stop to it. He was walking back and forth in the bar, looking out the windows. It was pretty obvious he was waiting for someone, and it didn't take a genius to work out who, especially after that private detective contacted the office. So I went and hid. I figured he wouldn't want her to use the front door – the kitchen was the obvious choice.'

'What did you do when she got there?'

'They went through to the bar, so I sneaked out….' He let out a guttural snort. 'I must've looked like an idiot crawling on my hands and knees across the kitchen and out to the bar, but I couldn't risk either of them seeing me. I overheard everything of course, how he was going to arrange for her to come out on tour with them, and how much he was looking forward to spending more time with her… Everything I was worried about really.'

'What happened when she left?'

Kasprak's face fell. 'If I'd known what was going to happen… I saw the taxi drop her off, you see. Through the window in the storeroom. So before I crawled through to the bar, I phoned the company and asked if a return trip had been booked. It had, so I said alternative arrangements were made, and they could cancel it. I just wanted to talk to her, to make her see that she had to wait, that she had to leave all of the family stuff until the New Year, at least until the European leg of the tour was done and we'd hit that Christmas number one spot…'

'Did you use your car?'

'Yes.'

'Where is it now?'

'Here. I mean, it's in the car park round the corner. Next to that carriage museum.'

Barnes eyed both men. 'We're going to need your car keys, Mr Kasprak. And you might want to make alternative travel arrangements for the next few days.'

'That's preposterous,' Javernick spluttered. 'You can't

do that. My client has attended this interview voluntarily, and—'

'Your client is currently the main suspect in the brutal slaughter and maiming of Tansy Leneghan,' said Barnes. 'So yes, we can. Keys, please.'

Kasprak's brow furrowed, and then he withdrew his keys from his pocket with a shaking hand and handed over the car fob from the keyring. 'I want a receipt. And if it comes back damaged, I'll...'

'You'll get a receipt, don't worry.' Barnes slid the fob to Kay and turned his attention back to the band manager. 'So, how did you persuade Tansy to get into your car?'

'I guess she was too tired by then to argue,' said Kasprak. 'I parked down the road and flashed my lights when she came out the pub, so she couldn't see me until she opened the back door. She sort of laughed, and then got in and asked me if I'd heard their conversation. I said I had, and wondered if she'd at least hear me out while I drove her wherever she wanted to go.'

'Did you know where she was staying?'

'No, and she never told me. She told me to drop her off on that stretch of road by the retail store and that hotel, so I presumed she was staying there. There's nowhere else around there, is there? I mean, for all the cloak-and-dagger stuff that night, she wasn't exactly being smart about it.'

'What did you talk about?'

'I just tried to make her see sense, that's all. She wouldn't have any of it though.' Kasprak's gaze dropped to the table. 'I'm not proud of it, not after what happened, but I lost my temper with her. She was just so infuriatingly naïve about the whole damn thing.'

'Did you hit her?'

The man's head shot up. 'No. Of course I didn't.'

'Did you lash out and strike her? Is that what happened?' Barnes's voice didn't waver. 'We've seen it before, Brian. Tempers frayed, frustration… you name it. One punch is all it takes. Maybe when that knocked her out, you panicked. Perhaps decided to finish the job and choke her, except she wasn't dead yet, was she?'

'No. No, no – I didn't kill her.' Kasprak's voice rose in desperation. 'I just… we just shouted for a bit. And then she said she wanted to see where her dad was playing later that day. I told her there was no way I was going to give her a backstage pass, not there of all places. She said I had to, that she couldn't get a ticket, and when I said no again that's when she told me to drop her off. As soon as I stopped the car, she got out, slammed the door and stormed off.'

'And you just left her to walk alone.'

Kasprak paled. 'Hey, if I'd known that was the last time I was going to see her alive, I would have insisted on taking her to wherever she was staying. I swear.'

Barnes sat back in his seat for a moment and then gestured to Kasprak's jacket. 'Could you take off that for a moment, please?'

'What?'

'Your jacket. Could you remove it please?'

The band manager looked at Javernick, who gave a nonplussed shrug in response.

'Oh, okay. Whatever.' Kasprak stood, then eased his arms from the jacket and held up his hands. 'Anything else, detective? Would you like me to do a song and dance routine next?'

'Show me your arms please.'

The man rolled his eyes, but then twisted his arms left and right.

Kay bit back a sigh.

There wasn't a scratch mark in sight, not even any sign that such an injury had been concealed with the same make-up as the shaving scratch.

Her heart slammed into her ribs.

'Mr Kasprak, could you remove the make-up on your neck please?'

'What?'

She reached out for a box of tissues next to the recording equipment and slid it across the table at him. 'Remove the make-up please.'

She held her breath while he scrubbed at his jawline, then leaned closer. 'How did you get that scratch?'

'I caught myself shaving this morning.'

'Do you do that often?'

He glared at her. 'My hand was shaking. I guess I had a lot on my mind.'

'I'll bet you did.' Kay returned to her seat, and gave Barnes a nod.

Her colleague cleared his throat, and then turned to the recording equipment, his hand hovering above the "stop" button. 'Interview paused at eleven forty-three.'

Before he had a chance to stop the tape, Javernick was launching himself from his seat. 'My client has important business to attend to this afternoon, detective.'

'He's right,' said Kasprak, desperation in his voice.

'I'm due to talk with the promoters in Poland about financing for the tour there. We've been trying to schedule this for three months.'

'Oh, you're not going anywhere, Mr Kasprak,' said Barnes. 'Not until we've corroborated *all* of your phone numbers with the taxi company. And we'll be inviting you to provide a DNA sample as well.'

FORTY-ONE

Kay hurried into the incident room, saw Laura by the kettle, and beckoned to her while she headed for her desk.

'I need you and Gavin to bring Melanie Cranwick in for questioning,' she said, picking up the message transcripts from Tansy's hidden social media account that Kyle had left in a neat pile under her computer mouse. 'And for Christ's sake make sure you caution her.'

'Sure, guv.' Laura turned to swish her jacket off the back of her chair and flipped her hair over the collar. She glanced over her shoulder as Barnes swept in. 'I take it there's been a breakthrough then?'

'Kasprak was the one who cancelled Tansy's taxi ride back into Maidstone,' he said. 'And he was the one who drove her back, although he swears she was fine when he dropped her up the road from the hotel.'

'Did you get the DNA swab?' said Kay.

'Already bagged and with Hughes on the front desk for the courier,' he said. 'I've phoned the lab to give them the heads up it's a priority.'

'Bet they were pleased. How long did they say it'd take?'

'I called in a favour, so we might – *might* – get it before the weekend.'

'Jesus, I hope so. I don't fancy trying to persuade a magistrate to sign off on keeping Kasprak in custody beyond the standard thirty-six hours as it is. Not without something concrete to charge him with.'

'Is he a flight risk, guv?' said Laura.

'I hope not,' Kay replied. 'And you're still here because…?'

'I'm gone.'

The detective constable scurried away, dragging Gavin away from the photocopier as she passed and steering him towards the door.

'Are those the transcripts from Tansy's phone, guv?' Barnes said, peering over her shoulder. 'Wow. They were really chatty once she contacted Joey by the look of it.'

'Yeah, I know.' Kay scanned the texts, passing each page to Barnes to finish reading while she sifted through the rest in date order. 'And it looks like he wasn't kidding – once he got over the shock, you can hear his enthusiasm in these about organising that meeting, can't you?'

'When was the last one sent?'

Kay turned to the last messages, and swallowed at the poignancy. 'Here, at one oh five Saturday morning: "Just leaving to meet the taxi. See you soon! XX". Then he replied: "Meet you round the back of the pub. I'll unlock the kitchen door. Can't wait to see you at last. XX".'

Barnes took the page from her, and sighed. 'And she was dead within a few hours of this. Jesus, guv.'

'Okay, so we've probably got half an hour until Laura and Gavin get back here with Melanie. Let's make it count. I want you to review the band's social media accounts, and I'll take hers. Let's work up a better profile than the skeleton one we've currently got for her and make sure we make this next interview count.'

'Right you are, guv.'

Kay rapped her knuckles against the door of interview room number three and opened it to see Melanie Cranwick dressed in a cream sweatshirt and blue jeans.

She was sitting beside a familiar duty solicitor who had been appointed for her. At such short notice, and with scant funds for the sort of legal representation Brian Kasprak had engaged, the woman had taken Gavin's advice and accepted the help of a local firm of criminal defence solicitors whose offices were only a stone's throw away from the Palace Avenue police station.

The man wore a cheap dark grey suit and a look of permanent weariness, loosening his tie and giving Barnes a nod by way of greeting as her colleague sat and started the recording equipment, repeating the formal caution that had been given to Melanie less than an hour before by their colleagues.

'Melanie, we'd like to begin by asking you about your relationship with Brian Kasprak,' said Barnes. 'Can you tell us how you started working for him?'

'I guess I was about twenty-one, twenty-two perhaps. Not long divorced anyway, and sort of wondering what to do with my life.' Her gaze turned wistful. 'God, they were good times though. I was sharing a flat in Islington and working as a temporary secretary at a bank in the city. I was earning good money too so most nights I was out at gigs around the city. One of the local bands didn't have a clue about how to market themselves and I'd seen enough by then to figure out how to do it for them so I started running their fan club. They split about six months later but I'd sort of got to know Brian on the music scene by then and was bored in my job so I offered to go and work for him instead.'

'He paid that well?' Barnes said, raising an eyebrow. 'Compared to a bank?'

Melanie bit back a mischievous smile. 'Well, there were other benefits I suppose. Joey being one of them. I was sort of seeing him by then too.'

'How has your role with Brian changed over the years?'

'Oh my god, so much.' She threw up her hands. 'I mean, where to start? The internet was still in its infancy compared to where it is these days, the social media sites were... I mean, people talk about them with a sense of nostalgia now, but honestly they were crap. It's so much easier to promote the band now and keep in touch with their fans. I've been running that side of things for the band for all of that time—'

'And Brian's social media? How long have you been managing that?'

'Just this year, since the reunion was announced. You see, there's just so much to do with a project like this. He's juggling financing for the album and tour, speaking to tour promoters around the world at all hours, as well as marketing the band through his own social media accounts to help drum up interest from investors.' She leaned forward, lowering her voice conspiratorially. 'Did you know there's even talk of him appearing on the judging panel of one of those TV talent contests later this year? He'd be perfect – he's so photogenic, and he knows *so much* about the music industry. Having him mentor a rising star would be amazing.'

'What did you do while the band were on hiatus?'

Some of the enthusiasm left her face. 'I had to find another job. I mean, I kept the fan club going, the website and the newsletter, but Brian couldn't afford to pay me while there wasn't any money coming in – did he tell you the royalty payments were drying up? So, yeah – I got a job down the road from here on the industrial estate at Aylesford, working for a biosciences company until they made me redundant a few years ago, and then I got another job working in a tiny insurance company's office here in town.' She shook her head, emitting a theatrical sigh. 'I can't tell you how happy I was to tell them where to stick *that* when Brian phoned me up at the end of January and said about the band's plans to get back together. He offered me my old job back there and then, saying they couldn't do it without me. Of course, Joey had given me a heads-up it was probably going to happen after he and Thommo met in secret, but it was still good to hear Brian's voice again.'

'When did Brian find out about Tansy?'

'What?' Her eyes widened.

'What did Brian do when he found out she'd asked a private investigator to find her father, Joey Twist?'

'I... I don't know. I didn't know he knew about her. Joey told me when she got in touch.'

'When did Joey tell you?'

'Last week. Wednesday, I think.'

'But you knew before then, didn't you, Melanie?'

She jutted out her chin. 'I don't know what you're talking about.'

'Brian told you that Tansy employed a private investigator to track down Joey. Was it his idea to set up the secret social media account to send her a message telling her to keep her distance, or yours?'

'I... I don't know.'

'Did you find out Brian's password to the secret account and send a threatening message to Tansy telling her to "back off"?' Barnes opened the manila folder and slid across the photocopied screenshot. 'This one here. Did you send this from Brian Kasprak's social media account?'

'I-I'm not sure.' She kept her hands clasped, as if afraid to touch the page. 'I can't remember.'

'Think, Melanie. It's important. One of you knows the band's social media accounts inside out. One of you was panicked enough about Joey's daughter getting in touch to threaten her. And one of you is lying.'

He leaned closer. 'And currently, you're both under suspicion for her murder.'

FORTY-TWO

The sounds of Melanie's broken sobs filled the interview room while Kay watched dispassionately, her jaw set.

Barnes slid across a box of paper tissues, and kept his own counsel while the duty solicitor checked his watch.

'Perhaps my client could have five minutes to compose herself,' he said in a bored monotone. 'And I'd like a word with her.'

'Fine.' Kay pushed back her chair as her colleague paused the recording equipment, then traipsed after her into the corridor. Closing the door, she leaned against the plasterwork wall and crossed her arms. 'All right, what do you think?'

Barnes's mouth twisted. 'I dunno, guv. I reckon she sent that message, but I'm struggling to get my head around the fact she might've murdered Tansy. I can't see it myself.'

'What if she knows who did though? Could she be protecting Kasprak?'

His shoulders rose and fell, and then he turned as the door opened and the duty solicitor peered out.

'My client would like to make a statement,' he said.

Kay cocked an eyebrow at Barnes, then followed both men into the room, waiting while the recording equipment was started once more, then rested her arms on the table and looked at the woman before her. 'We're rapidly running out of patience, Melanie, so let's hear it. No more lies.'

'Okay,' the woman whispered.

'And please speak up. We need to make sure the recording can pick up your voice.'

Clearing her throat, Melanie sat upright although her gaze never left the table. 'I did send that message to Tansy telling her to back off. I never meant for her to get killed – I didn't kill her. When Brian told me about the private investigator, he didn't tell me Tansy was Joey's daughter. He just said that someone was trying to track down Joey from his past, and that if she got too close too fast she could jeopardise the whole reunion project. He banned me from telling Joey he knew about this woman from his past, and from telling anyone else in the band. I think he thought she would just give up if she couldn't find a way to contact Joey direct. He – we both – thought that she'd give up once Brian shut down any possibility of an introduction.'

She paused to dab at her eyes with an already sodden tissue, and then took a deep breath. 'I thought Tansy was someone who Joey knew romantically, you know, from way back. People do that, don't they? Realise they should've taken a chance on someone twenty or thirty years ago and want to see if it's possible when they get older, and try to rekindle something. I guess I got jealous, that's all. I found out about that secret social media account of Brian's by accident because it popped up in the notifications on my usual one saying "do you know this person?", probably because I manage all the band ones. Brian's like the rest of them, not very good around technology and social media,' she said with a sly smile. 'The lot of them are dinosaurs around that stuff, believe me.'

'How did you know it was his account though? It's not his photo on it, and it's set to private.'

'See that avatar he's used on the message?' She raised her eyes and reached out to tap the printed out transcript. 'It's the same design as the tattoo on his upper bicep. He keeps it covered with his T-shirt sleeve most of the time.'

'And you managed to log into that account?' said Barnes.

'Yeah.' She snorted. 'He uses the same password for everything, so it wasn't difficult. But there was nothing in those messages to say she was Joey's daughter, right? So I figured she was trying to barge in on what me and Joey have. You know, they're about to hit the big time again with this new album and tour, and so of course everyone's going to come out of the woodwork now and try to get in on the action, aren't they? So I told her to back off. I didn't want her fucking up the tour, the music, the… the…'

'The relationship you have with Joey?' Barnes prompted.

'Exactly. And then you go and tell me she's his daughter, she turns up in secret on Friday night—'

'And was murdered,' said Barnes. 'Let's not forget that, shall we?'

'I had nothing to do with that,' she said, holding up her hands. 'I didn't. All I did was send that message.'

'Have you logged in to that account again since you sent it?'

'No.' Melanie slumped back in her seat and crossed her arms, a petulant turn to her mouth. 'Brian changed the password late last week, and I couldn't work out what it was.'

Barnes eyed the duty solicitor while he collated the screenshots and closed the manila folder. 'We're going to need a DNA sample from your client before she leaves here today. I'll let you explain the procedure to her.'

FORTY-THREE

Kay shoved her hands in her pockets as the deluge eased, and peered into the gully between her garden and the orchard while a torrent of water gushed past.

The stream level was only inches from the base of the makeshift bridge she and Adam had dropped across it a few months before, and was threatening to breach the bank as it passed under the fence towards the neighbouring property.

Pulling her hood over her eyes, she smeared away the rain that splashed at her cheeks and chin, squinting through the orchard until she spotted Hovis sheltering under one of the large apple trees.

He bellowed a guttural bleat, and glared back.

'No use moaning at me,' she said. 'Besides, you could always go in that new shed of yours if you were that fussed.'

Hovis turned his back on her and stalked away.

'I think by the morning this will have gone down a bit.'

She shuffled to her left at Adam's voice, careful not to

slide in the mud that was congealing around her waterproof boots, and gave him a cautious smile. 'As long as it doesn't rain tonight.'

'It's not forecast.' He joined her, and then squinted up at the sky. 'Another few minutes and this'll pass over anyway. Kevin's got some sandbags in, just in case though.'

Kay glanced across to their neighbour's property, remembering that the garden across the fence was lower than theirs. 'Do you think he'll be okay?'

'I've told him to knock on the door if he needs a hand but it'll take more than this to burst the banks – I took a look at the historical record for the stream this afternoon and it hasn't flooded in our lifetime.'

She turned her attention to the orchard to see Hovis peering at her from within the confines of the shed, his pale eyes unblinking. 'At least this'll put him off trying anything until we've got a gate up or something.'

'Yeah, although we're going to have to wait until this ground dries out now before I try sinking any posts in. I don't fancy trying it in this.' Adam poked a wellington boot at the mud. 'Do you want to go and get dried out? I just phoned for a Chinese takeaway and it'll be here in half an hour or so.'

Kay's stomach rumbled in response. She laughed. 'That'll be a yes. Have we got any Verdelho in the fridge?'

'Yeah. Do you want some?' He led the way back to the house, pausing at the threshold to toe off his boots, then held out a hand to steady her while she did the same.

'Just the one – I said to Barnes I'd stay on call tonight

because he's taking Pia out to dinner at that new Moroccan restaurant.'

'I'll give you fifteen minutes, then I'm pouring.'

'I can take a hint.'

She took off out of the kitchen while pulling her blouse over her head, jogged upstairs and threw that and her suit trousers into the wash basket and five minutes later was standing under hot jets of water in the en suite shower.

Massaging shampoo into her scalp, she wondered if Harriet's lab team were already working on the DNA samples per their promise to Barnes, and whether either of them would prove to be a match for the blood splatter found on Tansy's arms.

There were too many variables in the case, too much forensic evidence to sift through from the crime scene, and not enough manpower to do anything about it.

She knew she couldn't push her team any harder than they were already working. Each and every one of them was doing overtime without claiming it – she had had her suspicions, but confirmed it earlier that day when she saw the time stamps on the reports being uploaded to HOLMES2.

And she knew better than to ask them to rest, to pace themselves, because she knew they were as desperate as she to find Tansy's killer.

A grim determination seized her while she rinsed the soapy suds from her hair. Whatever happened, she knew she would keep going until she had all the answers she sought. Even if headquarters refused to provide more staff, or sent in a case auditor to sift through her efforts to date.

As she was towelling herself dry, she heard the

doorbell and then Adam whistling as he made his way along the hallway.

'Shit, they're early,' she hissed under her breath, and pulled on jeans and a sweatshirt.

Scrubbing at her damp hair with a towel, she made her way downstairs and walked into the kitchen, the rich aroma of Szechuan sauce filling the room.

Adam winked, and slid a glass of white wine across the central workbench.

'Fourteen minutes, seven seconds,' he grinned. 'Not bad.'

FORTY-FOUR

Blinking back sleep, Gavin reached out and smacked his hand against the flashing phone screen on the bedside table, cutting off the blaring brass section mid-song.

Dappled sunlight shone through a crack in the blinds, warming his legs, and he wiggled his toes while listening to the coffee machine downstairs bubble to life.

'I think I preferred the klaxon,' Leanne grumbled, rolling away from him and burying her head under the pillow. 'And we have to sort out our shifts so we start at the same time.'

'Good luck with that,' he said, yawning.

He stretched his arms over his head and listened as a robin chirped merrily on the guttering above the bedroom window, the faint *swish* of traffic carrying from the junction at the end of the street mingling with a soft coo from a wood pigeon.

'If you're making coffee, I'll have one,' Leanne said, tossing the pillow to one side and pushing her thick curls from her face. 'I'm wide awake now.'

'Sorry.'

'Good job I love you.' She gave him a light punch on the arm. 'This training course of mine should finish early today. Want to go out for something to eat tonight?'

He smiled, throwing back the sheet and swinging his feet onto the carpeted floor. 'Yeah, sounds good. I ought to be able to get out by about seven latest so I could meet you in town. Where d'you fancy going?'

'I need carbs, so anything Italian works for me.'

'Okay. I know just the place.' He leaned over to kiss her. 'Coffee's on its way. Don't nick the shower before I get in there though – I wanted to go in early to try and get a head start on some paperwork before the boss gets in.'

His phone buzzed then, the vibration echoing through the pine bedside table, and he glanced over his shoulder, groaning as he saw the familiar name on the screen. 'Talk of the devil.'

Kay's voice cut him off before he had a chance to greet her. 'How soon can you get yourself over to Mote Park?'

He did a quick calculation in his head, then: 'Twenty minutes?'

'Make it fifteen if you can.'

'What's wrong, guv?'

'Someone's found a pair of jogging bottoms and a sweatshirt in a council bin by one of the entrance gates. The clothes are covered in blood stains.'

Smoothing a hand over damp hair before extracting a plain cornflower blue tie from his jacket pocket, Gavin hurried along the uneven pavement towards a line of Kent Police patrol cars.

Two of them blocked the eastern access to the park while a plain grey panel van that he quickly identified as belonging to Harriet's team was slewed at an awkward angle to the kerb alongside the closer of the cars.

Securing the tie under his collar, he buttoned his jacket and approached a young constable beside a stretch of blue and white crime scene tape that blocked his access. He glanced at the name on the stab vest, and shot him a grateful nod as a clipboard was thrust into his hand.

'Thanks, Greaves.'

The accompanying black biro was warm from the youngster's nervous grip, and Gavin resisted the urge to wipe his hand across his trousers after scrawling his name. Instead he jerked his chin towards a party of six figures all clad in identical biohazard suits.

'That's obviously the SOCOs,' he said. 'Where's DI Hunter?'

'Here.'

He turned at the voice to see Kay sidling between the van and the car, her jacket sleeves rolled up to her elbows. 'Harriet's lot didn't hang around getting here then, guv.'

'They were on their way back from a job in Ashford,' she said. 'Come on, you're just in time – I'm about to interview the bloke from the council who found the clothes.'

She led the way over to a stocky man in his early sixties who was dressed in a bright lime green high visibility jacket and matching trousers despite the rising temperature.

He wore what appeared to be a permanent frown given the lines that criss-crossed his forehead, and tossed a cigarette butt into the gutter with an apparent lack of irony when they approached.

''Bout time,' he rasped, then emitted a phlegm-laden cough.

'Sorry to keep you, Mr Wells,' said Kay. 'We appreciate your time. This is my colleague, DC Gavin Piper.'

Gavin gave the man a curt nod, then took out his notebook and thumbed to a fresh page.

Wells continued scowling at them. 'I got over fifty more bins to empty before the end of me shift, and I gets a report at the end of the month if they ain't done, so hurry up like, yeah?'

Kay didn't miss a beat, and seemed to be blatantly ignoring the man's attitude. 'What time did you start your shift this morning?'

'Six, same as I always do during the summer.'

'And where did you start it?'

Wells jerked his thumb over his shoulder. 'T'other side of the park. Over by Park Way.'

Craning her neck past him, Kay frowned. 'Did you walk here?'

'Nah, the truck's parked down the hill. I has to walk up here picking up the litter first, then I start on the bins. Easier to carry the bags down when they're full, see?'

'Right, so which bin was the first one?'

'That one,' he said, pointing to where Harriet's team worked. 'So that's buggered up the rest of the morning, ain't it?'

'How often do you empty these? Weekly?'

'Yeah. Usually on Mondays, except your lot have had this pavement closed off since Saturday so the schedule's fucked anyway. Today's the first day we've had a chance to get near it.' Wells gave a theatrical roll of his eyes. 'And it ain't like the company pays overtime. Can't get the extra money off the council, or that's what they tell us.'

Gavin eyed the detritus lining the verge and hedgerow separating the pavement from the park boundary fence. 'Is there always this much rubbish lying around?'

'Yes and no. Doesn't help that there was that festival. I mean, they put bins out for people to chuck their crap in all around the site, but they still drop it out here. Then we 'ad that storm, and that's blown stuff everywhere too.' Wells tutted. 'It's going to take me the rest of the day just to get through this bit.'

'I wouldn't bet on finishing anywhere near here today, Mr Wells,' said Kay, extracting a business card and handing it to him. 'And if your boss has a problem with that, get them to call me.'

He beamed, exposing a missing front tooth, and tucked the card into his trouser pocket. 'I will, ta.'

'Tell me what happened when you found the clothing.'

'Got the shock of m'life, I tell ya.' Wells scratched his chin, his gaze travelling to where the CSIs worked. 'I mean, I see the news about the girl's murder, and then when I opened the bin lid to empty it, there's a sweatshirt shoved in there with blood down the front of it. There was crisp packets and stuff stuck to the material, like, but I knew straight away there was something iffy about it.'

'How did you know it was blood?' Gavin said, looking up from his notes.

'I cut me finger a few weeks ago, bad like, and even though I was wearing black jeans at the time, it still stained 'em.' The man shook his head, staring at his feet. 'I knew what I was looking at all right. So I phoned your lot.'

'Did you touch the clothing?' said Kay.

'No. Didn't need to. I saw enough as soon as I took the bin lid off. Besides, even if I did I was wearing me gloves.' Wells waggled fingers encased in a pair of thick black gloves that were smeared with stains. 'One of them over there took me fingerprints anyway though.'

Kay raised an eyebrow at Gavin, but he shook his head. 'Right, Mr Wells. As I said, I doubt very much you'll be continuing your shift along this stretch of road today, but thank you for your quick thinking. You've got my card – if you think of anything else that might help us, give me a call.'

She led the way back to where Gavin had parked his car, then leaned against the door while eyeing Harriet's team.

'Do you think it's Tansy's clothing, then?' she said.

'It's got to be, hasn't it? But what's it doing out here? Why didn't her killer dump the clothing in one of the park bins, or even somewhere in the park?' Gavin tucked his notebook away. 'Hell of a risk carrying it out to here, surely?'

'Perhaps they did it to break up any evidence trail, given this one is a council bin – all the others in the park were due to be emptied by festival volunteers or the clean-up contractor employed by Crusader Events. I presume

Tansy was wearing that dress under the sweatshirt and jogging bottoms – if we're assuming it *was* her you and Sean saw in the CCTV images, that is.' Kay pushed herself away from the car and sighed. 'I suppose if we work on the hypothesis that she dressed in the dark clothing to access the park without being seen, and wore the dress underneath so she blended in with the crowd once it got light, that would work.'

'And all because Kasprak didn't want her to see her dad play live... I don't know, guv. Something isn't adding up.'

'Detective Hunter!'

They both spun round at the sound of Harriet's voice to see the CSI lead beckoning them back to the cordon.

When Gavin got there, he could see the excitement in her eyes.

'What've you got for us?' said Kay.

'This.' Harriet held up a sealed evidence bag. 'It was in one of the pockets.'

Gavin emitted a surprised grunt when he saw what was inside. 'That's Brian Kasprak's business card.'

Kay took the bag from Harriet and turned it over, exposing a handwritten note scrawled across the back. 'And that isn't the mobile number we've got for him. It's different.'

FORTY-FIVE

Some of the polish had left Brian Kasprak's appearance the next time he entered the interview room ahead of a thick-set uniformed constable.

He shuffled towards the chair beside his solicitor, nodded curtly to the man, and then slumped back and eyed Kay while Barnes started the recording equipment.

Without his trademark aviator sunglasses and after a few hours spent in one of the station's stark custody cells, there were dark circles noticeable under Kasprak's eyes, the whites of which were bloodshot.

His collar-length hair curled in different directions, adding to Kay's growing hunch that he straightened it first thing in the morning, and now showed signs of having been ruffled with worry at regular intervals while he had been a guest of the on-duty custody sergeant.

He had left his jacket in the cell, and now rubbed at his bare arms as the air conditioning rippled goosebumps across his skin. As he did so, Kay noticed the frayed edges of a tattoo, no doubt the one Melanie stated he had used as the avatar for his once-secret social media account.

After the formalities were complete, she wasted no time and slid across a photograph of the business card that had been discovered that morning.

'Is this your writing?'

'No, it isn't.'

'Do you recognise whose writing it is?'

'I don't.'

'Whose phone number is this, Mr Kasprak?'

He squinted, evidently ruing leaving his reading glasses in his jacket pocket, then leaned closer. 'I'm... I'm not sure. I don't recognise it.'

'Is it someone associated with the band? Are you trying to protect someone perhaps?'

'Look, I have all sorts of numbers in my phone, all right? I can't remember them all. I'd be delighted to check.' He paused, and gave a satisfied sneer. 'But you've got my phone.'

'DC Barnes, would you mind retrieving Mr Kasprak's phone for him?' said Kay. 'Perhaps it will jog his memory as to what the hell his business card was doing in Tansy Leneghan's pocket.'

The band manager reared back in his chair. 'What did you say?'

'Let the recording note that DC Barnes left the room,' Kay said, then snatched back the photograph and tucked it under the manila folder beside her. 'Think carefully, Mr Kasprak. The next few minutes are going to be crucial for you. At the present time, you're one of two suspects in the mutilation and death of Tansy, and your DNA sample will also be tested against the blood-stained clothing that was discovered in a council rubbish bin outside Mote Park this morning.'

She watched as the man's face paled further, a fine trace of sweat beading at his brow.

'I don't understand,' he mumbled, wiping his face with the heel of his palm. 'That's not what happened…'

He fell silent then, his attention turning to the chipped surface of the table while the seconds ticked past, until the door opened and Barnes reappeared, mobile phone held out.

Kasprak snatched it from him with the enthusiasm of a toddler getting its hands on a favourite toy. He held his breath while it powered up, then emitted a grateful sigh when the screen lit up and pressed his thumb to activate the passcode.

'Before you're tempted to check emails or anything, let's see your contact list please,' said Kay, holding out her hand.

Kasprak's top lip curled, but he lowered the phone and slid it across the table towards her with force.

She stopped it just before it toppled over the side, and began scrolling through the extensive list of names that were displayed.

The only sound that penetrated her concentration was the incessant *click* of the second hand on the clock above the door while she worked, her jaw clenching tighter with every passing moment.

Finally, she pursed her lips and turned to Barnes,

giving him a slight shake of her head before sliding the phone back to the band manager.

The relief in his eyes did nothing for her rising frustration and seeming to sense this, he held up his hands.

'Look,' he said, his voice calm. 'I gave out *dozens* of those cards at that festival. You can't imagine the number of people who were trying to get to the band, trying to get exclusive interviews, or trying to find out what the album was going to be called so it could be leaked to the press before we're ready... and those were just the sane requests. It was bedlam there from the moment we arrived on the Thursday and held an initial press conference.'

'You must have some idea,' said Kay. 'I can't imagine you give out those cards to members of the public as a rule, do you?'

'No, but look at how many people were involved behind the scenes. Your lot must've had to interview all of them, right? So you know how difficult it is for me to remember.'

Kay jabbed her finger on the bag and glared at him. 'This number doesn't match any of the contact details we were given in any witness statements to date.'

'So, you must've missed someone,' Kasprak insisted. 'Or one of them gave you a wrong number.'

A silence followed his words, and then Kay pushed back her chair, the metal legs scraping across the tiled floor with a tortured squeal. 'Interview paused at two seventeen.'

Five minutes later, heartbeat racing, she followed Barnes into the incident room, her shoulders tense.

All around her, phones rang, fingers tapped on keyboards and a steady hum of activity filled the air.

No one looked up from their work as she passed, almost as if they could sense the tension that trailed in her wake and instead kept their eyes firmly on computer screens or made an effort to find something to do on the other side of the room near the photocopier rather than be within her orbit.

'There could be another explanation, guv,' said Barnes as he got to his desk and reached across for a water bottle.

'Let me hear it, because I'm all out of ideas.'

'Kasprak could be telling the truth.' He took a swig, letting his words sink in, then shrugged. 'Someone could've been given one of his cards over the course of Thursday or Friday like he said, and then used it in the absence of anything like notepaper to pass on their number to Tansy if she didn't want to put it straight into her phone. It could just be a coincidence that it was Kasprak's card that was used.'

Kay narrowed her eyes at him. 'That doesn't bear thinking about.'

'I'm just saying.'

'Fuck.' Kay threw the manila folder onto her desk and rested her hands on her hips before turning to her colleague.

'Sorry.'

'Not your fault. It's a fair point. Have you tried calling the number?'

'Yes, and all I get is an automated message saying the phone's been switched off.' He jerked his chin towards the whiteboard. 'So, what do we do now? The phone company's dragging their feet about telling us who the number belongs to.'

'There's nothing we *can* do now. Not until we get those DNA results.' She checked her watch. 'And they need to come through tonight, or we're really in the shit, aren't we?'

FORTY-SIX

Kay tucked a loose strand of hair behind her ear, blinked to ward off the stinging sensation in her eyes and forced herself to focus on the next email that popped up on her computer screen.

She had sent Barnes and the rest of the team home an hour ago, aware that if they were as exhausted as she by the time they reached a frustratingly short afternoon briefing, then they would be no good to her over the weekend.

Biting back a yawn, she typed in a curt response to an email from the personnel department at Chatham headquarters, and glanced down as her mobile vibrated on her desk.

Despite everything, she smiled when she saw Adam's number displayed.

'Evening,' she said, switching it to speaker phone so she could continue working. 'Don't I know you from somewhere?'

'I was going to ask you the same thing,' he said, not

unkindly. 'How're you doing? I presume you're the only one working this late?'

'I am, don't worry – I wouldn't do that to them. Besides, I think by the time the briefing ended they wanted to be as far away from me as possible.'

'I'm sure that's not true. I'd imagine they're all feeling the strain right now.'

She heard him take a slurp of something, and then the musical warble of a blackbird resonated in the background. 'Are you outside?'

'In the orchard. I was just checking Hovis's shed stayed watertight these past few days but it seems okay.'

'What about the gate across the bridge?'

'Don't worry, I've got the timber I need on order. It should turn up next week.'

Kay's fingers hovered above her keyboard, and she narrowed her eyes at the phone. 'That water will be going down in the stream fast though, won't it?'

'Yes, but he doesn't seem interested in crossing the plank over it—'

'Still, I'd be happier if we could put up something temporary.'

He yawned. 'Okay, I'll take a look tomorrow if I have time. Oh, and Scott phoned earlier – they need me back at the surgery tomorrow to help him with an emergency procedure, and I might go in Sunday to give him a break. You'll be working all weekend, won't you?'

She took one look at the emails lining her screen and sighed. 'I reckon I will, especially the way this case is going.'

'What time do you think you'll be back tonight?'

'Give me another hour to clear some emails and I'll be there.'

'I'll put some pasta on.'

'Love you.'

'Love you too.'

Smiling, she ended the call and then began stretching her arms above her head, her shoulders protesting.

She froze halfway when her desk phone trilled and a single red LED flashed above her direct line number.

Snatching the receiver from the cradle, heart pounding, she cleared her throat before speaking. 'Detective Inspector Kay Hunter.'

'DI Hunter, it's Grahame Tanner at the forensics laboratory,' said a warm voice. 'Sorry to call so late, but Detective Barnes asked us to put a rush on some DNA samples for him and I thought you might want the results as soon as possible.'

Heart pounding, Kay reached out for her notebook and hurriedly flicked through to a clean page. 'Grahame, that's great – thanks for doing this for us.'

'Just don't tell anyone else,' he said, chuckling. 'Ian only got away with it because he thrashed me at golf a few months ago and I made the mistake of betting he wouldn't. I'm probably going to rue this for the rest of my career.'

She smiled, biting back the urge to tell him to hurry up. 'Sounds like the Ian I know.'

'I know, right?' He shuffled some paperwork, and then she heard him switch the phone to speaker, his voice becoming a little more brittle. A radio station played quietly in the background, emanating some sort of jazz ensemble that did nothing for her nerves. 'That's easier.

Okay, so we had DNA results from three people – Tansy Leneghan, your victim, and then Melanie Cranwick and Brian Kasprak. Then we have the business card. That was a mess by the way – lots of trace evidence smeared all over it.'

Kay closed her eyes for a moment, anticipating the problems that lay ahead. 'Go on.'

'Both of your people handled this card at some point,' Tanner confirmed. 'Kasprak's being the most dominant, which makes sense given it's his name on the front of it.'

'But you say Melanie Cranwick's prints were on it as well?'

'They were, but – how to explain this? – more like background noise.'

'So she handled the card at some point, but not recently, something like that?'

'Exactly. For example, if the cards had been ordered by her and then unwrapped when she took delivery of them before passing them on to Kasprak to use.'

'Okay, I understand.'

'That's not a definitive reason of course, but it gives you an idea of the sort of thing you're going to have to consider.'

'Got it.'

He turned a page, the swish of paper carrying through to where Kay sat, her heel tapping nervously on the carpet. 'Then there's a fourth print.'

The phone slipped in her grasp, and she caught it just before it hit the desk, then switched it to speaker. 'What did you say?'

'There's a fourth print on the card, in the top right-hand corner. A thumb, and partial finger I would say. It definitely doesn't match any of the samples provided.'

'Is it in the system?'

'Not that I can see, but I'll send it over so you can double-check.' He paused, and she heard the smile in his voice. 'There's something else too that might help you. We try to be thorough here when we're testing, to save going back and forth if any of our clients require additional information.'

'What do you mean?'

'I can sense your impatience from here, Detective Hunter, so I won't prolong the agony further. I tested this for all trace evidence, not just fingerprints. I can confirm that there's a tiny – and I mean, minuscule – sample of blood in the left-hand edge of the card.'

'It was found in the pocket of some bloodstained clothing we believe belonged to our victim. Didn't Ian tell you that?'

'He did, but that's the thing. This blood doesn't match your victim, nor is the DNA a match for Melanie Cranwick or Brian Kasprak.'

'Shit,' murmured Kay. 'Somebody else killed Tansy…'

FORTY-SEVEN

The next morning, Laura dropped her sunglasses over her eyes and gave a nod of thanks to the barista before elbowing her way out the door of the café.

She was assaulted by blinding sunlight that bounced off the stark concrete paving slabs lining Jubilee Square, an architectural misstep that had resulted in a bland expanse with no shade save for a bus stop facing the High Street.

Squinting, she hoicked her handbag up her shoulder then shifted the takeout cup from hand to hand while pushing her jacket sleeves up her arms, simultaneously eyeing the pale skin that poked out and envying Gavin the ease with which he tanned.

'I need another bloody holiday,' she muttered. 'I'm starting to look like a vampire again.'

Turning right and walking down Gabriel's Hill, the gradient clutching at her calves, she scuttled into the scant shade afforded by the shop awnings on the left-hand side of the cobbled street, picking up her pace as she neared the police station.

Above her head, gulls cried and squabbled while doing their best to outsmart the myriad of pigeons that cluttered the rooftops and swooped onto spilt takeaway wrappers. Piles of discarded fast food joined the litter that lined the gutters, yet to be swept away by a team of council workers who were huddled outside the entrance to the shopping centre, talking in low voices and enjoying a cigarette or vape before continuing their morning shift.

The twin lanes of traffic that snaked around Palace Avenue at the foot of the hill was already nose to tail, with a steady stream of cars turning off towards the multi-storey car park, and tempers were fraying judging by the honking horns sounding from farther along the queue.

Zigzagging between a stationary white van and a pair of large motorcycles that roared with a throatiness that shook her eardrums, Laura waited while a liveried patrol car exited the police station car park then ducked under the barrier before it closed.

She spotted Barnes ambling towards her, and grinned when he opened the security door for her.

'Good timing, Sarge.'

'Got one of those for me?'

'Sorry – the place was heaving. I got glared at for ordering this as it was.'

'Ah, the delights of tourist season.' He swiped his card against the panel beside the inner door and led the way up the stairs towards the incident room. 'Did you hear from Kay last night?'

'I got a text message.' Laura paused on the landing to take a sip of coffee. 'Not good, is it?'

The older detective shook his head, his hand on the bannister. 'No, it isn't. At this rate, Sharp will be over here asking what we're playing at. Or worse, someone else.'

'Shit.'

The door at the top of the stairs opened outwards and Kay peered down at them.

'Briefing in two,' she said, then turned and let the door swing shut behind her.

'I swear she's got a sixth sense when it comes to coffee,' Laura muttered.

'And when we're talking about her.'

Laughing under her breath, she followed Barnes into the incident room, hurriedly drained her takeout cup and tossed it into the first recycling bin she passed before switching on her computer.

Shrugging off her jacket while the machine whirred to life, she nodded a greeting to Gavin and Kyle, then rolled her chair towards the whiteboard where the rest of the team were already gathered.

A few more stragglers entered the room but Laura kept her attention on Kay, who paced back and forth in front of the team with a palpable energy.

The effect created an electric atmosphere as Debbie handed around briefing agendas fresh out of HOLMES2 and voices began to subside.

'We have a problem,' Kay said, pausing in her steps to stand in front of Tansy's photograph. She looked at each team member to ensure she had their full attention before continuing. 'Late last night, the DNA results from

Kasprak's business card came through, and although he and Melanie Cranwick's fingerprints were confirmed to be present, alongside Tansy's there was a fourth set of prints. Worse for us, there are also traces of blood, and it doesn't belong to our victim.'

Laura's heart slammed into her ribs, her jaw slackening. 'Guv, is the lab saying we've got DNA evidence from her killer?'

'We have, but that DNA doesn't match with anything on the system,' said Kay. 'Which gives us a bigger problem than some of you will appreciate, because you were probably still at school when the changes came in.'

Sean Gastrell looked up from his notebook. 'What changes were those?'

'Before the law changed in 2012 here in the UK, DNA results could only be kept for a maximum period of five years for anyone charged with an offence. These days, the results are kept indefinitely, which is how we manage to match repeat offenders to any new crimes. Prior to 2012, once someone gave a DNA swab, the clock started ticking.' Kay ran a hand through her hair, and Laura saw then how much strain the detective inspector was under. 'So we have three scenarios we now have to consider. Whoever killed Tansy has never been arrested before, or has but it was prior to 2012 so the record is lost, or—'

'They've killed before, but never been caught,' Laura finished. 'Shit.'

The DI pointed at her. 'Exactly. Shit.'

'And given the way in which Tansy was killed, we have to assume her killer had experience,' said Barnes. He jerked his chin at the photographs taken at the post mortem. 'Given the injuries she sustained.'

'I agree.' Kay dropped the agenda onto a nearby desk and sighed. 'In the circumstances, I'm inclined to release Brian Kasprak and Melanie Cranwick with no further action to be taken. Does anyone have an issue with that?'

The room fell silent.

'Good,' she continued. 'Next steps then. We take a closer look at the other people around Joey Twist. That means everyone who might've come into contact with Tansy, including the private investigator she employed. Kasprak was contacted by him, so he should be able to give us the bloke's details. He might've come across something during his enquiries and doesn't realise the significance of it. *We* might, if he lets us have it – which I'm sure he will, if he wants our cooperation in future.'

Laura ran her gaze over the photographs behind Kay as she listened, fighting back an overwhelming sense that Tansy's murderer was slipping away from them while the DI's voice washed over her, issuing instructions and encouragement in equal measure.

She remembered it then, a story that had been central to the band's implosion and subsequent reunion, a story that had become part of the band's mystique and legend. A story that—

'Guv?' Her hand shot up to get Kay's attention. 'What about Thommo?'

The DI stopped talking to Gavin, her full attention on Laura. 'Explain.'

Taking a deep breath, Laura rose from her chair and walked over to the whiteboard, peering up at the official photograph of the band that had been taken to launch the news of the impending album and tour.

The guitarist posed to the right of his bandmates, his hip thrust sideways at a nonchalant angle and his mouth in a theatrical sneer while he peered down his nose at the photographer's lens, oozing attitude.

'I'm just trying to think of anyone else who would want Tansy out of the way,' Laura said. 'Kasprak's told us that Thommo was the joker in the band, always up to mischief, but what if there's a vindictive side to him too? I mean, we know he can be violent – we've all heard about him and Joey laying into each other backstage fifteen years ago. He didn't hold back then, did he?'

'There's a long way between having a fight on stage to killing your mate's daughter,' said Gavin.

She spun on her heel to face him. 'But Joey *isn't* his mate, is he? They're only talking to each other again because they need the money from this tour. Kasprak said so. And looking at each of their careers since the split, Thommo's the one who probably needs it more than most – the others got session work or things like that over the years. Thommo didn't. He's been relying on benefits in between casual jobs. He needs this tour to go ahead.'

'So, you reckon he found out about Tansy and decided to meet with her to make sure she didn't wreck their plans, is that it?' Kay picked up a pen and wrote Laura's suggestion on the board. 'Do you want to bring him in for formal questioning as a potential suspect on that basis?'

Seeing it in black and white, the DI's looping handwriting formally committing her thoughts to the investigation, Laura paused a moment before answering.

Was she sure?

Would she stake her place in the team on it?

'Yes,' she said eventually. 'Yes, I do. Because then we can demand an up-to-date DNA sample from him as well, can't we?'

She heard Nadine's sharp intake of breath from where the young constable sat in the front row of seats, but kept her gaze firmly on the DI.

A slow smile began to form, and then Kay waggled her pen at her.

'I always knew you had the makings of an extraordinary detective, DC Hanway.'

FORTY-EIGHT

Despite spending twenty-four hours in custody, or perhaps because of it, when Brian Kasprak stalked into the reception area beside Thomas "Thommo" Smith, the manager's appearance resembled his usual attempt at looking fashionably bedraggled once more.

Tie askew, hair damp from where he had no doubt made use of the men's showers within the past hour, his unshaven jawline only served to accent his ruggedness.

And yet it was nothing compared to the lanky guitarist.

Fifteen years out of the spotlight had done nothing to dim Thommo's charisma, and Kay watched with interest as the young constable behind the custody desk blushed while she went through the various pieces of paperwork with the man, making sure he understood what was about to happen next.

His tight blue jeans and black vest top accentuated skinny limbs that probably had more to do with a poor diet and good genes than any form of exercise, while his silhouette was lengthened further in appearance by dark brown hair that reached the middle of his spine. Tattoos entwined his forearms and biceps, bright colours creating stark pinpricks against the aged darker blue tones.

When he turned to face her after scrawling his trademark signature across the final pages of documentation, she saw a greyness in his features that no amount of hair dye could erase.

'Do you have a solicitor?' she said by way of greeting, 'or do we need to appoint one for you?'

'She'll be here soon,' Kasprak replied. 'Don't worry.'

'I'm not worried. Your client is entitled to the same rights as everyone else who's been interviewed today, and if he couldn't afford legal representation then we can phone a local solicitor to act on his behalf.'

'That won't be necessary, Detective Hunter.'

She turned at the sound of a haughty voice to see a dark-haired woman of a similar age to her own stalking towards the small group, her entrance into the room turning heads amongst the younger male constables that milled about.

Dressed in a black mini skirt and matching jacket, she oozed confidence – and money.

'And you are?' Kay said, arching an eyebrow.

'Me wife,' said Thommo, and grinned. 'Ain't she a corker?'

―――

'How the fuck did we not know his wife is a bloody barrister?' Kay hissed to Laura as she watched the pair settle into the hard plastic chairs on one side of a Formica-covered table in interview room four.

Laura had turned three shades paler upon Felicity Smith's arrival, her movements clumsy.

Within the space of thirty seconds, the once confident detective had morphed into the probationer that Kay had nurtured from an early introduction to the team, and her nervousness was palpable.

'I don't know, guv,' she stammered in a barely audible whisper. 'I mean, obviously with her job and everything the two weren't connected at all on social media, and without him being charged we couldn't delve much deeper into his background over and above what's available through a basic internet search, so…'

Kay held up her hand. 'Take a deep breath. Maybe three. Go on. We've got time.'

Her colleague gulped in air, a little colour returning to her cheeks. 'Sorry, guv.'

'Nothing to be sorry about. If nothing else, the financial team at headquarters are going to want to know why he's been claiming unemployment benefits if he's married to a barrister, aren't they?'

She winked, then turned and led the way into the interview room, hearing the door slam shut behind her colleague and then waiting while Laura started up the recording equipment and recited the formal caution.

By the time that was done, the younger detective's face had regained some colour, and her voice had grown in confidence.

Kay took a moment to flick through the papers in the manila folder in front of her, and wondered what she should order from the Chinese takeaway on Spot Lane when Adam got home that evening.

Not that Thommo or his wife would know that.

All they would see was a detective taking her time reviewing the evidence – however flimsy – and wondering why she had been insistent on a DNA sample being taken the moment Thommo had arrived at the station.

'Tell me about Tansy Leneghan,' she said eventually, folding her hands together and eyeing the man. 'When did you meet her?'

Kay heard a sharp squeak from her colleague, which was quickly turned into a cough.

Thommo emitted a surprised grunt. 'I never said I did.'

'No, but you *did* meet with her, didn't you? What happened?'

After glancing at his wife, who gave a curt nod in response, he turned back to Kay. 'It was a complete coincidence, fate… whatever. I didn't know who she was to start off with. I just found her lurking around one of the main gates into the park late Friday night.'

'Hang on, what time?'

'I dunno. It was more like Saturday morning – you know when you start to sense the sky getting lighter? Say after three, at least. I don't wear a watch, see? So I'm not sure.'

'What were you doing there? I thought Kasprak had you all staying at the pub?'

'I didn't want to. I don't sleep much before a big gig like that – never did. I need to double-check stuff, get a feel for the place, so I walk about a bit. Brian had me tucked away in one of the posh tents but had it put up behind the main stage, out of sight of the public.'

'Go on.'

'It's just like I said, I was out for a walk and I saw this girl in a dress lurking around one of the gates – she just appeared out of nowhere after I'd seen one of the security blokes go past so she must have hidden until he'd gone and thought the coast was clear. I gave her one hell of a fright, I tell you.' He gave a soft chuckle. 'I asked what she was doing, and she... She looked sad, like. Not desperate, not one of them types who try it on just to say they've slept with someone in the band. Not that that happens these days.'

Kay watched with amusement as the man shot a sideways glance at his wife who sat in stony silence, her gaze firmly on the legal pad before her. 'What did you say to her?'

'I asked her what she was doing. Got the shock of my life when she told me she just wanted to see her dad play live later that day but couldn't get in. I thought she meant one of the support acts or something like that, and she obviously just wanted to talk so I asked her who he played with. Got the shock of my life when she told me it was our Joey.'

'She just told you?'

'Yeah. I think she'd given up by then, but I could tell it meant a lot to her.' He kneaded his hands together. 'I wish I hadn't, now that... now that she's dead, but I wanted to help. So I told her to stay where she was, and I legged it back to my tent. I had some old track suit bottoms and a sweatshirt that were reasonably clean so I lobbed them over the security fence to her.'

'She wore your clothes into the park?'

'Yeah, I waited until the next security bloke had gone past, then said I'd spotted that some of the houses on the next road over backed onto the park so she could probably get in that way, and then hide. I figured if she was wearing dark-coloured clothing she could sneak along the fringes of the park, wait until it was properly light and then ditch my clothes – she was still wearing her dress and a cardigan thing underneath them, see, so she'd blend right in with the rest of the ticket holders.'

Kay let Laura catch up with her note-taking then turned back to the guitarist. 'Didn't you have a problem with Tansy trying to get in touch with her dad?'

'Fuck knows I've made some mistakes during my lifetime,' he said. 'Especially with that fiasco fifteen years ago. Least I could do to make it up to Joey would be to help his daughter, right?'

'What about the tour and the implications it could have had if Joey invited her along?' said Kay.

Thommo shrugged. 'Couldn't see a problem myself. Would've been the same as Flick here coming along, and Kasprak ain't said nothing about her not touring with us.'

'Why not just give her a backstage pass?' said Laura.

The guitarist snorted. 'Are you kidding me? Kasprak guards those like they're made from fucking gold. Besides, if he'd already told her there was no way he was letting her have one, that's that. He never changes his mind once he makes a decision. Chances are, he'd given them all out to people he thought could help us get the new album some airtime and sales anyway.'

'So, the plan was for Tansy to sneak into the park overnight and then what, get down to the front when your lot got on stage?'

'Yeah, or whatever she was planning to do. I mean, I told her not to try and get backstage or draw attention to herself. She seemed happy enough just to get in though and see her dad play live.'

Kay looked up from the manila folder and frowned. 'Hang on. If you got her into the park, then why didn't she stay with you until it got light?'

Thommo's jaw tightened under his fashionable stubble. 'Because I had other matters to attend to. And before you say something, yeah, it's been on my mind ever since that if I hadn't left her on her own, chances are she'd still be alive now.'

'Other matters? Such as?'

'Look, I'm not proud all right, especially after what's happened an' all, but someone managed to score me some... something to help me with me nerves. Been a while since we played a gig that big and I was worried, that's all.'

'I take it we're talking recreational drugs rather than prescriptive?'

He nodded, lowering his gaze, and twisted the signet ring on his finger. 'Yeah.'

'Whose phone number did you write on Kasprak's card?'

'I told you, I wasn't happy about leaving her on her own, but I needed... Anyway, it's me brother's number. He was working that weekend and I figured if Tansy did need anything, he was the best person for her to speak to in an emergency.'

'Your brother works with the band as well?' Kay flicked through her notes. 'We don't have him listed as part of your entourage.'

'Nah, he don't work for us,' he said, smiling. 'We ain't that close. He works for Crusader Events.'

'The lot that organised the festival? Doing what?'

'Well, he owns it.'

Kay frowned. 'What's his name?'

'Alistair Featheringham.' Thommo shrugged. 'He kept the family name. Joey wasn't the only one who decided his name wasn't right for the band when we were starting out, see?'

Ten minutes later, after the interview formally ended, Kay and Laura stood in the corridor and watched while a uniformed constable showed Thommo Smith and his wife to the exit.

The barrister's disdain for the entire process was palpable, her voice carrying across the heads of a pair of administrative staff who scuttled out of her way as she stalked out ahead of her husband.

Laura watched as the outer door swung shut behind them, and then turned to Kay, who wore a watchful expression.

'How did you know he met Tansy that night, guv?'

'It was just a hunch.' Kay smiled. 'And luckily for us, it paid off.'

FORTY-NINE

Over the course of the afternoon, the remaining three band members were reinterviewed under caution one by one and then subsequently freed without further enquiry after each provided a solid alibi.

Finally, at half past four, Brian Kasprak walked into the reception area with his solicitor in tow and one of Gavin's cans of energy drink clutched firmly in his hand.

He sidled up to Kay while Danny, the singer, was released by the latest incumbent behind the custody desk, and nudged her elbow. 'Look, Hunter, no hard feelings okay? We all know you're just doing your job. We want you to find Tansy's killer as well. Joey's a mess, and the sooner you find the fucker who did that to his little girl, the better.'

Kay murmured her thanks, then made her way back to the incident room with a renewed determination in her stride.

'All right, that's the rest of the band in the clear,' she

said, crossing to where her tight-knit group of detectives waited for her beside the whiteboard. 'So what've you managed to find out about Alistair Featheringham?'

'Apart from the fact he's a model citizen, nothing,' said Barnes, pouting. He jerked his thumb over his shoulder at the board. 'He's active on social media, supports a lot of charity fundraisers through things like five-kilometre runs, things like that, and appears to be closer than Thommo to their parents. They live in Hastings, by the way. Both in their early nineties.'

'What about previous? Anything?'

'Not even a speeding fine, guv,' said Kyle. 'And looking at the sorts of cars he likes to drive, that's saying something. Sorry.'

Kay's shoulders sank. 'Dammit, I thought we might be onto something there. What about his statement – did you double-check that in case anything was missed when he was interviewed last Saturday?'

'I did, and I didn't think of anything else the team on site could've asked him,' said Barnes. 'And unless we've got something definitive to work with, we're not going to be able to pull him in for questioning, let alone demand a DNA sample to test against that business card of Kasprak's.'

'Yeah, I know – we were pushing our luck doing that with Thommo.' She rested her hands on her hips and glared at the whiteboard, unwilling to admit defeat. 'Any suggestions?'

'He only lives in Charing, doesn't he?' said Kyle. 'What if we went and spoke to him?'

Kay turned. 'What, now?'

'Yeah.' He grinned. 'If anything, it'll throw him having us turn up unannounced on his doorstep, especially when you formally caution him. You never know what we might find out that way, guv.'

'I like his style,' Barnes murmured, then reached into his trouser pocket and threw his key fob across to the probationary detective constable. 'Best you go with her, then.'

The man who opened the front door to the converted flint stone barn wore fashionable wire-rimmed glasses and a perplexed frown.

'There's a sign on the gate post that says no uninvited guests,' he said. 'That includes the postman, so... Wait, I met you at the festival on Saturday, didn't I?'

Kay held up her warrant card. 'Detective Inspector Hunter, Kent Police. This is my colleague, DC Kyle Walker. Can you confirm that your brother is Thomas Smith?'

He blinked. 'Is Thommo all right?'

'He is. May we come in?'

'Why?'

'Probably better if we explain inside, Mr Featheringham.'

'I'm in the middle of cooking dinner. We're expecting guests at—'

'The sooner we talk, the sooner we'll be gone.' Kay smiled maliciously, and nodded towards the scruffy pool car that had been assigned to the team that week. 'Unless you'd like us to wait for your guests to arrive? We're okay parked there, aren't we?'

The man took one look at the vehicle, and baulked. 'Come in. We'll have to use the reception room – my wife's taken over the living room with her sister's kids.'

Kyle shot her a curt nod, then followed her along a wide hallway and into a large rectangular room that had been painted a daring shade of amber.

Three white sofas were placed in a U-shape facing patio doors at the far end, affording views across an impossibly green lawn. An empty hearth stretched along the left-hand wall, above which an enormous television played silently, its screen displaying a cricket match from overseas offering little hope for the current England squad.

Featheringham paused in the centre of the room and turned to face them, crossing his arms over his chest. 'All right, you're in. Make it quick please. I take it this is about the young woman who was found dead last weekend? You do realise I've already provided a statement?'

'It is, and I am,' said Kay, eyeing the framed photographs and awards that adorned the wall beside her. 'However, I'm surprised you didn't mention your brother was the headline act.'

'It didn't seem relevant at the time.'

'And now?'

'Now I'm getting annoyed,' he said. 'Did you have anything you wanted to ask me, or do I have to tell the media I'm being harassed by the police after already spending most of this week talking to my insurance company? Do you have any idea the damage your lot have done to my organisation's reputation?'

'Frankly, I couldn't care less,' Kay snapped, and took a step closer. 'Did Tansy Leneghan call you?'

There was a fraction of a pause, and then Featheringham blinked.

'What?' His eyebrows shot upwards. 'Who?'

'She did, didn't she? When?'

'I… I'm not sure.'

'When, Mr Featheringham? It's important.'

'I didn't say she did.'

'You didn't have to.' Kay raised her chin, glaring at him. 'I've been doing this long enough to know when someone's lying. When did Tansy call you? We know Thommo gave her your mobile number when he saw her within a few hours of when she was killed, so—'

'It was about four fifteen,' Featheringham blurted. 'I only know that because I was back here, getting my head down for a few hours' sleep and the phone woke up my wife. She wasn't happy about it, I can tell you – especially when she overheard another woman's voice. Not many people have my direct number.'

'Speaking of which, we've been trying to call it. Why has your phone been switched off?'

'Because I needed a break from all the calls I've been getting about the event being cancelled, that's why. At least until I've had a concrete answer from my insurers as to what they're going to do about compensating all of our suppliers.'

'What did Tansy want?'

He dropped his gaze to the ornamental rug beneath

their feet, scuffing at it with the toe of his suede loafer. 'I don't know.'

'What do you mean? You spoke to her, didn't you?'

Kay watched in silent amazement as tears filled the man's eyes, his voice shaking with his next words.

'I didn't get a chance. I asked who it was, because I didn't recognise the number. It was a mobile phone, and like I said, very few people have my direct number. Anyone from around here is saved to my contacts list so their name would've popped up instead.'

'So you *did* speak to her. You just said you didn't—'

'I didn't though. I asked who it was, like I said, but there was no reply. There was… sort of a scuffle at the end of the line, and then it went dead.'

'What?'

'It cut off. I tried redialling it, but the first time it was busy, and the second time I tried it five minutes later, it rang out. Nobody picked it up.' Featheringham wiped at his eyes, and glared at her. 'And now you're here. It was her, wasn't it? Tansy. It was her trying to phone me. Why was that, Detective Hunter? Why was Joey Twist's daughter trying to phone me?'

———

At Kay's suggestion, Alistair Featheringham's wife had taken charge and cancelled their dinner party plans for that evening.

The woman had swiftly ushered her sister and children into her car and taken them out to a nearby gastro pub, her pale complexion belying her shock despite her brusque efficiency.

Featheringham now sat on a chrome-framed bar stool in the couple's expansive kitchen, his fingers cradling a mug of sweet tea that Kyle had made for him before retreating to the hallway, his notebook and phone in his hand.

Kay had already spoken to Featheringham's wife, who had confirmed that Tansy had only asked to speak to Alistair and seemed out of breath.

She was unable to provide any other information simply because she had walked out of the bedroom in a huff while he had tried to elicit a further response from the caller.

'Guv?' Kyle said, beckoning to her from the open door to the hallway. 'Can I speak to you for a minute?'

Following him, she waited until they had reached the foot of the staircase and then raised a quizzical eyebrow. 'What've you got?'

'It's about that mobile phone that was used to call him,' he said. 'Laura's looked into it, and the number matches one that was reported stolen from a tent on the fringes of the campsite on Saturday morning.'

'That explains how Tansy managed to phone Featheringham when she'd left hers at the hotel then. Okay, thanks. Let's go and see what else he can tell us.'

Walking back to the kitchen, she eased into one of the bar stools opposite the events company owner.

'How long have you run Crusader?' she said, steering Featheringham back to safer, familiar territory. 'It's been going a while, hasn't it?'

'Twenty-four years.' His hand shook as he brought the mug to his lips. After taking a sip, he sighed. 'Although I've only been more hands-on again these past four years or so. We were obviously on hiatus for a while, with a smaller team just working from home while we waited to see whether there'd still be a business after all the lockdowns and everything, and I haven't yet managed to extract myself again.'

'Don't you get involved in the events?'

'I try not to. I have staff for that. For the past fifteen years, I've been concentrating on the investment and expansion side of the business, working with overseas partners and securing corporate sponsorships. We've got some pretty big investors you know. They all require my time in ensuring each feels that they're getting value for money. I only went along at the weekend because that festival was on the doorstep, so to speak. I don't want my staff to think I'm checking up on them all the time – I'm all for empowering them to fulfil their potential.'

Kay smiled as the man settled into corporate-speak once more, his voice growing stronger as he expanded on his subject. 'You must be incredibly proud of what you've achieved.'

'Oh, you know… it keeps me out of trouble.' He managed a smile. 'And pays for the petrol.'

'Yes, I'd seen you're quite the classic car enthusiast.'

'It's just a way of letting off steam.'

She looked around the kitchen, at the gleaming appliances and granite worktops, the light beyond the windows slowly dimming as a burnt ochre sunset began to colour the horizon, and then back to Featheringham.

'Is there anything else you can think of that might help with our enquiries?' she said, hating the desperation that saturated her words. 'Anything at all?'

'I wish there was.' He pushed away the hot drink, then shook his head. 'I really wish there was.'

FIFTY

A soft sunset had turned into an indigo-stained twilight by the time Kay ended the team briefing.

As she ran her gaze over the tired faces in front of her, she could sense the frustration emanating from the group and almost hear the grinding of teeth as they revisited the evidence time and time again.

And yet, there was nothing.

Nothing at all.

She glanced at the clock on the wall as Barnes stifled a yawn. 'Look, take a break, all of you. Go home, and get something to eat, and get some sleep. Maybe we'll have a different perspective on things in the morning.'

She noticed a reluctance in the way they slouched out of the room, and a sense of pride sent a shiver across her shoulders.

None of them wanted to admit defeat, she could see that, but eyeing the myriad of theories now streaming across the whiteboard, she bit back a sigh at the realisation that the investigation was slowly but surely slipping away from her grasp.

Whoever killed Tansy was too good, too practised – and lucky.

Ignoring the hunger pangs that pinched at her stomach, Kay crossed to her desk and opened the file that Barnes had left for her.

After a few moments, she closed the folder with a sigh, her gaze travelling to the blind-covered windows and wondered when she and Adam might get away next.

She would give her all to see Tansy's killer arrested and charged with her murder, but she was also well aware that her energy levels were starting to ebb with the effort of making sure her team stayed focused on the investigation.

Gavin's desk phone trilled from the workstation alongside hers, and she peered over the low partition screen to see a Gravesend number displayed.

'DI Hunter.'

'Detective Hunter, it's DC Paul Solomon over at HQ,' said the familiar voice. 'Is Gavin there?'

'I've just sent them all home for the evening,' she said, snatching up a sticky note. 'Do you want to leave a message for him?'

'Actually… I guess I could tell you, to save him repeating himself.'

'Oh? What is it?'

'When Gav was over here last week he mentioned about that festival murder you've got on your hands. He said you wanted to find out if I knew of any similar open cases – he said the current theory is that your victim's killer has done this before, right?'

'Going by the state of her injuries and the fact they've got away with it – so far – I'd say yes.' Kay stopped waggling her pen between her fingers and sank onto her colleague's chair. 'Why, have you got something?'

'I don't know… maybe.'

'Try me. Despite what Gavin might've told you, I don't bite. Not at the weekend, anyway.'

Paul laughed. 'Good to know, guv. Okay, well I couldn't find anything on our patch but something rang a bell so I made a few phone calls to colleagues in other forces across the south I've become familiar with over the years. Essex, East and West Sussex, and Hampshire, to be exact.'

Kay leaned forward, staring at the number displayed on the phone screen. 'You *have* found something, haven't you?'

'Maybe. Got a pen handy? I'll email this lot over to you in a bit but I've got a late briefing I need to attend in ten minutes. We've got an armed gang we're trying to arrest in the morning.'

'Go ahead. Ready when you are.'

'So, nothing came up in East Division. As far as I can tell, without further information, Tansy's death is the first one like this in Kent. However, there's an open suspicious death in Hampshire from a mid-sized folk festival near Winchester eight years ago that sounds similar – the victim there was a man in his early twenties who was cut, then strangled and left in woodland nearby. His fingertips had been removed, as were his ear lobes.'

Kay winced. 'Ear lobes?'

'He wore quite distinctive earrings – the sort that are embedded in the lobes, rather than piercings.'

'Okay...' She heard the horror in her voice, and blinked to clear the image. 'Anything else?'

'Yes. Four more across the south – once I'd spoken with my contact in Hampshire, they then raised the matter with people they know in Dorset, and Devon and Cornwall force as well. Guv, we're looking at six further suspicious deaths across twenty years. And those are the ones we know about. In each case, the fingertips were removed post mortem, and sometimes other body parts too if there were distinctive features. But in most of these, there weren't the associated cuts and strangulation you've got with Tansy's murder. Four were suspected drugs overdoses, with the subsequent mutilations written off as some sick bastard interfering with the corpse before the body was reported to authorities. The mutilations were never made public in those cases, which is why it took some digging around to get the details.'

'Jesus.'

'You're definitely onto something, guv.' His hand covered the receiver, and she heard muffled voices in the background before he returned. 'Sorry, got to go – but I'll email this over after the briefing, and you'll have my number on the system if you need me. Is that okay?'

'Absolutely, and thanks, Paul. Owe you one.'

'Just get the bastard, guv. Before they kill someone else.'

FIFTY-ONE

Jaw clenched, Kay jiggled a dozen coloured pins in her hand while she eyed the freshly printed map that now stretched across a cork board by her desk.

A dreary overcast morning cloaked the county town, a dull light filtering through the window blinds of the incident room promising more of the same.

The overhead strip lighting cast a sickly yellow sheen across the whiteboard to her left, its presence a permanent reminder of what was at stake if she failed now.

'Come on, Hunter. Focus,' she muttered.

She had spent the time since arriving an hour ago plotting out the six crime scene sites for the unsolved cases that bore a remarkable resemblance to Tansy's murder.

Paul Solomon's email had appeared as promised, together with the case file reference numbers for each investigation that had gone cold due to lack of information or solid leads to progress them.

She hadn't slept since reading it, and had lain awake imagining the pain of six more families like Tansy's parents who remained desperate for answers, desperate to understand why their loved ones had been taken from them so cruelly.

Kicking off her shoes and wiggling her toes on the thin carpet, she cricked her neck and tried to concentrate once more.

'Okay,' she said, running her gaze over the pins in the board. 'Six suspicious deaths, six different locations, six completely different events. What connects them? Roads? Ease of escape? What?'

Except no two murder scenes were within a one hundred-mile radius of each other.

Each was scattered across counties, a seaside resort on the Dorset coast here, a farm in Hampshire there, a theme park in Sussex…

So, where was the killer?

'Shit,' she muttered, and tossed the pins onto Gavin's desk.

Her own desk was hidden under all the case documentation she had printed out from HOLMES2 moments after reading through Solomon's email again when she had first arrived that morning.

Rolling up her jacket sleeves, she sifted through the paperwork, even though she knew most of its content by heart now.

Surely there was something, some fact she had missed.

She bit back a yawn, knowing that her exhaustion was contributing to her frustrated efforts but unwilling to let go of the sensation she was close… so close…

'Morning, guv.'

Laura's bright greeting threw her from her fogged

rumination and she looked up to see the detective constable switching on her computer, and then Kyle and Gavin appeared at the door already engaged in a friendly argument about the previous night's football match on television.

Barnes was last through the door, but shot her a grin and handed her a takeout coffee cup as he passed on the way to his desk, frowning as he took in the mess strewn across hers.

'I take it the cleaners gave yours a wide berth last night, guv,' he said. 'What've you been up to?'

'Blimey, guv,' said Gavin, dropping his backpack onto his chair. 'Wait until Debbie finds out you've single-handedly depleted our paper supply.'

'I think she'll forgive me,' Kay said with a tired smile. 'Your mate Paul over at HQ came through.'

'Please tell me you haven't been here all night, guv,' said Barnes. 'Have you?'

'Not quite, but don't worry. I did get home for a few hours.'

He nodded, but didn't look convinced. 'Okay, want to tell us what you've been up to then while the rest of us have been getting our beauty sleep?'

She took a deep breath. 'I don't want this theory leaving this room until we've got more evidence to support it, understood?'

Four faces stared back at her, and then Kyle spoke.

'Guv, I haven't worked with you for long, but if you need to ask us that, I reckon we're doing something wrong.'

'Yeah, true. So, here's the thing. All this time, we've

been looking for someone who targeted Tansy before the festival. Someone who was close to the band,' she said, pacing the carpet. She stopped, then looked at each of them in turn. 'I think we were wrong.'

'Do you mean we've been approaching this from the wrong way, guv?' said Barnes.

'I do, yes. Maybe this has nothing to do with the reunion tour, or Joey, or Tansy even.' Heart racing, she eyed the whiteboard, her gaze roaming over the different streams of information and photographs. 'What if there was a practised killer *inside* the festival looking for their next victim? And what if Thommo Smith inadvertently put Tansy right in the killer's path?'

A stunned silence filled the incident room, broken only when the photocopier decided to recalibrate with an earth-shattering rumble.

'Er, guv…?' said Gavin tentatively. 'Are you suggesting that Tansy was murdered by a serial killer?'

Kay turned around to see him and the other detectives staring back at her, their eyes wide. 'That's exactly what I'm saying. I think we're dealing with a serial killer who's been using events like this across the country to stay hidden for a long time. Perhaps for more than twenty years.'

FIFTY-TWO

Ian Barnes ran his hand across his jaw and eyed Kay with a growing sense of anticipation.

He had worked with her for a number of years now, trusted her judgement, and had watched her grow with confidence as she had settled into her role as detective inspector.

And he had never once known her to jump to conclusions.

'What makes you so sure?' he said, knowing he was likely the only person on the team brave enough to pose such a question, but with the knowledge that she expected it.

A faint smile crossed her lips before she answered. 'Because the same events company, Crusader Events, was involved at every single one of these festivals.'

Barnes rocked back in his seat, heart thudding. 'Do we get Alistair Featheringham in for formal questioning, then?'

'Yes, but not as a suspect.' Kay picked up a sheaf of

documentation off her desk and waved it at him. 'I've already done the OSINT checks – like he said to me and Kyle last night, he doesn't get involved on the ground when there's a festival because there's so much else going on in that company. Except for one instance – Tansy's. And, as he said, that's only because the festival was here, close to where he lives. We speak to him again all right, but this time it'll be because I want all his employment records for the past twenty years.'

'Christ, guv, I can't see him wanting to do that without…'

Kay glanced over her shoulder as Gavin's mobile phone vibrated on his desk and held up a finger to silence the rest of them while he took the call.

Barnes turned to Laura, and raised a questioning eyebrow at the look of astonishment on her face. 'Having fun yet?'

'Jesus, Sarge,' she whispered. 'A serial killer? Seriously?'

'I think she's onto something, don't you? And what about—'

'That was Harriet,' said Gavin, his voice cutting through theirs. 'They've found Tansy's missing cardigan.'

Barnes automatically reached for his notebook. 'Where?'

'In one of the biohazard bins they've been sifting through since Saturday.'

'What about DNA? Any traces?'

'Blood splatter, so they're getting that tested right now against the sample taken from Kasprak's business card that was found in Tansy's pocket too.'

'What took them so long?' said Laura. 'I mean, it's been a week.'

'Their first priority was to process all the evidence gathered where Tansy's body was found, and then of course the council bin where the clothing was discovered,' Kay explained. 'The biohazard bins were collected from various points around the festival site – they're the ones used to collect needles and stuff, which is why it's taken so bloody long. Harriet's team had to be really careful how they dealt with all of that – the last thing we needed was for one of her CSIs to get a needle prick through carelessness.'

Barnes moved closer to the whiteboard, running his gaze over the various photographs from the previous weekend's crime scene. 'Gav, did Harriet happen to mention which biohazard bin the cardigan was found in?'

'She said it was one of the ones used in the volunteers' tent. They kept a couple in there every day over the festival to collate anything that was handed in.'

Barnes grinned at Kay as a smile formed on her lips. 'And one of those volunteers manages that tent every time Crusader Events is involved in a festival, right, guv?'

FIFTY-THREE

'Are you absolutely sure about this, Kay?'

DCI Devon Sharp peered through the blinds in his old office, the slats bent out of shape with age and dusty from lack of use.

'Honestly?' Kay sighed, then joined him, watching while Dana Schuldberg was led from a patrol car across a rain-soaked car park and through the back door of the police station. 'Yes. Yes, I am. I think.'

He chuckled. 'What did Featheringham have to say about this?'

She turned away, busying herself with gathering up some of the discarded office paraphernalia that had been tossed onto Sharp's old pockmarked desk and shoving it into an already-overflowing filing cabinet with a dent in the side of it. 'He was shocked, understandably, but he's been very cooperative in the circumstances. Kyle took three of our uniformed officers over to the storage unit that Crusader Events uses to keep all its old documentation in to keep their costs down, and they've come back with all the personnel files.'

'All of them? What, from the past – what is it? – twenty-odd years that the company's been in business?'

'Apparently Featheringham is a bit of a stickler for keeping a hold of things,' Kay said, kicking shut the filing cabinet drawer with her shoe. 'I was chatting with his wife while he was on the phone to the storage company, and she reckons their attic is a nightmare.'

'Well, thank goodness for that.' Sharp turned from the window. 'Anything in those records to support your theory?'

Kay huffed her fringe from her eyes and grinned. 'Yep. Dana was in attendance at every single one of those six festivals where we've got a suspicious death.'

'Really?'

'And we've drawn up a list of every festival where she's been in charge of the volunteer tent so we can share that with forces up and down the country to find out if there are more cold cases.'

Sharp gave a low whistle under his breath. 'No wonder you called me.'

'I didn't want to face the media on my own if this story breaks before we're ready, guv. And that's why only a small percentage of my investigation team knows what's really going on at the moment – we can't afford any leaks.'

'I agree. Okay, well it won't take long to process her through the custody suite so you'd best show me what you've pulled together.'

Kay led the way back out to the incident room, handed

him a manila folder containing the team's evidence and watched while he started to read.

It included everything they had managed to glean within the space of two hours about Dana Schuldberg, together with an executive summary Barnes had typed out with their suggestions.

It was brutally short, merely pointing out that the woman appeared to be immersed in her career and charity work. Save for a six-year relationship that had turned sour three years ago, her social media posts were full of photographs taken with friends and their families, some of the festivals she'd attended over the years – both as an employee and others where she had purchased a ticket – and of holidays spent in sunlit exotic places.

'Hang on,' Sharp said. 'It says in her statement that she's only been working with Crusader for four years, so how do you explain her being around for those six murders?'

'I spoke to Alistair Featheringham about that, and he's confirmed that she was a volunteer for a number of years before applying for the full-time role she's got now. Here, have a look.' Kay reached over and flicked through to a stapled list towards the back of the file. 'This is a complete list of every event she's attended over the years, both as an employee and as a volunteer. Crusader Events have to keep these for insurance purposes, albeit not as long as he insists on storing them.'

'Thank goodness for his hoarding habit then,' Sharp murmured, running his eyes down the list before turning the page. 'And your six suspicious death sites are on here, are they?'

'Yes, and that's the list I've shared with other forces although Kyle's gone through and tidied up the version sent out so it only shows the ones relevant to each force. I didn't want to overburden them at short notice.'

'Probably wise.' Sharp slapped the folder shut and handed it back. 'Who's interviewing her with you?'

'I thought maybe you might want to, given this one could have wider implications countrywide.'

'Agreed. Okay, let's go and find out what Ms Schuldberg has to say for herself, shall we?'

Dana Schuldberg sat with her hands clasped firmly together, her knuckles white while Kay read out the formal caution and requested the woman's solicitor introduce himself for the record.

'Andrew Gillow,' he intoned with a bored inflection.

Kay watched as Dana fidgeted her weight in the uncomfortable plastic chair and drew her cardigan around her shoulders to offset the cool air conditioning, which Sharp had set four degrees colder than usual.

It was a trick Kay had watched him implement from time to time working with him over the years, and one which no doubt had been learned from his time with the military police.

A plastic cup filled with water stood untouched in front of the volunteer leader, despite her solicitor requesting it be fetched for her after she had provided a DNA swab forty-five minutes ago.

Immediately after that, Gavin had couriered away the

same DNA sample towards the forensic laboratory with his trademark lack of respect for other road users.

Kay resisted the urge to check her watch or look at the clock on the wall behind the solicitor.

Surely the test was underway by now, wasn't it?

'Dana, can you please start by confirming how long you've been working for Crusader Events?' Sharp began.

'Four years.' The woman's gaze shifted from him to Kay, then back. 'You don't honestly think I killed that woman, do you?'

'Being in charge of all the volunteers for the festivals must give you certain powers,' Sharp continued. 'Such as access to backstage areas, secure zones, places like that, right? Do you find it easy to move around a festival site, or do you have to have additional security privileges?'

'No, I... I, um... I suppose I can pretty much come and go as I please. I've never really thought about it, to be honest.'

'How did you first start with Crusader?'

'I was a volunteer, just helping out when I could so I didn't have to pay for a ticket to their festivals.'

'How long did that go on for before you applied for a role with the company?'

'Nearly twenty years, I suppose. I volunteered for other festivals though, not just theirs. Around Bristol, where I'm from, there are loads of festivals over the summer so I was spoilt for choice really. It's just that the job with Crusader came up and I was able to do what I love full-time.'

Kay lowered her gaze to her notebook, a chill crossing her shoulders at the thought that Tansy's killer had cast a wider net than she and her team had first thought.

How many other unsolved murders were there yet to be discovered?

Opening the file, Sharp slid across a photograph to Dana. 'Tell me about this man. Where did you meet him?'

The woman's brow puckered as she peered at the image. 'I... I'm sorry, I don't know who this is. I've never met him.'

'He was murdered at a festival in Hampshire two years ago. At the time, it was treated as an accidental overdose but his family always insisted he wasn't a drugs user and requested a second coroner's enquiry be held.' Sharp shrugged. 'Unusual, but understandable in the circumstances, and just as well – it was later found that foul play was involved. Specifically, a trauma injury that had first been thought to have been caused by him falling and hitting his head. It turns out that injury was inflicted by a third party. Someone murdered him.'

Dana blinked. 'That's awful.'

'Then there's Alicia Scotsman,' said Sharp, flipping another photograph across the table at her. 'Nineteen, found dead in her tent the morning after the final night of a festival in Sussex. And this woman was murdered at a festival in Weymouth nine years ago...'

'I don't understand,' said Dana, glancing at her solicitor. 'What's this got to do with me?'

'You were at each of these events,' Sharp said.

'I work at lots of events. That's my job. It's what I do. I told you before – I'm in charge of the volunteers at everything Crusader hosts.'

'And you're able to move freely about every festival site, as you've previously confirmed, without question.'

Sharp flicked through the folder, taking his time. 'In fact, according to Crusader's records, you rarely leave the site once there and are often seen helping out suppliers and festival-goers alike. "Indispensable" is how one of your annual reviews puts it. That responsibility must weigh heavily on you. How's your personal life holding up?'

'What?' Dana rocked back in her seat at the sudden change in direction the DCI was going with his questions. 'What the hell has that got to do with you?'

'Answer the question please, Ms Schuldberg. Are you seeing anyone in between single-handedly running the volunteer aspects of Crusader's business?'

'I-I am. Sort of.' She blushed, and looked at her solicitor. 'Do I really have to answer him?'

Andrew Gillow inclined his head slightly in response, and Dana turned back to Sharp.

'I find your questioning intrusive.'

'I find your reluctance to answer intriguing.'

The woman squirmed in her seat before replying. 'I see one or two men, yes. Neither live with me, and our arrangement suits our busy lives.'

'We'll need their details.'

'That's prepos... oh, whatever.' She flapped her hand impatiently. 'I suppose you can do what you want, right? You're the police after all.'

Kay looked up at the woman's tone, but only saw a tired acceptance in Dana's eyes.

'Why did you kill Tansy Leneghan?' Sharp continued. 'Did you hear about her being linked to Joey Twist and reckoned on targeting someone more high-profile this time around, or was it just her bad fortune to be out in the park alone last weekend?'

'I didn't kill her. I told you that. Why would I?'

Sharp said nothing, and Kay followed his lead, letting the silence grow while watching the woman twist a single silver ring on her little finger.

'I didn't kill her,' Dana reiterated quietly, dropping her gaze to the table. 'You've got this all wrong.'

'How did you single out your other victims?' said Sharp. 'You have access to all the ticket holders' names as volunteer leader don't you, in case you need to notify their next of kin in the event of a medical emergency. Is that how you picked them? Did it ever occur to you how much pain you put those next of kin through every time you took a life?'

'Stop it!' Dana rocked back in her chair and wiped at the tears streaming down her face, mascara blurring to create black streaks that zigzagged over her cheeks. 'Stop.'

'Detectives, I'd like to request a break for my client,' said Gillow, unbuttoning his jacket and pulling a packet of paper tissues from an inside pocket. 'At least twenty minutes, I think, don't you?'

Sharp gathered the photographs together and shut the folder before nodding to Kay.

'Interview paused at eleven forty-five,' she said, then stopped the recording equipment and followed him from the room.

FIFTY-FOUR

'She's good, I'll give her that.'

Sharp finished the last of the water in the plastic cup, then shoved it under the filter tap for a refill while Kay alternated between checking her watch and then her mobile phone.

There was a frantic energy within the incident room now that clutched at her heart and sent goosebumps rippling across her skin.

'Come on, Gav,' she muttered. 'Let's have that result, and quickly.'

'How many favours did you call in for this?'

'Too many, guv. But the lab's been on standby for the past forty-eight hours and they're working two murder enquiries for East Division this weekend as well, so for a change they've got enough staff on hand to help us.'

'Good to know.'

'Guv?'

Kay turned at Kyle's voice to see the probationary detective advancing towards her with an open folder stuffed full with freshly printed pages. 'What have you got there?'

'It's the cleaned-up list of volunteers that have worked continuously with Crusader Events for the past twenty years,' he said, flicking through the documents. 'I just wanted to confirm that Dana appears in every single one of these, and I've tied in her name to two more festivals where there were suspicious deaths. There's one in North Somerset from 2015 and another in Cornwall in 2017 that we should probably include.'

'Christ, so we're looking at one murder a year at least.'

'Seems that way, guv. I'll keep digging but I'm waiting on other forces to phone back and that might not happen until tomorrow or Tuesday, depending on rosters and things like that.'

'Okay, thanks, Kyle. Do what you can, and add those deaths to the board, will you? Make a start on victim profiles, social media, that sort of thing. I take it the next of kin details are on HOLMES2?'

'They are, and I've also checked that the SIOs at the time are available if we need to talk to them at short notice. One of them retired three years ago but his email address and mobile are on file, so I'll get clearance before contacting him.'

'Good work.'

She spun on her heel to face Sharp. 'Jesus, how many more are we going to find?'

'I'll get onto HQ and light a rocket under their arses about getting you some more staff,' he said, already pulling out his mobile phone. 'You should've had extra help days ago. This is a big one, Kay – we'll need to start strategising how we're going to handle the media too, given this is going to be a nationwide case. I'm sure our colleagues in other counties are going to want to ensure we don't cast them in a bad light.'

'Sounds like a good plan, and thanks for the help with the extra staff. What about—?' Her phone vibrated in her hand, and she automatically answered it. 'Gav?'

There was a chuckle at the other end of the line, and then: 'Jonathan Aspley, *Kentish Times*. Have I caught you at a bad time, Detective Hunter?'

'Jonathan, any time is a bad time,' she said. 'What do you want?'

'I'm hearing a rumour that Tansy Leneghan's killer might've done this before. Would you like to comment?'

'Not at this time. I'm in the middle of an investigation. Could I call you later?'

'I'll hold you to that.'

Ending the call, she met Sharp's gaze and sighed. 'The vultures are starting to circle. I don't know how long I'll be able to—'

'Guv!'

Laura's voice carried across the incident room, and when Kay saw the sickly pallor to the detective constable's face, her heart sank.

'What is it?'

'I've got Gavin on the phone, guv. He couldn't get through on your mobile.' Laura pushed past one of the administrative staff members with a hurried apology to join them. 'He's at the lab, and they've just finished testing Dana's DNA sample, guv. It's not her.'

'Not her?'

'The sample isn't a match for either the blood on the clothing or the trace evidence on Kasprak's business card,' Laura said, wide-eyed. 'What do we do now?'

'Fuck.' Sharp spun away, running a hand over his closely-cropped hair.

Kay swallowed, dread crawling across her belly and twisting her guts. 'Are they sure? Have they checked?'

'They're running it again, guv, but they're ninety per cent certain. Dana Schuldberg didn't murder Tansy Leneghan.'

'And so likely didn't kill these other victims, either.' Kay squared her shoulders and stalked over to the whiteboard.

Kyle was staring at the list, fresh pen marks still glistening from where he had added the names of the two other victims to a horrifying tally that was steadily growing in length. Jaw set, he flipped open the folder and started flicking through the pages once more.

'Jesus, Kyle, don't tell me you've thought of another victim,' she said.

He said nothing for a moment, then crouched and set the folder on the floor beside her, fanning out the pages around his feet, muttering under his breath.

'You have, haven't you? Where? Local, or further afield?'

She watched as he grabbed at one of the pages, and then he looked up at her, eyes wide.

'There's another name that appears on each of these lists of volunteers for the festivals that Crusader Events organised,' he said. 'It's Lewis Molton.'

'Molton?' Barnes wandered over. 'Isn't that the older

bloke we saw in the volunteer tent before we first spoke to Dana?'

'It says here that he's an ex-army medic,' said Kyle, straightening before handing over the page.

Running her eyes down the details, her hand shaking, Kay felt a renewed burst of adrenaline surge through her. 'I think you're onto something.'

Sharp beckoned to Laura. 'Tell Gavin to get back here as soon as possible – without breaking the speed limit if he can help it. And I want you to take Kyle to this address on file for Molton. We'll work up a profile for him while you're doing that and arrange to release Dana but Molton's now our number one priority. I want him in custody within the hour.'

'Understood, guv.'

'If you have any concerns, then call for backup.'

'I will.'

'He means it, Laura,' said Kay. 'If we're right and he is our killer, then he's dangerous. Especially if he knows we're onto him.'

FIFTY-FIVE

Laura eyed the tired-looking bungalow fifty metres away and drummed her fingers on the steering wheel.

Lewis Molton's home was tucked away in a nondescript cul-de-sac in one of the older parts of Maidstone, with an unkempt privet hedge shielding the front garden from view. From her position she could see cream-coloured render peeling away above a bay window frame that was pockmarked with rot, and the roof guttering was sunken in places with telltale green mould splatters adding to an already forlorn-looking façade.

Misshapen black metal gates blocked access to a concrete driveway to the left of the bungalow that led to a garage with a dark blue aluminium door that remained resolutely closed.

She exhaled, trying to calm a thundering heart rate that accompanied the tension in her shoulders.

Beside her, Kyle had his phone in his hand while he peered at a maps app, pinching and pulling at the satellite image of the property.

'There's a side access between the garage and the house, according to this,' he said. 'Behind the house, it looks like there's a garden mostly laid to turf, and there's a shed – more like one of those garden office things – in the back corner, diagonally opposite to the rear of the garage.'

'Which car is his?'

He flicked from the map back to his messages app, then pointed to a grey estate car parked farther along the street, its paintwork chipped and rusting around the wheel arches and door seams.

'I'm guessing he's in, then.'

'Maybe. Haven't seen any signs of movement yet.'

'Do you think he's spotted us?'

Kyle shrugged. 'Hard to say.'

'Okay, let's find out.' Laura pulled the door latch, then glanced over her shoulder. Her colleague hadn't moved. 'You all right with this? I mean, after—'

'I'm fine.'

'Come on, then.'

Her colleague launched himself from the car after her, crossing the road and matching her no-nonsense pace along the pavement and through the front gate.

'Hang on,' he said, catching her sleeve before she reached the front door. 'Get behind me in case he's expecting us.'

She nodded, unwilling to admit that her heart was thrashing about between her ribs so hard that she thought he could probably hear it. Palms greasy, she stepped aside and watched while he hammered on the door with his fist.

There was no answer, and when she peered across to

the front window, she saw no shadows behind the yellowed net curtain.

Kyle shielded his eyes with his hand and looked through the frosted glass panel in the door, then shook his head. 'I can't see any movement.'

'Let's try round the back. Maybe that garage is unlocked too.'

'Can we go inside?'

She ran through the details of the planned arrest in her head, then nodded. 'I reckon so.'

'If his car's parked down the street, he should be in though, right?'

'Maybe he walked to the corner shop or something.' She followed him back along the path then across four chipped paving slabs to the driveway, and paused at the corner of the bungalow. She pulled out her phone as it vibrated. 'We're here now, guv. No, no sign of the backup yet. Yes, I'll let him know.'

Kyle cocked an eyebrow. 'Wait, or proceed?'

'Proceed.' She managed to inject a modicum of aplomb to her voice, then winked. 'With caution, of course.'

'If you're sure?'

'We can just have a look before they get here, right?' She brushed past him and strode towards the garage door, slipped on a pair of protective gloves from her trouser pocket, then bent down to toggle the rusting latch.

It didn't move.

'Locked?' said Kyle.

'Either that or stuck solid.' She wrinkled her nose. 'God knows when that was last opened.'

'Probably why his car's out on the road then.'

'Yeah.' She straightened. 'Wonder why he didn't just park on the driveway though?'

'Maybe it's easier to park out there if he's going out later, especially if people have a habit of blocking the driveway.'

'Maybe.' Turning, she made her way past the garage along a narrow path that ran adjacent to the side of the bungalow.

As they passed each of two windows, she tried peering in through the net curtains, but could see nothing save for a washing up liquid bottle and a can of fly spray on the window sill of the second in what was evidently the kitchen.

There was still no sign of movement though.

A shiver crossed her shoulders, goosebumps stippling her forearms at the sudden thought that Molton could be watching them, watching her as she crept by.

When they reached the back of the bungalow, she could see a doorway at the rear of the cinderblock garage that was accessible from the garden. It was closed, but she could hear a low incessant hum from within.

Raising her gaze, she saw a power cable stretching from the house to the garage.

'What are you up to?' she murmured.

Then Kyle tapped her elbow, and she let out a muffled yelp.

'Shh,' he said, then pointed to a squat chalet-style outbuilding that took up the back corner of a neatly trimmed lawn. 'He's in the garden office, look.'

She froze, eyeing the pale blue timber-framed structure with its two shallow steps leading down to a neat gravelled path that curved around the lawn to the garage and then onwards to the house.

There were Venetian blinds at the window instead of net curtains, and she could just make out the familiar blue hues of a computer screen.

The door of the garden office was ajar, a man's voice just audible, but as she strained her hearing, she couldn't hear anyone else.

'I think he's on the phone,' she said.

'Try the garage door while he's busy, then,' said Kyle, already hurrying over to it. 'Might as well take a look in here if we can.'

'Okay.' Laura glanced over her shoulder at movement at the end of the driveway, and exhaled as she saw two uniformed constables walking towards them. 'At least they're here. I couldn't see any other way out of the garden, could you?'

'No.'

'All right,' she said, pulling open the door. 'Well, at least he can't get away while we take a look in—'

A swarm of flies enveloped her.

Waving her hands in front of her face in an attempt to bat them away, she then peered into the gloom beyond the sunlight that filtered through the opening.

'What the—'

Six large chest refrigerators lined the walls, one blocking the locked up-and-over style door to the front of the garage. Rust speckled the corners of two of them, the rectangular structures humming with efficiency despite their evident age.

The concrete floor had been swept clean, and there were no other items of furniture visible.

Laura exhaled, swatted another fly away from her eyes, and stepped closer, her heartbeat thrumming in her ears. A pervading sense of dread enveloped her, all her focus on the refrigerator closest to her.

The one with a shiny new manufacturer's badge, and a bright clean white rubber seal around the lid that remained resolutely closed.

'Now or never, Hanway,' she muttered.

Taking a deep breath, she then flipped up the lid and peered inside.

For a brief moment, her brain refused to comprehend what her eyes were seeing.

There were trays set out in tidy lines, row upon row layered one on top of the other, all with neat little coloured labels that were at odds with the horrific display.

Rows of coloured fingernails, ear lobes that had shrivelled over time with dull silver or black discs pinched to the remnant skin, tattoos that had been sliced from limbs, and was that a—

She felt the first spasm clench her stomach before dropping the lid back into place, and raced to the open door.

'Stay there,' she blurted to Kyle as she shot past him. 'Don't go inside.'

She made it to the far side of the lawn before her stomach convulsed violently, and retched into a ragged collection of overgrown shrubs.

Breathing heavily, she closed her eyes and tried to fight

the sheer horror that was threatening to override her training.

'Got him,' called one of the constables, his voice carrying across the lawn to where she remained doubled over.

Straightening, she saw a spritely pensioner at the officer's side dressed in a black cotton shirt and olive-green trousers, his gaze shifting from the open door of the garage to the two detectives.

A shiver crawled up her spine when his eyes found her, an almost reptilian alertness gracing them before a smile formed on his lips.

'Found my little collection, have you?' he said in a lilting voice.

There was no remorse, no fear, no attempt at denial.

Instead, he squared his shoulders and set his jaw, as if proud to share his gruesome work with an audience at last.

Laura took a paper tissue from Kyle with a curt nod of thanks and dabbed at her lips, gulping in fresh air. 'Phone Kay. Let her know we're going to need Harriet's team here, and get Molton into custody – we're going to be in for a long night.'

FIFTY-SIX

Kay placed a cup of sweet tea beside Laura and rested her hand on her colleague's shoulder.

'How're you holding up?'

The other woman shuddered, but took the drink with a murmur of thanks. 'Just getting my report written up, guv. Shouldn't be long.'

'That's not what I meant, and you know it.' Dropping into a spare chair beside the young detective's desk, Kay checked over her shoulder to make sure the rest of the team were out of earshot. 'From personal experience, I'd recommend you speak to a professional early next week. You're on your own at home at the moment, aren't you?'

Laura nodded, putting down the cup with a shaking hand. 'Yeah. The last toe-rag moved out a few weeks ago.'

'Right, so tomorrow night I want you round at mine and Adam's for dinner, okay? Don't panic – we'll keep it low-key rather than have the whole team there, even though Barnes is dropping hints about a barbecue soon.

But I need to make sure you're not bottling up what you've gone through this afternoon, all right?'

'Okay.' Her colleague sniffed. 'I reckon I've got about ten more minutes on this, and then it'll be in HOLMES2 and I'll print out copies for the interview. I got Harriet to take some initial photos when she and Patrick first got there too.'

'Great thinking, thanks.' Kay looked over her colleague's head as Sharp walked into the incident room, and patted Laura's hand. 'Got to go.'

'Guv?'

She looked over her shoulder to see a renewed look of determination on Laura's face. 'What?'

'Don't let him get away. Nail him to the wall, all right?'

'I will, don't you worry.'

Hurrying over to where the rest of the team stood around the whiteboard with the DCI, she rolled up her shirt sleeves. 'Ian? Are you ready?'

'You bet.' He handed her two manila folders, giving an identical set to Sharp. 'The observation suite is set up for you, guv. Gavin's going to join you there.'

'Good.' The DCI flicked through the bullet-point summary that Barnes had pinned to the inside of the top folder, and gave a curt nod. 'Right, I'll get HQ onto this so they can coordinate with other forces as we go. That way, if we need to correlate something Molton says with regard to another open unsolved case, we can hopefully get the information fast-tracked. I don't imagine everyone's going to be working the same hours as us tonight.'

Kay glanced over her shoulder as Kyle walked into the

room with a stack of takeout pizzas in his hands that he distributed amongst the uniformed officers who had volunteered to stay late. She tried to ignore the rumble in her stomach, then grinned as he flipped open the lid of the last box and handed it over.

'Best you and Barnes get some of that down you, guv, before it all disappears,' he said. 'Can't imagine you're going to get another chance.'

'Thanks.' She sank her teeth into a slice, then nudged him away from the group. 'Do me a favour? Keep an eye on Laura for me.'

'Don't worry, I will.'

'How are you doing? Are you okay?'

'Yeah, I did what she said and didn't go inside.' He peered past her to where Laura sat at her desk, head bowed while she quietly put the finishing touches to her arrest report. 'I wish I had though, instead of her.'

Kay wiped her hands on a napkin. 'Don't think of it like that. She was the lead on the arrest, and she made that decision. Neither of you could have had any idea what was in that garage.'

'I suppose so. Have you heard from Harriet?'

'Not in the past thirty minutes, no. I'd imagine they're going to be there for a few days yet.' She moved back to where Barnes was helping himself to a second slice of pizza. 'Have that, and then we'll make a start.'

'Molton's solicitor is here, guv,' called Debbie from her desk. 'And the DNA sample from Molton's just been taken over to the lab by Dave Morrison – he was on duty tonight anyway, so I've sent him. And don't leave here without this folder – it's got the information from the Crusader Events file in it.'

'Thanks.'

Barnes shot her a grim smile. 'Ready to do battle?'

'Lead the way.'

FIFTY-SEVEN

Kay flipped open the first of the manila folders, and despite a rising repulsion for the man sitting opposite, edged her chair closer to the table.

Lewis Molton watched her with cool interest while Barnes recited the caution. The killer's manicured hands were clasped together on the table, his posture relaxed. He kept his shirt sleeves rolled down while the air conditioning emitted a soft hum in the silence that followed the formal introductions.

The antibacterial wipe that Molton had been handed after providing both a full set of fingerprints and a DNA sample was now crunched up on the table beside his elbow, and a pervading smell of antiseptic wafted across to where she sat. His aftershave mingled with the scent, and sent a curious mixture of citrus and sandalwood her way that she knew she would recall for days to come.

'How long have you been volunteering for Crusader Events?' she began.

'About twenty-two years.'

'Which organisations did you volunteer for before that?'

'One of the big first aid ones.' Molton smiled. 'They appreciated my skills.'

'You were a medic in the army, weren't you?' Kay lowered her gaze and sifted through the documentation. 'When did you leave the army?'

'I was in the Territorial Army, so I only did that for about ten years. Then work got... busier, so I had to leave.'

'And what work was that exactly, Mr Molton?'

'I was a landscape gardener at a large property south of Staplehurst. They decided to expand into rewilding before it became fashionable, and then opened it up to the public. I was integral to the project design and management until I retired six years ago.'

Kay paused to make a note to herself, wondering how many of Molton's victims might have ended up in the ornamental gardens without the owner's knowledge, while simultaneously fighting back a growing sense of repulsion at the man's lack of emotion.

'Tell me how you started volunteering with Crusader Events.'

'Oh,' he waved a hand in front of his face. 'You don't want to really hear about that, do you?'

'Mr Molton, answer the question please.'

'All right.' He pouted, leaned back in his chair and crossed his arms. 'They put an advert in the local paper. It was advertised online as well, but there was still a regular free paper back then. There was a folk festival they were organising about twelve miles away from here, and they were short of volunteers over the summer months. First aid training was one of the preferences they listed, so I applied.'

'Why did you apply? You already had a busy job as a landscape gardener.'

He shrugged. 'I still had to take time off. I had twenty days of annual leave to use up, and no family to spend it with so I figured I'd see some live music instead. Amongst other things.'

'What sort of things?'

'Crusader organises beer festivals, car shows, caravan and motor home shows. Anything like that, really.'

Kay paused as Barnes began to scrawl hurriedly in his notebook, the page angled away from the killer's gaze. She could only imagine the list of tasks he was concocting for the already overworked team upstairs. With Molton's confession, they would now have even more past events to scour for potential victims.

She fought hard to keep the mounting disgust from her face and turned to the second manila folder. 'Your personal file with Crusader doesn't mention first aid duties until four years ago. What did you do when you first signed up with them?'

'Handing out sunscreen, festival maps, answering questions,' he said in a bored monotone. 'Trivial things.'

'You used those trivial things, as you call them, to seek out your victims, didn't you?' she said, extracting a series of images from the folder. 'Such as these men and women, all young festival-goers, all innocent. What made you target these in particular?'

'Oh, I don't know,' he sighed. 'Sometimes I liked what

they were wearing, sometimes it was the way they smiled at me or spoke to me – I could tell straight away that they trusted me, of course. And, why not?' He spread his hands expansively. 'I was there to help them, wasn't I?'

Kay's gaze rested for a moment on each of the photographs spread across the table, and she swallowed. Molton was right – there was no obvious pattern to his choice of victim, no similarities between the accusing eyes that bore into hers from each image.

A sadness pierced her heart at the lives cut short by someone who spoke with so little emotion, so little compassion.

All those daughters, sons, mothers, fathers, sisters, brothers... all taken by the monster who sat across from her, his complacency palpable.

Barnes's pen stopped scratching the surface of his notebook and he cleared his throat expectantly.

'When did you start using the events to murder your victims?' she said, blinking to clear the stinging sensation at the corners of her eyes.

'Almost straight away,' Molton replied, a malicious smile forming. 'It was easy, really. People get drunk and do stupid things all the time. Sites are often close to the countryside so as not to disturb the neighbours... plenty of wildlife to explain away some of the little nibbles and missing bits and pieces. And it wasn't like I had to worry about disposal. Did you know, on at least four occasions, it was *three days* before anyone discovered them? Everyone else was too busy partying, doing drugs, getting drunk, dancing... What does that tell you about humanity, detective?' He leaned forward. 'Nobody cared.'

'Why keep them?' Kay said, biting back the vile taste in her mouth at his words. 'Why take Tansy's fingernails? Did she scratch you? Were you afraid you'd left part of yourself behind?'

'God, no. I wasn't afraid.' Molton laughed, a raucous bark that echoed off the plain plasterwork walls. He leaned forward. 'They were pretty. Did you find them? So pretty. I wanted them.'

'Why Tansy Leneghan?'

'I couldn't sleep that night. I was too excited. All those people, all those *choices*.' He ran his tongue over his lips. 'I decided to go for a walk. And then I saw her.'

'Where?'

'She thought she was being clever.' A sly smile formed, his eyes taking on a dream-like quality. 'I was walking along the top of the hill when I saw a figure emerge from the hedgerow. She'd obviously managed to climb over a fence to avoid the security patrol. I didn't know who she was of course, just that I'd been presented with an exquisite opportunity that I couldn't possibly resist.'

'Tell me what happened,' said Kay, aware of the silence that followed Molton's words. Her mouth dry, she forced herself to clasp her hands and affect a non-threatening posture, knowing this would be her only chance to discover the truth.

'Oh, there's nothing much to say,' he replied, leaning back in his chair and sighing. 'I've had a bit of practice, you see. Although I really didn't expect her to put up such a fight.'

With that, he undid the cuff buttons on his cotton shirt and rolled up the sleeves.

A series of track-like scratch marks clawed his skin between his wrists and elbows.

'She was feisty, I'll give her that,' he said, a sadness to his voice. 'Not that it did her any good. It never does.'

'Why did you move her after you'd killed her?'

He snorted. 'The silly bitch refused to die. I thought she was dead after I strangled her until she started struggling when I began removing her fingernails.'

Kay fought back a shudder. 'Why dump the sweatshirt and trousers in the council bin, and her cardigan in a biohazard bin?'

'To confuse you, of course. Why else?' Molton's face hardened. 'I didn't come this far to make it easy for anyone. You just got lucky, Detective Hunter, that's all.'

'How many? Do you bother to keep count? Do you even wonder how many lives you've ruined over the years?'

'Three hundred and four.'

She heard both Barnes and the solicitor's sharp intakes of breath.

'What?'

'Three hundred and four.' Molton rolled his shoulders, and then sighed. 'I didn't manage to catalogue all of those, of course. It would've been impossible, space-wise. I mean, you've seen my garage. And besides, time ravages all. Even some of the most beautiful specimens became tarnished over the years, and I couldn't have them sully the pretty ones. So they had to go. But, yes, three hundred and four.'

Kay gathered the photographs together, and closed the folder. 'Then I can assure you, Mr Molton, that you won't be seeing the light of day again.'

'I don't mind. I've always wanted to write a book.' He smiled. 'And now I'll have the time to do that.'

Kay's jaw dropped. 'A book?'

'I'm sure there are a lot of people who will want to read about me.'

She looked from Molton to his solicitor, who wisely kept his gaze firmly lowered to his notepad, his pen hovering above the page.

Beside her, Barnes stifled a snort of disgust.

Eyeing the killer in front of her, Kay squared her shoulders, and uttered the words her team had worked so hard to hear.

'Lewis Molton, you are charged with the assault and unlawful killing of Tansy Leneghan…'

FIFTY-EIGHT

Kay ran her tongue across her lips, savouring the faint trace of brandy that lingered, and followed Barnes over the road towards the police station.

After Lewis Molton had been processed through to the cells to await transportation to a remand centre, her colleague had suggested they walk to a quiet pub on the fringes of the High Street.

It was an offer she accepted without hesitation.

Over a stiff drink, they had murmured their disgust and disbelief at the killer's confession.

Shellshocked at his words, already overwhelmed by the sheer amount of work ahead of them, they had spent a few moments contemplating the fallout from their investigation, before sombrely raising a silent toast to his victims and their families for the justice that would swiftly follow.

'Here,' said Barnes once they were safely across the road. 'Just in case.'

She took the packet of mints from him and popped one

in her mouth with a nod of thanks. 'I reckon a short briefing tonight, Ian, and then we'll send everyone home. I'll tell them to make sure they're in for nine o'clock tomorrow – they're going to need a lie-in after this one.'

'Sounds good, guv.' He glanced up at the darkening sky. 'It's going to be nice over the next couple of days for a change. Want to try and organise a barbecue after work sometime this week? Pia's been nagging me to get everyone together.'

'Yes, that'd be good. I think I'm on call but the rest of you should be all right. I'll check the roster with Debbie in the morning.'

She led the way through the security door and up the stairs, a fatigue settling over her with every tread as the frustration and fear of the past days gave way to relief.

It was this, this knowledge that she could rest tonight with Tansy's killer behind bars, unable to harm anyone else, that sustained her in her darkest times, that kept her going when all else seemed lost.

She paused at the top of the stairs and smiled. 'Thanks, Ian. We got him. We bloody got him.'

'We bloody did.' He grinned. 'Not a bad team in there, are they?'

'They'll keep.'

Her smile widened when they walked into the incident room.

An almost festive atmosphere enveloped the team, with everyone talking at once, laughter filling the space where only hours before a heightened tension had gripped them.

Now, as she crossed to where her younger detectives were gathered around Gavin's desk, she felt the familiar sense of pride in their work, and nudged her way past one of the administrative team to join them.

Except they didn't look up from Gavin's screen.

Instead, Kyle and Laura peered closer and continued an animated discussion over an email they were reading.

'What's going on?' Kay said, perplexed.

All three of them visibly jumped.

'Didn't see you there, guv,' said Laura, blushing.

Kay craned her neck. 'What's that?'

'The sweepstake,' said Gavin.

'What—?'

'The one for Hovis,' Kyle explained. 'We had to start a spreadsheet. I asked him to see how much we're up to. What've you got, Gav?'

'Four hundred quid,' said the detective constable. 'Paul Disher's lot from the tactical firearms team got wind of it somehow and decided they wanted in, and so did Harriet. Then there's the forensic lab and some of Paul Solomon's team at Northfleet—'

'You're kidding me…' Kay sighed. 'All right, enough of that. Come on, briefing – and then you lot can bugger off.'

She turned her back on the sound of laughter, and focused on the whiteboard for the final time.

'Here you go, guv. One more to keep you going for a little while longer,' said Debbie, handing her a steaming mug of coffee.

'Thanks. How're we doing for supplies?'

The constable winked. 'I'll put in a new order tomorrow, don't worry.'

Once the uniformed staff and administrators had joined

them, she beckoned to Kyle. 'Do we have the DNA test results from the lab yet?'

'Yes, guv. They've confirmed Molton's blood is a match for the samples taken from Thommo's clothing that was found in that council bin, and for the blood stain found on Kasprak's business card.'

'We've got him.' Kay clenched her fist. 'That, plus his confession – the CPS will have their hands full, but at least it's a start.'

'What about all the other victims, guv?' said Debbie, her eyes wide. 'What do we do about them?'

'We'll have to work with Molton's solicitor to see if his client will give us names – if he knows them – and we'll have to pull out all records for suspicious deaths up and down the country.' Kay exhaled. 'It's going to take time, but believe me, we'll charge him with as many as we can so the CPS can advise he lives out the rest of his life behind bars.'

A collective sigh filtered through the team.

'Next, I need a media statement drafted to go out first thing tomorrow. Gavin, would you mind doing that please? It'll need to go over to headquarters in case they want to add anything about the ongoing investigation into other cases, but for now just concentrate on Molton being charged with Tansy's murder.'

'Will do, guv.'

She continued to delegate the different tasks around her team, working through the outstanding matters on the whiteboard one by one before holding up her hand for silence. 'I'm proud of you all for your dedication during this investigation. It hasn't been easy, and I realise for some of you, the repercussions of what we're dealing with will stay with you for a long time. I've said it before, but if you need to talk just come and find me. I'll always be here for you, and there's professional help available too in confidence, so don't be afraid to ask. It doesn't reflect on your abilities as police officers, and sometimes we can't talk about these things with our families. Is that understood?'

There were nods and murmurs of acquiescence through the room, and she smiled before picking up her mug of coffee. 'In that case, finish whatever you can over the next half an hour or so and get yourselves home. We'll reconvene here at nine tomorrow so you can have some semblance of a lie-in, and I want—'

She broke off as Barnes's desk phone began to trill, and frowned when he answered it and started laughing.

Confused, she watched as he murmured a response to the caller, then wiped tears from his cheeks, wheezing while he tried to catch his breath. 'Yes, of course – I'll let her know.'

The incident room fell silent as he replaced the receiver, and then he looked across at her and grinned.

'That was Adam, guv,' he said. 'He says you might want to buy some more rose bushes in the morning.'

'What?' Kay lowered her coffee cup. 'You mean Hovis…'

Her colleague checked his watch, still grinning. 'Yup – and according to our sweepstake, I'm four hundred quid richer, thanks.'

She looked around as the rest of her team began to

laugh, glaring at each of them before turning back to Barnes.

'That bloody sheep. I swear he won't make it to Christmas at this rate.'

THE END

ABOUT THE AUTHOR

Rachel Amphlett is a USA Today bestselling author of crime fiction and spy thrillers, many of which have been translated worldwide.

Her novels are available in eBook, print, and audiobook formats from libraries and retailers as well as her website shop.

A keen traveller and accidental private investigator, Rachel has both Australian and British citizenship.

Find out more about Rachel's books at: www.rachelamphlett.com.

ABOUT THE AUTHOR

Rachel Amphlett is a USA Today bestselling author of crime fiction and spy thrillers, many of which have been translated worldwide.

Her novels are available in eBook, print, and audiobook formats from libraries and retailers as well as her website shop.

A keen traveller and accidental private investigator, Rachel has both Australian and British citizenship.

Find out more about Rachel's books at www.rachelamphlett.com